KW-482-626

The No. 2 **FELINE** Detective Agency

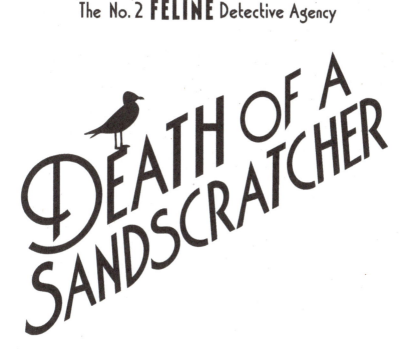

DEATH OF A SANDSCRATCHER

MANDY MORTON

Farrago

This edition published in 2025 by Farrago,
an imprint of Duckworth Books Ltd
1 Golden Court, Richmond TW9 1EU, United Kingdom

www.farragobooks.com

Copyright © Mandy Morton, 2025

The right of Mandy Morton to be identified as the author
of this Work has been asserted by her in accordance
with the Copyright, Designs & Patents Act 1988.

All rights reserved. No part of this publication may be reproduced,
stored in a retrieval system, or transmitted, in any form or by any
means, without the prior permission in writing of the publisher.

This book is a work of fiction. Names, characters, businesses,
organizations, places and events other than those clearly in the
public domain, are either the product of the author's imagination
or are used fictitiously. Any resemblance to actual persons,
living or dead, events or locales is entirely coincidental.

Printed and bound in Great Britain by Clays Ltd, Elcograf S.p.A.

The authorised representative in the EEA is Easy Access System
Europe, Mustamäe tee 50, 10621 Tallinn, Estonia.

Print ISBN: 9781788425193
e-ISBN: 9781788425209

MIX
Paper | Supporting
responsible forestry
FSC® C018072
FSC
www.fsc.org

Praise for the No. 2 Feline Detective Agency series

'**Original and intriguing...** a world without people which cat lovers will enter and enjoy.' P. D. James

'**Deliciously clever and a true delight**.' Laura Thompson

'**I loved it.** The whole concept is just so "real"!' Barbara Erskine

'Mandy Morton's Feline Detective Agency instigates a new genre, both **wonderful and surreal**.' Maddy Prior

'There's **so much heart** in this book as well as a **cracking good plot**. Can't wait for the next one!' Barbara Nadel

'The world that Morton has created is **irresistible**.' *Publishers Weekly*

'Witty and smart. **Prepare to be besotted**.' M. K. Graff

'Mandy Morton's series is both **charming and whimsical**.' Barry Forshaw

'Hettie Bagshot might be a new face at the scene of a crime, but already **she could teach most fictional detectives a thing or two**.' *The Hunts Post*

What readers are saying about the series:

'This series is **the perfect warm, fluffy cosy mystery read** for fans of Agatha Crispy-style mysteries and cat-lovers alike.'

'**True escapism into a world of pies, cakes and cats** while somehow smuggling a truer reflection of the real world than much human detective fiction.'

'A deceptively nasty murder wrapped up in a cardigan, and served by the fire with tea and cake. **A delight from beginning to end**.'

'**Hilarious and captivating**.'

'**The cat world's answer to the cosy crime novel**, with bags of charm and characters you don't want to leave behind.'

'**I love this series** and am waiting with a warmed pastry, a hot mug of something, and a crackling fire for the next in the series.'

By Mandy Morton
The No. 2 Feline Detective Agency
Cat Among the Pumpkins
The Death of Downton Tabby
The Ghost of Christmas Paws
The Michaelmas Murders
Magical Mystery Paws
Beyond the Gravy
The Ice Maid's Tail
A Pocket Full of Pie
The Cat and the Pendulum
The Windmill Murders
The Suspicions of Mr Whisker
Murder on the Santa Claws Express

In memory of Squeak, an extremely fine cat, and Michael, who never turned anyone on four legs away. Both very sadly missed but remembered with love.

Chapter One

The town's second literary festival promised to be as big a disaster as the first. Back then, the murder of several authors, including Downton Tabby, had given Hettie Bagshot and Tilly Jenkins from The No. 2 Feline Detective Agency a real headache. Their skill and ingenuity had finally triumphed as they sifted through the evidence, putting themselves in grave danger to bring the killer to justice. In Hettie's not-so-humble opinion, a second festival should never have been attempted whilst memories of the body count at the first were still raw.

Tilly felt very differently. She was a lover of books and consumed them as keenly as she did her favourite pastries from Betty and Beryl Butters' high street bakery. She had only recently had to have a clear-out, as her books had begun to overwhelm the small bed-sitter at the back of the bakery that she and Hettie shared, and from where they conducted their detective business.

It was surprising that Hettie had agreed to attend the festival at all, but she had been coerced into helping Betty and Beryl set up the refreshment tent on the promise of a free lunch and a cream tea. Tilly had signed up to several of the events, whilst Hettie moved between a deckchair in the sun and her own reserved table in the refreshment area, from where she could observe the goings-on without getting involved in the festival itself.

It was day two of the planned week-long procession of authors talking about themselves and their latest books, and the disasters had already begun to emerge. World famous Queen of Crime Agatha Crispy had to cancel at the last minute after being incapacitated by a swarm of bees, much to Tilly's disappointment as she regarded Miss Crispy as one of her almost-close friends. Saveloy Daily could no longer present his latest book of life drawings thanks to a court hearing brought by one of his models, who claimed he'd spiked her lemon barley water with high grade Canadian catnip. Florence Brulee-Smythe had backed out of her cookery demonstration due to health and safety issues and the fact that one of the recipes in her cookery almanac had poisoned at least ten cats in the last month. Luckily, no one had suffered more than three days of extreme discomfort and Florence was last seen boarding a flight to the Bahamas.

'You look a bit lost sitting there on your own,' said Betty, banging a pasty down in front of Hettie. 'Get your teeth round that while it's hot. Sister is bringing you a milky tea when she's finished arguing with Garfield Blunt.'

Hettie looked across to the counter, where Beryl was standing her ground with a cat dressed in black from head to toe except for a bright yellow cravat. 'Who on earth is Garfield Blunt?' she asked, eyeing up her pasty appreciatively.

'He's one of the authors Turner Page has booked for the festival. He writes science fiction, evidently. He's complaining about there being no breakfast this morning here in the tent. We've had to point out that we have a bakery to run in the town, as well as lunches and teas here, but as you can see that's only made his tantrum worse. Turner came in for a frothy coffee earlier and told us that the science fiction event hadn't gone well on account of no one turning up, so I think that's at the bottom of his attitude.'

The cat in question was now slamming his paw down on the counter and upsetting the two romantic novelists behind him in the queue. 'Would you like me to go over and have a word with him?' suggested Hettie.

'Bless you, but I think Beryl can handle him. There's nothing like a steak and kidney pie to calm rough seas.'

Betty was right: the moment that Beryl jammed a pie into Garfield Blunt's paw, the waters were instantly calm again. Grudgingly, he paid up and slunk out of the tent.

Beryl left the novelists in the queue to bring Hettie her tea, pleased to have got rid of at least one difficult customer. 'Milky with two sugars,' she said, putting the mug down next to Hettie's pasty. 'I don't mind saying, the sooner this week is over the better I'll like it. Why we ever agreed to this nightmare I'll never know. Nothing but complaints from all these so-called authors, while Turner Page hides in the library keeping his head down. Not ideal for the festival director – it seems that the only tickets he's sold are for the events that have been cancelled. That cat couldn't organise a quarter of toffees in a sweet shop.'

Betty nodded in agreement. 'And I gather the Morris Dancing display is now off due to the cat who plays the concertina refusing to appear as they're serving the wrong sort of beer in the beer tent.'

'Too much gas and not enough draught,' added Betty, 'which could easily be one of those metaphors for the whole festival if we're being literary.'

'Then there's that disaster yesterday,' continued Beryl. 'That reading we had in here with a cream tea, now what was it? Ah yes, *Lord Peter Whoopsie and Harriet Stains* read by Nova Pilchard. She won't be invited back. She was sick halfway through her first chapter and caught all the cats in the front row. Delerium Treemints did her best to clean up but the tent emptied very quickly.'

'I'm pleased I missed it,' said Hettie, sipping her tea. 'I don't think any events have gone smoothly yet and it's only the second day. At least the last festival had proper authors, even though most of them ended up being murdered.'

'That's true,' said Betty, 'but most of this lot should have been drowned at birth. Polly Hodge is the only decent one among them now that Miss Crispy has had to cancel. That Nicolette Upstart won't be bringing her merch tent this year either as her latest effort, *Shot With Crimplene*, has been put back until the autumn on account of them giving the plot away on the back cover. No great loss there; she was a damn nuisance at the last festival, swinging her blonde fur about and smiling at every cat that passed her.'

Having delivered their critique on the festival so far, the sisters returned to their counter to battle through the lunch queue. Hettie savoured the first bite of her pasty and washed it down with several mouthfuls of milky tea. At least the festival came with a selection of the Butters' bakery delights, she thought, but several more days of sitting around waiting for Tilly to emerge from her various events was beginning to seem like purgatory.

She looked up from her lunch as Tilly made her way across the tent to join her, flushed from Polly Hodge's intensive creative writing workshop. 'I wasn't sure what you'd want,' said Hettie, 'but the pasties are really good.'

'I don't think I could eat a thing – I'm too hot and too excited,' said Tilly. 'Polly Hodge says if I keep at it I could find myself on the bestseller list.'

'Well, that *would* be something, then we could retire from being detectives and buy a house as big as the one Polly Hodge lives in. What would you write about?'

Tilly thought for a moment as she clawed a large piece of pastry off Hettie's plate and put it in her mouth. 'Polly says you should try and write what you know and observe everything around you. She says travelling about is good and can be a real source of inspiration. The trouble is, everywhere we go there's always a murder to solve, and I don't really want to write about that as it's work and usually nasty.'

'You certainly seem to have been inspired by my pasty,' observed Hettie. 'As you've eaten most of the pastry, I'll go and get us two more before the rest of Polly Hodge's workshop devotees fill the tent.'

Having fought her way to the front of the queue, Hettie returned minutes later with a tray full of delights. The Butter sisters had done the festival proud by providing enough cakes, pastries and pies to content any bookworm; in the absence of some of the authors booked to appear, the refreshment tent was proving the most popular event by far.

Tilly eyed up the selection that Hettie put in front of her and suddenly realised that she was hungry after all. She had absent-mindedly finished Hettie's pasty while her friend was at the counter and now her attention rested on a cheese scone and a milky tea to wash it down.

'I've been thinking about what you said about travelling,' said Hettie, before taking a substantial bite from her replacement pasty. 'You're right – we never go anywhere that isn't work, except for those few days at Marley Toke's B&B in Southwool the summer before last. This festival is on its beam end and the weather is set fair so why don't we take a holiday by the sea?'

'What, now?' said Tilly excitedly, spilling her milky tea. 'Where would we go? It's probably busy everywhere at this time of year.'

'I'm sure we can find one of those guest houses to stay in. A week away from the town would do us both good – fish and chips, sandcastles, sea air and maybe even a funfair. I think we need a good old-fashioned holiday at the seaside. You might even find some inspiration for that book you want to write.'

Tilly reached for a cream horn from the tray and noisily sucked the filling out of it before eventually responding to Hettie through a mouthful of flaky pastry. 'Betty and Beryl have one of those guidebooks on places to stay. We could borrow it when we get home tonight. I'm so excited about our holiday I can hardly eat.'

Hettie smiled at her friend as Tilly poked the final piece of cream horn into her mouth. The prospect of several more days at the literary festival had now been dispatched into the unclaimed ticket box. When there were only crumbs left on their lunch tray, the two cats left the tent to sit in the sunshine until their friend Bruiser arrived to drive them home.

Chapter Two

Bruiser was an important part of The No. 2 Feline Detective Agency. He drove Hettie and Tilly's motorbike and sidecar and could always be relied upon to sort out any trouble they encountered along the way. Some of their cases had required more than diplomacy and Bruiser had had to use his paws and claws on several occasions to dig them all out of trouble. He had proved to be invaluable to the Butters as well, becoming their odd job cat, and they had rewarded him by building a rather fine shed at the bottom of their garden, where he lived with Miss Scarlet – the name that Tilly had given to the motorbike in celebration of her favourite board game.

On the dot of six o'clock, Bruiser arrived to take Hettie and Tilly home. While they were waiting, they helped Betty and Beryl load up their car with the few pies and pastries left over from the refreshment tent, then the five cats set off together, with Miss Scarlet leading the way and the Butters' Morris convertible following on behind.

The sun was still warm when they arrived back at the bakery and Betty suggested that they all sit out in the garden to eat their suppers. Beryl had roasted a large chicken earlier in the day, and insisted that Hettie, Tilly and Bruiser share it with them. Betty added some freshly cooked chips and a substantial strawberry and peach trifle to the feast, and the cares of the day melted away in a very pleasant evening of excellent food and good company, all washed down with a glass or two of fiery ginger beer.

When the sun had finally put herself to bed behind Bruiser's shed and the last chicken bone had been sucked clean, Betty and Beryl made a move. 'We'd better get ourselves to bed, sister,' said Betty. 'We've got another busy day tomorrow. It's wearing me out, opening the bakery in the morning and doing the festival in the afternoon.'

'Before you go up to your flat, I was wondering if we could borrow your book on places to stay?' asked Tilly. 'We thought we'd treat ourselves to a week by the sea.'

'What a good idea,' said Beryl. 'It's time you had a break from all those murders you solve. Come up with us now and fetch it.'

Tilly wiped the cream from her paws on her deck-chair. The trifle had refused to be contained in her bowl and had spread its love all over most of the long-haired tabby fur that peeped out from her T-shirt. She loved her food and it loved her back in the most demonstrative of ways.

Now, she followed the Butters through the back door of the bakery and up to their flat, leaving Hettie and Bruiser to fold up the deckchairs. 'Do you fancy a week away with us?' asked Hettie. 'It's so hot in the town at the moment and there's nothing much to do round here except sleep in the sun.'

'Nothin' wrong with that,' said Bruiser, 'an' I got several *Bikers' Monthly*'s ta catch up readin', but I'll take you an' fetch you back if you like. Me an' Dolly thought we'd 'ave a few days out if the weather stays nice.'

Bruiser was sweet on Dolly Scollop, who helped run the café in the high street with Molly Bloom. Molly hailed from Ireland and Dolly from Cornwall, and the two cats had created one of the most successful businesses in the town. Molly's mixed grills were legendary and Dolly's rapport with the customers and her colourful Cornish tales made the two hard-working cats a winning team.

With the deckchairs neatly stacked under an old apple tree at the bottom of the Butters' lawn, Bruiser said goodnight and made his way to his shed while Hettie returned to the room at the back of the bakery that she and Tilly called home. When Betty and Beryl had moved south from Lancashire to seek their fortune, they had bought the bakery as a going concern. The back room had been little more than a dusty storeroom then. Hettie had inadvertently boosted the success of the bakery by recommending the Butters' pies to the proprietors of Malkin and Sprinkle, the local department store in the town, who – at Hettie's suggestion – decided to stock them in their food hall. The pies were a runaway success and helped to put the sisters' bakery on the map. When Hettie subsequently found herself homeless, the Butter sisters – in appreciation – offered her their storeroom for a very small rent and a daily choice of pie from their ever-extending range. To say that Hettie snapped their paws off would be an understatement. Shortly after moving in, she befriended Tilly, and she too became a grateful lodger under the protective eye of Betty and Beryl, who could never bear to see a cat down on her luck.

As time passed, the four cats had become much more than landladies and tenants. Since the success of Hettie and Tilly's detective agency, they could easily have afforded a house of their own but they regarded the Butters as family and the feeling was mutual. As Tilly often said, they had everything they could ever want in their little room at the back of the bakery.

That little room was stifling when Hettie reached it. The heat of the day had made the space stuffy. She opened the window into the yard to let some fresh air in as Tilly bounded through the door waving the Butters' guidebook. 'Betty says we should try and find somewhere in Felixtoe, as there's lots to do even if it rains,' she said, settling down on her blanket. 'They had a few days out there last summer and rented a beach hut right by the sea. I wouldn't mind one of those.'

'But if we had a beach hut, we'd have to make our own dinners or eat out all the time,' Hettie pointed out. 'If we find a guest house, we'll have breakfast and dinner on tap. I feel like being waited on and having a proper holiday.'

'Good point,' agreed Tilly, 'so let's look at guest houses in Felixtoe, although I don't know how we'll get there.'

'That's not a problem. Bruiser says he'll take us and fetch us home. I suggested he could come with us, but he has other plans with Dolly.'

Hettie and Tilly shared a knowing look regarding Bruiser's amorous expectations before Tilly turned to the section on Felixtoe accommodation in the guidebook. 'There's a lovely bit here before you get to the guest houses,' she said. 'Shall I read it to you?' Hettie nodded and climbed up into her armchair to fill her catnip pipe while Tilly began.

'The old port of Felixtoe is on the Suffolk coast and offers a wide range of entertainment and pastimes for cats of all ages. Take a nostalgic walk along the promenade, venture onto the pier to try your luck on the fruit machines or dine out in one of the many seafood cafés. Take a carefree wander across the sandy beach or picnic in the sand dunes at Gobbles Point. No seaside is complete without a fair and Meakins Mewsments, situated only a spit from the beach, offers traditional family fun with exhilarating rides and sideshows to make the fur stand up on your head. Get spooked in the Ghost Train, try your luck in a Boxing Booth or sample the tasty delights from the fair's food stalls. Once you've had a holiday in Felixtoe, you'll never want to go anywhere else.'

'Not sure about that last bit,' said Hettie, blowing a perfect smoke ring. 'Do they mean you'll never want to go anywhere else because the holiday was so awful, or that you'll always want to go back *there*?'

Tilly giggled and pressed on with the guest-house entries. She read through several of them before choosing two that she liked the sound of to read out to Hettie. 'This one is at Gobbles Point. It's called Gobbles Rest, run by Mrs Shrimpton. Six double rooms, two with sea views, a day room for guests to relax in, a choice of English or continental breakfast and a hot evening meal from Mrs Shrimpton's extensive range of traditional family receipts. Gobbles Rest nestles in the sand dunes of the Gobbles Point Golf Course and...'

'Let me stop you there,' said Hettie. 'The last place I want to spend a week's holiday is in the middle of a bunker with a load of cats waving sticks and wearing plus fours. What's worse is they'll all be staying at Gobbles Rest and we'll have to sit down to breakfast and dinner with them. It's an abomination to have our countryside plundered by cats who want to spend their time dressing up in ridiculous outfits and knocking balls into holes.'

'That's a no to Gobbles Rest, then,' said Tilly, who was more than used to Hettie's rants. 'How about this one? Sandscratchers Villa, perched high above Felixtoe's sandy beach, in walking distance of the funfair, the famous Spa Pavilion Theatre and the pier. Miss Minnie Meakin offers ten rooms, six with sea views, a full English breakfast and a cooked evening meal. Miss Meakin is a member of the celebrated Meakin family, who have run the funfair on Felixtoe beach for over ten years.'

'Well, that's a possibility,' said Hettie. 'I like the bit about everything in walking distance. As long as the food is good, we should have plenty of time to do very little.'

'The picture looks really nice,' said Tilly, forcing the book under Hettie's nose. 'It's quite a big place and look at those verandas – really posh. I could sit and read a book up there watching the world go by.'

'I'd have thought you'd had enough of other cats' books this week. You should be making notes on writing your own book or just sitting and enjoying the sunshine. You'd better give Miss Meakin a ring in the morning to see if she has space for us, but we must get some sleep now. It's been a long day and we might have to be up early to pack for our holiday.'

Hettie knocked her catnip pipe out in the fireplace and curled up in her chair. Tilly was far too excited to sleep and pulled her notebook out from under the sideboard. She turned to a clean page, amid all the notes she'd taken on a recent murder case, and scribbled the heading 'Holiday List'. For the next hour, she filled the page with all the essentials and non-essentials needed for a week away before falling into a deep sleep, in which she dreamt of a giant seagull carrying her across the water to a deserted island and leaving her there with only a cream horn and a packet of salt and vinegar crisps to eat.

14

Chapter Three

The Butters' bread ovens woke Tilly at four-thirty. They were situated just outside the door to her and Hettie's room and it was a familiar, comforting sound as the sisters set to work creating their pies and pastries. The roar of the ovens was accompanied by Betty's renditions of a selection of songs from the shows, with Beryl joining in on the choruses as and when she felt like it. Today's performance included hits from *Oklahoma* and *My Fur Lady*, although the lyrics seemed to meld into one big new musical. Betty was managing to combine 'feeling pretty' with 'a little bit of luck' to the tune of 'Surrey with the Fringe on Top'. Beryl obviously preferred the chorus to 'Get Me to the Church on Time', as she added that to each new verse her sister sang. The medley would have horrified the town's musical theatre society but – as Betty and Beryl had never shown the slightest interest in joining – their secret performances in front of the bread ovens were only privately admired by anyone silly enough to be awake at that time of the morning.

Hettie slept on, conditioned into not waking up until the smell of freshly made toast reached her food-sensitive nose. Since Tilly had moved in, it was understood that she would make the breakfast and the first cup of milky tea, a task she happily embraced with both paws. The room she shared with Hettie was the first proper home she'd had and every day, no matter what time it began, was a sheer joy to her. To be in charge of her own toaster and kettle was tantamount to winning the football pools, although waking her friend was never an easy business, even armed with a fresh slice of toast.

Tilly checked the time on her Top Cat alarm clock. It was far too early to call Miss Meakin at Sandscratchers Villa, but she was too excited about the holiday to go back to sleep. The dawn chorus was now adding to the cacophony coming from the Butters and she realised that she would have to be patient until at least eight o'clock. She struggled from her blanket and tiptoed past Hettie's chair, then filled the kettle from their small sink and switched it on, preparing a mug for herself. There was an open packet of custard creams in the cupboard which she helped herself to, thinking that they would only go stale while she and Hettie were away on holiday.

The milky tea and most of the biscuits were dispatched quite quickly. Tilly brushed the crumbs out of her fur and picked up her notepad to read through her holiday list. It was extremely comprehensive and she could see at a glance that her excitement had run away with her. As they were currently experiencing a heatwave, she crossed out two of her best winter cardigans, a pair of woolly socks, Hettie's best velvet jacket, several paperbacks by Miss Crispy, which she'd read numerous times, her Cluedo board game and her Top Cat pyjamas, which she knew needed a wash after an accident with an egg custard slice. Satisfied that the remaining items would fit into her tartan shopper, she padded across to the filing cabinet, where she and Hettie kept their business correspondence and their clothes.

She pulled the bottom drawer open, keeping her claws crossed that some unknown, unseen fairy had miraculously washed and ironed their T-shirts, shorts and other casual wear, only to be disappointed. The contents of the drawer resembled an almost insurmountable tangle of clean and dirty clothes, all fighting each other for prominence. Winter cardigans grappled with business slacks; shirts wrapped their sleeves around vests and brightly coloured socks and scarves hid in trouser legs, waiting to be discovered.

Tilly blinked at the mess and decided to take decisive action. Starting with the T-shirts, she began to sniff each one and make two piles, one clean and one that needed washing. By the time she'd finished, the drawer was empty except for a well-sucked barley sugar covered in fluff which Tilly had hurriedly stowed away in her best cardigan pocket last autumn at a line-dancing class.

The pile of dirty washing exceeded the height of the clean clothes by far and Tilly knew there was only one solution: the Butters' twin-tub. She gathered the washing in her arms and blindly fumbled with the doorknob until it allowed her into the back hallway, where the bread ovens and preparation area were situated.

'My goodness!' said Betty, as the pile of laundry came towards her. 'Are you in there somewhere or has this washing grown legs?'

Tilly's muffled reply made Betty and Beryl laugh. She abandoned her unruly burden on the flagstone floor. 'I was wondering if I could use the twin-tub to freshen some clothes for our holiday,' she said, as Beryl forced a hot sausage roll into her paw from a tray she'd just pulled out of the oven.

'Mind that, as it's hot, and of course you can use the washer. Looks like two loads to me,' said Beryl. 'You need to separate your cottons from your woollies. You don't want your cardies to shrink, do you?'

'You eat your sausage roll and I'll sort the washing,' offered Betty, wiping her floury paws on her apron. 'This lot will be dry in no time if we get it on now. Did you find a place to stay in Felixtoe?'

'We found a guest house we liked the look of but it's too early to phone them so I thought I'd sort out the packing instead. I seem to have got behind with the washing, so I'm panicking a bit.'

'And I suppose Hettie is still in the land of dreams?' suggested Beryl. 'Here, wave this sausage roll under her nose – that might disturb her sufficiently to greet the day. Our old ma used to say the earlier you wake, the better the hake – that's on account of her spending her early years living in a fishing village near Blackpool.'

Tilly was a little confused by Beryl's family wisdom, but gratefully accepted a second sausage roll for Hettie and returned with them to her room, leaving Betty to do battle with the twin-tub. Hettie was still fast asleep in her chair, on her back with her legs in the air. Tilly filled the kettle again and this time prepared two mugs for tea. It was now just gone seven o'clock and although she thought she might be skating on thin ice she decided to wake her friend. If Minnie Meakin could accommodate them, there would be much to do before they went away and Hettie would have to pull her not insubstantial weight in helping to get them ready.

Tilly was the organiser in their partnership and Hettie liked it that way. She had never been much of a homemaker herself, preferring the open road in the days when she'd travelled with her band, playing music venues across the country. At that point in her life, home was where she laid her head and the only possessions she'd cared about were her guitar, a motley selection of stage clothes and several rather fine pairs of boots. Now, older but not particularly wiser, she was pleased to have a fireside to call her own and a good friend to share it with. Tilly rejoiced in making their little room a comfortable home for them both. The No. 2 Feline Detective Agency had been born out of an urgency to pay the Butters some rent; it was still a great surprise to Hettie that she and Tilly had made such a success of it, their reputation spreading far and wide as detectives who solved some of the most difficult, high-profile murder cases of the present day.

As Tilly approached Hettie's chair with one of the sausage rolls, the last thing on her mind was murder – but the prospect of waking Hettie Bagshot at this time of the morning was almost as risky. She jumped up on the arm of the chair and dangled the sausage roll in front of Hettie's nose. There was no immediate response, but she persevered and was eventually rewarded by twitching whiskers, swiftly followed by one eye opening. It took several seconds for Hettie to focus on the sausage roll in front of her face; when she did, Tilly withdrew it immediately as Hettie rolled over to a sitting position, rubbing the sleep from her eyes with her paws. 'Don't tell me it's morning already,' she grumbled. 'I dreamt I was being attacked by a giant sausage roll.'

Tilly giggled and pushed the pastry into Hettie's paw. 'Betty and Beryl sent it and I'm making us a milky tea to go with it.'

Hettie made her first decision of the day, choosing not to wait for the tea. She dispatched the sausage roll in three large bites, then glanced at Tilly's alarm clock. 'Does that really say a quarter past seven!' she exclaimed.

'I'm afraid it does,' said Tilly, placing a mug of milky tea on the arm of Hettie's chair. 'I've been up since five sorting out the clothes for our holiday. I thought you might like to wake up early so we can get ready together.'

'Well, you know what thought did, don't you?' snapped Hettie.

'No,' said Tilly, looking slightly bewildered.

Hettie blinked and took a sip of her tea. She realised that she had absolutely no idea what thought did either, and decided to adopt a rather more reasonable tone. 'I wonder if Millie Meakin will have room for us? It's a bit of a long shot at this time of year, especially with all this good weather we're having. I bet every cat worth his salt will be heading for the seaside.'

Tilly was still wondering what thought did as she nibbled her pastry from around the sausage meat, but had to agree that they should be prepared for a disappointment. She looked across at the clock and was pleased to see that it was just coming up to half past seven. 'Do you think it's too early to phone?' she said. 'And it's *Minnie* Meakin, not Millie.'

'We'll get her name right if she has a room for us. That sausage roll went nowhere – let's have some toast and a cheese triangle. By the time we've eaten that it'll be nearly eight and that's a perfectly reasonable time to call someone.'

Tilly poked the final piece of sausage meat into her mouth and set about loading the toaster and making two more cups of milky tea. By the time they'd finished their second breakfast, it was ten minutes to eight and Tilly crawled into the sideboard, where she kept useful things, and pulled out the telephone which lived there, nestled in cushions because Hettie hated to hear it ring. She dialled the number and waited for quite some time before the call was eventually answered by an out-of-breath female cat. Before she had a chance to speak, the cat on the other end of the phone took over completely.

'You are through to Sandscratchers Villa,' the voice said. 'Minnie Meakin speaking and I do apologise for keeping you waiting on account of my arbour playing up again this morning. My hotplates have been on the blink for days. The fried eggs just sit there looking back at me and the bacon keeps curling up and looking the other way entirely – and don't get me started on the sausages.' Tilly stifled a giggle and moved the receiver so that Hettie could listen in. 'I've been in such a fix I haven't even had time to fill up my compliments. I've got the family in number five crying out for brown sauce, the two in number four want a packed lunch so they can eat espresso while the weather is nice, and the cat in number three has just paddled sand all over my Axminster. I must admit, I'm run rugged this morning.'

There was a slight pause and Tilly grabbed her moment. 'Miss Meakin, my friend and I were hoping to come and stay with you for a week and we wondered if you had a double room available, perhaps with a sea view?'

There was a clatter on the other end of the phone before Minnie replied, 'Whoops! I do beg your pardon. I've just pulled the payphone off the wall. Are you still there?'

Tilly just about managed to squeak out a yes as she was laughing so much. Minnie Meakin carried on regardless, now grappling with her reservations book. 'I could do you number seven for a couple of days with a sea glimpse, and then move you to number six for the rest of your stay, which has an unbroken vestige of the beach and my brother Marlon's Fun Fur. Meakins Mewsments is famous, you know. I don't want to rush you, but I can smell burning and I don't want to have to call out the fire brocade for the second time this week.'

'Number seven and then number six would be lovely,' said Tilly. 'We could be with you today by late afternoon?'

'Champion,' said Minnie, 'and will you be wanting dinner? We're having cod balls in batter, pomme frights and peas, followed by banana custard.'

'Yes please,' said Tilly. 'Would you like to take my name for the booking?'

'No time for that – I've got to get my extinguisher out of the wardrobe in number five. I'll see you later.'

Minnie Meakin ended the call and Tilly replaced the receiver. 'Well, I hope we've chosen the right place to stay,' she said, hauling the telephone back into the sideboard. 'It all sounds a bit chaotic.'

'I think Minnie Meakin's guest house is just what we're looking for,' said Hettie, wiping the tears from her eyes. 'I think we're about to have a holiday we'll remember for some time if we survive the week without being poisoned by the food or burnt in our beds. If we're leaving today, I'd better go and let Bruiser know. We'll need to set off around lunchtime if we're to get to Felixtoe in time for Minnie Meakin's cod balls.'

'I'll make him a milky tea and some toast while you're getting dressed,' said Tilly, heading for the kettle. 'I should think the first load of washing will be ready to peg out by now.'

Perfectly on cue there was a knock on the door and Tilly opened it to Betty. 'There you are,' she said, forcing a laundry basket into Tilly's arms, 'that's your cottons washed and spun. Your woollens are on at the moment but you'll have to see to them yourselves as we need to get the bakery open – we've a queue down the high street. Good news is Turner Page just phoned to say the festival is off for today, so we won't be needed.'

'Why, what's happened?' asked Hettie, joining Tilly at the door.

'Well, it seems that Delerium Treemints stuck the samovar into the wrong plug socket during Ronnie Spot's late night jazz session in the main marquee. Fused all the lights and gave the keyboard player such a shock that his fur is still standing up on his head.

The library is out as well and several houses in Sheba Gardens – on the same ring main, evidently. Turner says he can't get an electrician till tomorrow at the earliest, so he's had to cancel all today's events including Judi Drench's drama workshop and the Spine Chillers formation dance group.'

'At least no one has been murdered this time,' observed Hettie. 'It sounds like Turner should just stick to running the library and forget about literary festivals altogether.'

'You're right there,' said Betty. 'Anyway, did you get your holiday booked?'

'We did,' said Tilly, 'and we're leaving at lunchtime for a week.'

'Then you'd better get your washing pegged out or it won't be dry. I'm going to help Beryl but we'll wave you off later.'

Betty disappeared through the door that led to the bakery and Tilly returned to the kettle and toaster to make breakfast for Bruiser. Keen now to help with the holiday preparations, Hettie pulled on some clothes and took the basket of wet laundry out into the backyard, where the sun was already warm. It was a rare thing for Hettie to do anything domestic but, after she'd pegged the washing onto the line, she stood back, feeling rather pleased with herself.

Bruiser was also pleased with his breakfast and spent the rest of the morning cleaning and polishing Miss Scarlet, ready for the journey to Felixtoe.

Chapter Four

By midday, Tilly was able to announce that they were ready for their holiday. She'd phoned Turner Page to cancel the remaining events she'd booked for at the literary festival, braved the post office – and more especially the town's cantankerous postmistress, Lavender Stamp – to draw out some spending money, and packed her tartan shopper with a selection of clean clothes. Hettie added her catnip pouch and pipe, a couple of crossword books and her best jelly sandals, as she hated the thought of sand between her toes.

Bruiser drove Miss Scarlet round to the front of the bakery and helped Tilly to load the shopper into the sidecar. The sun was now high in the sky and it was a beautiful hot summer's day, so it was decided that Tilly and the luggage should ride with the sidecar lid open and Hettie would climb up behind Bruiser on the bike.

Tilly was overexcited and eager to get going, but Betty and Beryl were also keen to offer some holiday wisdom and left their counter to dish it out. 'Now then,' said Beryl, 'Bruiser, you make sure to drive carefully – no taking those hairpin bends at high speeds. And you two, don't go getting involved in any murders. You have to remember you're on holiday. As our ma used to say, all work and no play makes a dull old cat.'

'And mind you don't get burnt in this sun,' added Betty, passing a bag of chocolate brownies to Tilly. 'You have these with a nice cup of milky tea when you get there. I assume you'll have tea-making facilities in your room? A holiday isn't a holiday without facilities, is it, sister?'

Beryl nodded in agreement, handing another paper bag to Tilly. 'And if your dinner isn't up to scratch, there's some savoury lattice tarts in there for your suppers. You can never tell with these guest houses. We once stayed in one in Scotland – rained all week and we got served lumpy porridge and mashed potatoes and peas every day, with not a hint of gravy. The old cat who ran the place said she was one of those vegetarian types but we caught her tucking into a pork chop with sausages, roast potatoes and all the trimmings the night before we left.'

'So what did you do?' asked Hettie, clambering up behind Bruiser.

'We threatened to report her to the Feline Tourist Board for Scotland,' said Betty, joining in. 'She gave us a full refund and two tickets to a Highland Fling evening at the Haggis and Neep Hotel. Turned out to be the cheapest holiday we've ever had. Not so good for the cat playing the bagpipes, though.'

'Why, what happened to him?' asked Tilly.

'Choked his silly self on his blow stick during "Scotland the Brave" and had to be airlifted to Glasgow,' said Beryl. 'We had to make do with the greatest hits of Jimmy Shand and his Band on the landlord's Dansette for the rest of the evening.'

There was now a queue forming at the bakery as the lunchtime rush was beginning. Betty and Beryl brought their holiday memories to a conclusion, said their goodbyes and returned to their counter. Bruiser kicked Miss Scarlet into life and the three cats sped off down the high street, heading for Felixtoe.

The ride was exhilarating. Bruiser negotiated the narrow Suffolk roads with great skill as Hettie and Tilly enjoyed the rolling countryside, the small villages and the grass verges teeming with wild summer flowers. By the time they reached their destination, they were hot and dusty and ready for a cold drink.

Sandscratchers Villa was perched high up on a cliff overlooking the sea and commanded views of the old docks to the right, the pier in the middle, and a seaside fairground to the left. The beach was heaving with families, all enjoying the sunshine while picnicking or paddling in the sea, which today was a bluey green. The villa itself was Victorian, painted white and in three gabled sections with wooden verandas that ran across the front of the first floor, offering spectacular views.

'This is perfect,' said Tilly, struggling out of the sidecar with her tartan shopper. 'It's got everything you could ever want from a seaside holiday.'

'Looks pretty smart,' said Bruiser, brushing the dust off his goggles with his paw. 'I wish I'd booked in fer the week but maybe I'll bring Dolly fer a day out when I come an' fetch you back.'

'That would be lovely,' said Tilly. 'We could all go to the funfair together.'

'It's certainly impressive from the outside,' said Hettie, appraising the villa. 'I suppose we'd better get our stuff up to our room, then cold drinks and ice creams are on me.'

Tilly clapped her paws at Hettie's sudden burst of generosity. Keen to wash the dust out of his throat, Bruiser took control of the tartan shopper as Hettie and Tilly headed for the entrance to the guest house, situated at the side of the building.

The smell of burning greeted them as they opened the door. A black-and-white-tiled hallway with several doors on either side culminated in a dark, well-polished mahogany staircase, leading to the upper floor. Further down the hall, there was clear evidence of Minnie Meakin's recent phone call with Tilly: the payphone box was still lying on the floor, where Minnie had inadvertently pulled it off the wall. Just inside the door was a hallstand with a mirror, sporting an assortment of umbrellas and walking sticks, a visitors' book, and an old-fashioned brass bell which Hettie picked up and decided to ring. No sooner had she put it down again than a door at the end of the hall burst open.

The cat who responded was small but filled the hall with a tornado-like energy as she approached her visitors, swathed in a seagull print, wraparound pinafore which reached almost to the floor. She wore red slippers with white ankle socks and was wielding a feather duster, which she flicked along the dado rails as she danced up the hallway. Squinting at her visitors through a pair of round spectacles perched on her nose, she offered her welcome speech. 'Come in, come in,' she began. 'Don't stand on celery – my home is your home. I am Minnie Meakin and you are most welcome to Sandscratchers Villa. You must be the folk for number seven going into number six, but I thought there was only two of you?'

Hettie opened her mouth to explain that Bruiser wouldn't be stopping, but Minnie continued, 'Not that it's a problem – I like to think my guests find me immoveable when it comes to squeezing in an extra cat. I have to say, you find me at sevens and sixes today as the arbour is playing up and my youngest brother Matty, who's my occasional odd job cat, has been purloined by my oldest brother Marlon to run the gallopers down at the fairground for the next week, as he's had to move my nephew Monty on to hooking ducks and balls in a bucket on a temporary basis. He wanted the dodgems, but that was completely out of the question. I said to Marlon, you need to insert your sincerity with those youngsters.'

Tilly was laughing so much that she was shaking and had to hide behind Hettie as Minnie Meakin continued to offer her malapropisms to her newly arrived guests. 'If you'd be kind enough to follow me, I'll get you settled in number seven. You'll have to manage with a camp bed for one of you, unless you'd rather toe to top. My twins are substandard and have been known to accommodate three cats at a time. I like to think that we cater for all punctualities.'

Minnie led the way, with Hettie and Tilly following on behind, leaving Bruiser to bump the tartan shopper up the stairs after them. Number seven was on the left at the end of a corridor. 'I have to creep up on this doorknob as it sometimes comes off in my paw,' said Minnie, passing the feather duster to Hettie to hold as she approached the problem. The knob turned without any issues and Minnie swung open the door to reveal a sunny, twin-bedded room with a window that looked out on the car park. 'Here's your keys – one for the room and the other for the front door, although I don't lock it until after ten. If you crane your neck, you can see the sea out of this window. It used to have a dual upset, but my mother – who had this as her bedroom – had the other window bricked up because she hated seeing that cold North Sea in the winter. That's why she had the ceiling painted, so she had something nice to look at. My sister Marmalade painted it. She does all the artwork for the fairground rides and my mother asked her to paint something along the lines of the Pristine Chapel in Rome. Of course, my mother is completely gymnastic now and mostly lives in the kitchen as she can't manage the stairs. I'd leave the window open if I were you, as we're prone to condemnation up here on the cliff. I'll leave your keys here on the sill.'

Hettie, Tilly and Bruiser stared up at the ceiling, taking in Marmalade's astonishing brightly coloured mural, looking every bit as if it had been rescued from a funfair rather than a copy of anything inspired by Michelangelo. There was a sudden clatter behind them as both the inside and outside doorknobs fell to the floor. Bruiser abandoned the tartan shopper and proceeded to put them back. 'I'll go and fetch me tools an' get this fixed if yer like – needs tightenin', that's all.'

Bruiser disappeared down the corridor before Minnie could respond to his kind offer, leaving her to continue with her family's history. 'Of course, in my father's day we didn't take in guests. We had the villa all to ourselves as we're such a big family – five boys and three girls, we were. He left the villa to me on the understatement that I would look after my mother, and Marlon, my oldest brother, got the dodgems and runs Meakins Mewsments down on the beach. That includes the funfair and the pier. The rest of the family run the rides and stalls down there. My father died in this room but we've stopped being sad about it as he was very old. He never really recovered after being run over by one of his own dodgems. Good Friday, it was, although not so good for him as it turned out.'

Tilly looked around the room nervously, hoping that Mr Meakin senior had left no traces of himself. Minnie was finally silent, perhaps recalling something from the past, which gave Hettie an opportunity to speak. 'So where do the rest of your family live now that this is a guest house?'

'They all live in wagons down on the beach. First thing Marlon did after he inherited the Mewsments was to set up a camp of showcat wagons where the old big dipper used to be that got carried away in the famous floods of '53, along with the prefabs. Marlon likes to keep things eccentric, like in the old days when showcats travelled across the land bringing in the fairs. We were all born on the road in wagons, but my father had an eye for a bargain and he bought the Mewsments and the villa off old Gervaise Smith, who was a Sandscratcher.'

'What is a Sandscratcher?' asked Tilly, who by now was totally fascinated by Minnie and her stories.

'A Sandscratcher is a showcat who doesn't want to travel any more and settles down to run a permanent fair, mostly at the seaside. We all became Sandscratchers when father bought the Mewsments here in Felixtoe. It was strange moving into a house but we got used to it and we all worked the fair in the season.

I wish I still did – this place is hard work and no constellation for the days when I ran the penny slots on the pier. My sister Mary runs them now. We call her Mary Queen of Slots.'

Hettie and Tilly laughed out loud as Bruiser arrived with his toolbox – which he kept in the boot of Miss Scarlet's sidecar for emergencies – along with the two paper bags that the Butters had given them as they left. He passed the bags to Tilly for safekeeping in case the dinners at the villa weren't up to much. In seconds, the knobs were screwed and tightened back onto the door, much to the delight of Minnie who showed her appreciation by offering a whole list of jobs around the villa. 'I'm sure you won't mind me asking,' she said, 'but could you work your magic on the payphone downstairs? The TV plug in the guest lounge needs a fuse, the light bulb in number four keeps blowing for no good reason, and the arbour has got a blockage somewhere and keeps puffing out smoke at my mother, who insists on sitting right in front of it, even in a heatwave. She's frightened of getting frostbite, you see, and she's never liked the cold. The wagons were much cosier than this big old place.'

Bruiser was somewhat bemused by Minnie's maintenance requirements but took it in good heart. 'Right'o,' he said, putting his screwdriver back into his toolbox. 'I'll start with yer payphone.'

Minnie wasted no time in ushering Bruiser down the stairs, leaving Hettie and Tilly to settle in to their holiday accommodation. As Betty had suggested, the room had tea-making facilities and Tilly pounced on them, filling the kettle at a small sink in the corner of the room and preparing the two mugs set out on a tray with tea bags and milk from a jug stamped with the words 'Sandscratchers Villa'. The mugs matched the milk jug and left Minnie Meakin's guests in no doubt about where they were staying.

While Tilly was making the tea, Hettie busied herself in unpacking the tartan shopper. 'We've enough clothes here for the whole summer,' she pointed out, bundling them into a chest of drawers between the twin beds. 'They'll only end up covered in sand, ice cream and goodness knows what else.'

'Well, that's what holidays are all about, aren't they?' Tilly reasoned. 'If we went home with all our T-shirts clean it would look like we hadn't had a good time, but we'll have to keep some things nice for when we go downstairs for breakfast and dinner – it's a bit posh here.'

'I just hope the rest of the guests keep themselves to themselves,' said Hettie, helping herself to a brownie to go with her tea. 'The trouble with staying in a guest house is you're expected to mingle at meal times and the thought of watching TV with a bunch of cats we don't know makes my blood run cold. And there might be kittens, heaven forbid, climbing all over the place, screeching with excitement and being allowed to stay up long after their bedtime. Nasty little paws into everything while their parents turn a blind eye because they're on holiday, too. Discipline goes straight out the window, with no thought for the rest of us who just want a few days' peace and quiet.'

Tilly clawed a brownie out of the bag and nibbled on it thoughtfully, choosing not to respond to Hettie's rant. She was more than used to her friend's views on life in general and after several years of being together she felt completely qualified to deal with them. Hettie had a heart of gold, but made sure that very few cats knew about it. Her bluster was exactly that, an outward face that challenged the irritations of life whilst inwardly mourning the injustices dealt to those too weary or vulnerable to fight back. It was what Tilly admired about her, and what made Hettie Bagshot a wonderful friend and a very fine detective.

'Poor Bruiser,' said Tilly, deciding to move Hettie on from her dissertation on family seaside holidays. 'He shouldn't be so clever with his paws. He always gets stuck with fixing things and he's too kind to say no.'

'If Minnie Meakin has her way, he'll be staying for the rest of the season,' said Hettie. 'She obviously has plenty of jobs for him – this place must be like the Forth Bridge.'

'Why?' asked Tilly, looking confused.

'It's a really long bridge, and no sooner do the cats who paint it finish than they have to go back and start again because it takes such a long time,' explained Hettie.

'Why don't they start from either end and meet in the middle?' suggested Tilly as Bruiser came back into the room, meaning her question went unanswered.

'If yer don't mind, I think I'll 'ave ta stay tonight. Miss Meakin 'as found a few more jobs and I'm still tryin' to unblock 'er Aga. I can't understand what she's tellin' me 'arf the time as she's mixin' 'er words up. I don't know whether to laugh or cry when she starts, and 'er mother is worse – she's guardin' that stove as if 'er life depended on it.'

'It would be lovely if you stayed,' said Tilly. 'Hettie and I can share and you can have that bed to yourself, and we can all have dinner together. It's cod balls and chips, evidently.'

'It won't be if I don't get on with sortin' the Aga. It's puffin' out blue smoke at the moment.'

'Take one of these brownies with you,' said Tilly. 'They're really nice and you look like you need something sweet. If the cod balls are off, we could find some fish and chips later.'

'Righto,' said Bruiser. 'Miss Meakin has already mentioned fish and chips as a "consistency" plan!'

Chapter Five

The sun was still high in the sky and Hettie and Tilly's room was a little oppressive with the heat. The two cats changed into their favourite T-shirts and left the villa to do a recce of the immediate area. The beach was quieter than when they had arrived, with many families wending their way back to their accommodation. Long straggling lines of kittens carrying buckets full of shells, their fur matted with sand and salt water, padded after their parents. Some of the young cats were still wearing their rubber rings or dragging fish-shaped lilos, tired and cross at being forced away from the sandcastles they'd spent the day creating.

Elderly cats in sun hats were sitting on brightly coloured benches all along the promenade, some with ice creams and others just staring out to sea. There was an air of finality to the day as the cat who ran the donkey rides ushered his herd off the beach with the promise of apples and carrots and a straw-strewn stable for the night. The donkeys brayed and clopped along the promenade, pleased to be heading homeward, their reins jingling as they went.

The beach was littered with empty deckchairs, several abandoned picnic rugs and plastic bags full of rubbish, left behind by those who'd enjoyed their day and had given no thought to clearing up. 'What an awful mess,' said Tilly, choosing a green-and-yellow-striped deckchair to sit in. 'You'd think after a lovely day at the beach they'd take their rubbish home instead of spoiling the view for everyone else. There's broken bottles, half-eaten sandwiches, swimsuits and lots of socks, for some reason.'

'Well, that's just typical of your average seaside holidaymaker,' said Hettie. 'They're paying for the privilege of doing whatever they like for a week, including littering the beach and letting their kittens run wild. It's probably much nicer here in the winter, but we need to make the most of it. There's a kiosk over there and I think I promised you an ice cream.'

'Oh, yes please!' said Tilly. 'A Mister Whippy with a flake would be lovely.'

Hettie left Tilly sitting in her deckchair and made her way back onto the promenade, where there was a sizeable queue outside the ice cream kiosk. The cat serving took far longer than was necessary with each customer and it reminded Hettie of Lavender Stamp back in the town. Lavender took her time on purpose when serving customers in her post office because she liked making cats wait; it gave her the ultimate power and control over them.

Eventually it was Hettie's turn. She ordered two ninety-nines and waited patiently while the cat in the kiosk very slowly filled the cones with soft whipped ice cream from her machine, then even more slowly inserted two chocolate flakes, as if she were defusing a bomb. It seemed to Hettie that the cat had created some sort of art form out of dispensing ice creams and she was almost tempted to give her a round of applause, but she felt for the never-ending queue behind her and paid up instead of wasting any more time.

Hettie made her way back to Tilly as the sun began to melt the ice creams, dripping down the cones and onto her paws. A seagull offered to help by swooping low over her head ready to relieve her of her sticky burden but she was swift in her response and hissed at the bird, sending it high into the sky, but not before it had left a small present on her T-shirt.

'It's like taking your life in your own bloody paws!' she said, slumping down on a deckchair next to Tilly and passing her an ice cream. 'You'd better get on with this while there's some left, and watch out for the seagulls.'

There was much licking and sucking for several minutes as the two cats demolished their ice creams, much to the disappointment of the birds hovering overhead. As expected, Tilly's clean T-shirt had come off rather badly in the process and Hettie's hadn't escaped entirely. 'Oh dear,' said Hettie, 'we'd better make a move – that deckchair attendant is heading straight for us and he looks like he's on a mission.'

They left their deckchairs and scampered across the sand to the shoreline, where they washed their paws in the incoming tide. 'That must be the funfair,' said Tilly, looking to her left and shielding her eyes from the sun. 'It was so interesting what Minnie said about her family. I bet her mother's a character. I hope we get to meet her.'

'Judging by the ceiling in her old bedroom, I should think she's an absolute riot,' said Hettie, 'and as for Minnie, words fail me. She's definitely not your average seaside landlady.'

'It's just so funny when she gets her words mixed up. What's worse is she doesn't even know she's doing it.'

'I can only imagine what the rest of the family are like, and there seem to be a lot of "M"s involved.'

'What do you mean?' asked Tilly, flicking a squadron of sand flies away with her paw as they walked in the direction of the fair.

'Well, just think about it. We've got Minnie Meakin, and she's mentioned Marlon, Monty, Matty, Mary and Marmalade – all part of the family, and they work for Meakins Mewsments. I'm willing to bet that the other members of the Meakin clan have names beginning with "M", too.'

Tilly giggled at Hettie's observations. 'You're right,' she said. 'It hadn't occurred to me. I wonder what her mother is called and the rest of her brothers?'

'I dare say we'll find out during our stay. Minnie doesn't hold back when it comes to her family. She'd make a perfect end-of-pier afternoon stand-up for pensioner cats. With her command of the English "luggage", she'd have them rolling in the aisles.'

Hettie and Tilly laughed their way towards the funfair, arriving just as the lights over the entrance arch lit up and proclaimed that they were now entering Meakins Mewsments. There was still plenty of daylight, but the lights were obviously switched on at this time of day to attract an early evening clientele of young kittens and their parents, before the older cats descended as darkness fell to enjoy the more extreme rides that the fair had to offer.

'It's a bit quiet at the moment,' said Tilly, as she watched two small kittens being helped to the top of a miniature double-decker bus on a small carousel. There were no other takers for the ride and the cat in charge collected the money and made his way to the centre of the carousel, pulling a lever to set it in motion. The kittens screamed with delight as their parents looked on, waving their paws as the infants came round to where they were standing, over and over again until the ride slowed to a standstill and the kittens clambered off, a little unsteady and slightly dizzy from their treat.

Hettie and Tilly moved on through the fair, taking in the different rides and sideshows. The food stalls seemed to be more popular at this time of day, with families queuing for hot dogs, toffee apples and giant balls of candyfloss on sticks. Tilly was tempted by the candyfloss but decided against it as she didn't want to spoil her dinner – much to Hettie's relief; the thought of Tilly and candyfloss was quite possibly a combination forged in hell.

'I'm not sure that I actually like candyfloss,' Tilly reflected, as a kitten in front of them wailed while its mother tried to tease the sticky, gooey mess out of her wilful daughter's fur.

'I'd steer clear if I were you,' said Hettie, appreciating the smell of hot dogs on the air. 'I tried it once but it was just like chewing cotton wool. It's clever the way they spin the sugar, but give me a bag of toffee nuts any day.'

'It would be nice if we could come back later when it gets dark,' Tilly suggested. 'Half the rides aren't open yet and I'm sure Bruiser would like to come with us. I got Lavender Stamp to give me some pennies in our holiday money to spend at the fair.'

'How on earth did you manage that?' asked Hettie. 'It's not like her to be that obliging.'

'I asked her for notes only so she emptied her change drawer just to be nasty and took ages to count it out. I thanked her and ran before she changed her mind. I've got a lovely big bag of pennies in my tartan shopper, so we can play the slots as well.'

'I'm impressed,' said Hettie, 'but we'd better be making tracks back to the villa. I'm starving. I hope Bruiser has fixed the Aga by now. We'll come back here later when the fair's in full swing.'

The two cats made their way out of the fair and across the sand. As they were about to climb up the path to the villa, a cat dressed in a cowboy outfit leapt in front of them and forced a flyer into Hettie's paw. The cat then proceeded to twirl two silver cap-guns on his claws, eventually firing them as he pointed them up into the air, making Tilly jump.

'You two look like you're in need of a great night out,' the cowboy said, replacing his guns in holsters on a belt slung round his waist. 'Get yourselves over to the Marine Car Park at Gobbles Point for Wilt Dinsney's Wild West Show. It's the greatest show on earth, featuring Wild Bill Hiccup, Buffalo Lill, Marshall Wyatt Twerp and Crazy Paws, descended from Chief Sitting Bill. Quick on the draw, you'll shout for more.'

'But not at the moment,' Hettie pointed out. 'Just now we're heading back for dinner, but thank you for your flyer.'

Hettie and Tilly quickened their pace up the path, leaving the cowboy a little dejected. Seconds later they heard his cap-guns fire again at another unsuspecting holidaymaker as he continued to drum up custom for the Wild West show.

Chapter Six

Sandscratchers Villa seemed fairly peaceful when Hettie and Tilly arrived back and there was definitely a smell of fish as they entered the hallway and climbed the stairs to their room. Hettie regarded this as something positive as far as dinner was concerned and Bruiser – who was waiting for them – was able to confirm that the giant ball of wool he had removed from the Aga had left the stove in full working order.

'I reckon the old cat stuck it in the flue,' he explained. 'The ball of wool was in a mess but it looked like the same stuff she was knittin' with. Miss Meakin said it wasn't the first time she'd done it.'

'Did you manage all the other jobs she'd found for you?' asked Tilly.

'Yep, although this place needs more than a few odd jobs. It's in a bit of a state if yer ask me. A lick of paint would cheer things up and there isn't a chair or table in that lounge that 'asn't been propped up with a beer mat or a block of wood. I reckon Miss Meakin 'as fallen on 'ard times. It's a big old place ta run on yer own.'

'It's a pity she can't get more help from the rest of the family,' suggested Hettie. 'Heaven knows there's enough of them. We've just had a wander through the fairground and it was almost deserted, which was a surprise for this time of year. Maybe the Meakins are all going through a rough patch.'

'We thought we'd go back to the fair after dinner if you fancy coming with us?' said Tilly. 'That's if there's going to be any dinner?'

'Well, when I left the kitchin, old Mrs Meakin was dippin' cod balls in flour, so I think we got 'opes. Miss Meakin was entertainin' one of 'er guests at the kitchin table. Giant of a cat 'e is, dressed like one of them cowboys off the telly. She cut 'im the biggest slice of Battenberg an' 'e swallowed it all in one go. She's sweet on 'im, I reckon.'

'Ooh, I wonder if he's with the Wild West show?' suggested Tilly. 'Look – we met a cowboy just now and he gave us this flyer all about it. It sounds quite exciting.'

'Could be,' said Bruiser, looking at the line-up on the small poster. 'Come ta think of it, Miss Meakin was callin 'im Wilt, so maybe it's 'is show.'

Hettie was hungry and found all the talk about Minnie Meakin's cowboy a little irritating. 'I think we should go down to the lounge and look like we're expecting to be fed,' she said. 'I assume there's a dining room close by. If we're planning on going to the fair, I'll need a proper dinner first.'

Tilly giggled and pointed a claw at Hettie's T-shirt. 'If we're going down to dinner, I think you'd better change. It's hard to tell what is seagull and what is ice cream.'

Hettie looked down at the mess on her shirt, then across at Tilly's. 'I think you need a clean one too – and for some reason you've got ice cream on both your ears.'

The three cats laughed and Tilly ran some warm water into the sink to wash her paws and face, paying special attention to her ears, while Hettie pulled two more T-shirts out of the drawer for them to change into.

'I'll see yer down there,' said Bruiser. 'Now the phone's back on the wall, I'd better give the Butters a ring an' tell 'em I'm stoppin' over fer tonight, or else they'll be worried when I don't turn up.'

Bruiser left Hettie and Tilly to tidy themselves, ready to face their fellow guests for the evening meal. There were several cats ahead of him at the payphone so he waited patiently to put his call through to the Butters, who were pleased that they had all arrived safely. He was just putting the receiver down when Hettie and Tilly joined him, looking much more presentable. Bruiser led them into the lounge, where several kittens were bouncing up and down on a sofa, watching a cartoon on the television. The sound was full up – on the TV and also on the kittens – and Tilly could feel Hettie tensing as they walked through the door.

'Maybe we should have booked somewhere with room service,' she said, more to herself than to Hettie, sensing that communal family get-togethers were as far from her friend's idea of a holiday as the moon.

Hettie took matters into her own paws, striding across to the television and switching it off. The kittens screamed their disapproval, just as Minnie Meakin entered the room followed by a large cat in full cowboy gear wearing a Stetson. The kittens were silenced immediately when the cat approached them and drew a toy gun out of the holster on his belt, playfully pretending to fire it at them. 'Bang!' he said, making the kittens giggle nervously. 'You'd better pipe down or you'll scare the horses and no cowboy wants his horse frightened.'

The kittens, now wide-eyed, looked towards the door, expecting a horse to enter, but Minnie stole the moment by clapping her paws together and announcing that dinner was served in the dining room. The kittens bounced off the sofa and through the door, leaving Minnie to introduce the cowboy to Hettie and Tilly.

'This lovely cat is the one and only Mr Wilt Dinsney,' she began. 'King of the Wild West show and a regular guest here at Sandscratchers. I would go as far to say that he is my financier and we hope to marry at the end of the season.'

Wilt Dinsney looked a little confused for a moment at Minnie's description of their relationship, then shook

Hettie and Tilly's paws and nodded to Bruiser, whom he had already met in the kitchen. 'Pleased to meet you, folks,' he said in a pronounced American drawl, 'and what brings you to Felixtoe?'

'We're on holiday,' said Hettie. 'It's the first break we've had in ages.'

'You've chosen well with this gal of mine – she runs the best hotel in town. So what do you guys do for a living?'

'We run The No. 2 Feline Detective Agency,' said Tilly, puffing her chest out proudly. 'We solve murders and that sort of thing.'

'Say, that's a real humdinger of a profession,' said Wilt. 'I don't think I've ever met a bunch of real gumshoes before. We should talk some more while you're here. I just love hearing about English murders – they're much more interesting than the ones we have in the States. You've got Dr Crippen and Jake the Nipper – such great stories, although Crippen was a Yankie, of course.'

'We've just met one of your cowboys who gave us a flyer for your shows,' said Tilly. 'I suppose some of the old cowboys were famous murderers too, in America?'

'Sure were, but the Wild West was all about land grabbing and gunfights and prospecting for gold – not really the same as serial killers creeping round Victorian London. That cowboy you just met is Billy the Kit. I send him out to fire up cats for the show. He comes from a long line of gunslinging outlaws. His family goes back to the first Billy the Kit, who was sentenced to hang back in 1881 but escaped and was shot dead.'

Tilly was fascinated and about to ask more questions when Minnie intervened, 'Now then, Wilt, you're holding up the dinner. If you'd all like to come through to the dining room, I'll get you seated. My cod balls won't wait much longer now the arbour is working, thanks to Bruiser here.'

Bruiser beamed, showing a severe lack of teeth, and Minnie led them through to the dining room across the corridor from the lounge. The kittens, now wearing bibs, were seated at a table in one of the bay windows, next to their parents. There was an elderly couple reading newspapers at a table for two and another table of four middle-aged female cats, laughing loudly and looking like they may have stopped off for more than one lager and lime on their way back from the beach. Minnie bustled off into her kitchen, leaving her guests to find a seat.

There was an empty table laid up for four in the other bay window and Hettie, Tilly and Bruiser made a beeline for it. Unfortunately, so did Wilt Dinsney. 'Hope you folks don't mind me muscling in, but I got a show in an hour so I need to grab a quick bite from Minnie's chuck wagon.'

There was no time to argue, as Minnie returned almost immediately with a plate laden with a stack of cod balls in batter, peas and a mountain of French fries, which she placed in front of Wilt, much to the annoyance of the rest of the guests who had all arrived before him. The cowboy tucked a serviette into the front of his checked shirt, squirted nearly a whole bottle of tomato sauce on his dinner and began to eat at great speed, only stopping occasionally to offer a grunt of satisfaction.

Meanwhile Minnie returned to her kitchen and emerged minutes later with a tray of much smaller dinners which she distributed to the family in the bay window. The four female cats were next to be served, then the elderly couple, followed by Hettie, Tilly and Bruiser; the size of these dinners was bordering on derisory compared with the portions heaped on Wilt's plate, but no one complained and all agreed that the cod balls were excellent.

Hettie was grateful that there was very little time for conversation, as Wilt's mouth was fully occupied. No sooner had he pushed his empty, licked-clean plate away from him than Minnie replaced it with a bowl full of banana custard. The cat responded immediately by spooning the pudding into his mouth and noisily scraping up every trace as Minnie had served the rest of her guests with their desserts.

'Well, I must saddle up and mosey on out to Gobbles Point for tonight's show,' said Wilt, wiping his whiskers and abandoning his serviette on the table. 'It's been good sharing a table with you guys. It's a sell-out tonight but have these tickets for tomorrow's show. You won't be disappointed.'

He pulled three tickets out of the top pocket of his waistcoat and pushed them across to Hettie. 'That's really kind of you,' she said, trying to be appreciative, and was about to add that they would only need two tickets when Minnie entered the dining room to collect the empty dishes. Wilt stood up and swept Minnie off her feet, twirling her round like a ragdoll.

'Ain't she just the best cook in town,' he boomed. The guests, taken a little by surprise, all responded with varying degrees of enthusiasm as the cowboy brought Minnie down with a bump on her Axminster and left the dining room, removing his Stetson and offering an exaggerated bow.

'Oh, he is a one,' Minnie said, retying the wraparound apron that had come a little adrift. 'Life and soul of the season, his Wild West show – as well as Meakins Mewsments, obviously. Wouldn't want to cast nasturtiums on the family business, would I? My brother Marlon would have my guts for gaiters if I did that.'

The diners laughed nervously and all stood as one to go about their business: the four female cats headed out into the evening in search of a few cocktails before turning in; the family in the window retired to their room to put the kittens to bed; and the elderly couple wandered off into the lounge to watch some TV and finish a jigsaw they'd started earlier.

Chapter Seven

Hettie, Tilly and Bruiser returned to their room to collect Tilly's bag of pennies, leaving Minnie laying up the tables for breakfast.

'That Wilt Dinsney reminds me of Desperate Dan from one of my comics,' said Tilly, scrabbling to the bottom of her tartan shopper for the coins. 'He eats huge pies and he's sort of a cowboy.'

'You're right there about him being like a character from a comic,' said Hettie. 'Larger than life, loud and just a tiny bit embarrassing.'

'This Wild West show sounds good,' said Bruiser, reading the flyer. 'They got a real good line-up of gun-slingers. I've even 'eard of some of 'em, and they've got a proper American Indian called Crazy Paws. It says 'e's descended from Chief Sittin' Bill. That's quite somethin' – 'e defeated General Custard at the battle of Little Bigcat in 1876.'

'Does it say all that on the flyer,' Hettie asked, looking over Bruiser's shoulder, 'or is it one of your stored-up nuggets of encyclopaedic knowledge?'

'Actually, it was in me *Bikers' Monthly* a while back,' said Bruiser. 'It was an article on how indigenous Americans now ride motorbikes rather than 'orses. It went on ta talk about all the different tribes and the famous Chiefs and the wars they fought. Sittin' Bill was huge in North American 'istory.'

'You never cease to amaze me,' said Hettie. 'You are a walking mine of information.'

Bruiser grinned, enjoying the compliment. 'What does indignuss mean?' asked Tilly, reaching for her notepad from the shopper. 'I need to write that down as I like the sound of it.'

Hettie laughed. 'You're beginning to sound like Minnie Meakin. It's indigenous, which means cats who are native to where they live and have been there long before anyone else. I-N-D-I-G-E-N-O-U-S.' Tilly jotted the word down on a clean page of her notepad as Hettie spelt it out for her. 'I think we'll have to go to this Wild West extravaganza tomorrow night,' she suggested. 'I can't wait to see Buffalo Lill. She's a dead-eye shot with a rifle, according to this.'

'Ooh how exciting!' said Tilly. 'This is turning into the best holiday ever. Bruiser, are you sure you can't stay on for another night to use the third ticket?'

'If you two don't mind, I'd really like to,' said Bruiser. 'I'll 'ave ta give the Butters an' Dolly a ring ta say what I'm doin', but I wouldn't want ta miss seein' a show like that. Accordin' to me map, this Gobbles Point is quite a way along the coast. I noticed that when I was plannin' me route ta get 'ere, so we could take Miss Scarlet.'

Tilly clapped her paws, delighted that Bruiser would be staying for another night and thrilled to be having a trip out in Miss Scarlet, which was one of her favourite things to do. Hettie moved over to the window and looked out at the fair in the distance. 'It's getting dark. We should get going if you want to spend some of those pennies.'

'I think I'd better share them out,' said Tilly, giving a pawful each to Hettie and Bruiser. 'If I keep them all, they might fall out of my pocket on one of the rides.'

The three friends left the villa and made their way across the beach to the fair, which had now become quite magical as darkness fell: the music and flashing lights; the sound of humming generators that powered the rides; and the smell of sweets, roasted nuts, fish and chips, seafood and mushy peas melding together and permeating the air. It was the soundtrack of youth, a moment in time that no young cat would forget and an experience that they would repeat with their own kittens in later years.

'I just don't know where to start,' said Tilly, holding her pennies tightly in one of her paws. 'I can't decide whether I want a ride or a game first. There's so much to choose from.'

'Why don't we have a wander and decide after we've seen everything?' suggested Hettie. 'If you spend your pennies now you might regret missing something later.'

Tilly wasn't convinced that this was the best idea, as she was keen to have a go on as many rides as possible and it was the dodgems that beckoned first. Leaving Hettie and Bruiser to follow after her, she made her way through the crowds of cats and joined the queue for one of the brightly coloured bumper cars. The dodgems were flying across a shiny metal surface, powered by a pole of electricity fixed to the back of each car. The pole gave off sparks, which added to the excitement, as cats – many driving for the first time – crashed and bumped each other, overseen by a showcat who leapt from one car to another, disentangling the multiple pile-ups.

'That cat must be Marlon Meakin himself,' said Hettie, as she and Bruiser joined the queue behind Tilly. 'Minnie said he ran the dodgems. He even looks like her, except for the apron and white socks.'

Tilly giggled. The showcat riding the dodgems was older than his sister and wore a crisp white shirt, waist-coat and breeches tucked in red socks, with a jaunty neckerchief to match. He wore a money belt around his waist for collecting the fares. The dodgems began to slow down as the cars bunched up at one end of the ride and there was a mad panic as the cats in the queue rushed forward to claim one, giving the previ-ous occupants very little time to vacate their dodgem. Hettie, Tilly and Bruiser moved to the front of the queue but there were no cars left. 'At least we stand a good chance next time,' said Hettie, as the cars started to move again and Marlon swung from one pole to another, collecting money from his new customers.

Five minutes later, the rush for cars started again but this time Hettie, Tilly and Bruiser were ahead of the field. Tilly leapt into a blue car and Bruiser and Hettie chose red. Once she'd made herself comfortable, Tilly realised that she had no idea how to drive and, as all the dodgems around her began to move, she was stranded in the middle. Hettie and Bruiser were already racing round, bumping into each other, but Tilly's car did nothing and she began to get upset.

It was Marlon who came to her rescue, swinging into the car and sitting beside her. 'Come on my little darling,' he said. 'Let's get you moving. Push your foot down on the accelerator there.' Tilly did as she was told and the car began to move. 'That's it. Now off you go and don't forget to steer at the same time and keep your paws inside the car.' Marlon left Tilly to her first driving experience and leapt onto another dodgem behind.

Tilly found herself shrieking with excitement as the car reacted to the pressure from her foot. Being in control was a wonderful feeling. She looked for Hettie and Bruiser in the mêlée of cars and found them heading straight for her. She swerved to avoid them, but got bumped by a bright yellow car, pushing her to the side and boxing her in. Marlon came to the rescue once again, sorting out the cars around her and clearing the way for her to put her foot down again. This time, now that she was beginning to get the hang of the steering wheel, she managed to increase her speed and avoided several tricky situations, even managing to bump Hettie before the cars began to slow down as the ride finally came to an end.

Hettie and Bruiser jumped out of their cars as the mad rush of new customers engulfed them, but Tilly seemed to be going nowhere and stubbornly gripped the steering wheel of her blue car. 'I'm going round again!' she shouted to Hettie and Bruiser. 'I'm just starting to get the hang of it.'

Bruiser decided to try his luck on the rifle range, arranging to meet up later. Hettie waited by the dodgems for Tilly to finish her ride, but, when the cars came to a standstill once more, she announced that she was having one more go.

There was a penny rolling stall next to the dodgems and Hettie decided to try her luck while she was waiting for Tilly finally to give up the blue car. The first few pennies she rolled landed outside the squares, but then she got a ten and a six, and before she knew it she'd doubled her money. The cat running the stall reluctantly pushed Hettie's winnings across to her as Tilly joined her, waving goodbye to Marlon, who had clearly taken a shine to her.

'Did you win?' asked Tilly.

'I did, which is just as well, as I bet you're running out of funds after three goes on Marlon's dodgems.'

'Actually, he didn't charge me for the first go and he said if I come back tomorrow I can have another free one.'

'I bet he did,' said Hettie, 'but we're going to Wilt Dinsney's Wild West Show tomorrow, so Marlon will be disappointed. What shall we do next – a ride or a game?'

'I'd quite like a go on the ghost train if it's not too frightening. I saw it this afternoon. I think it's over there, next to the swing boats.'

Before Hettie could respond, Tilly was making her way towards the attraction and Hettie followed, beginning to feel like a long-suffering parent who stood and watched as their infant had the time of its life. She never begrudged Tilly her happiness: life had been cruel to her in her early years and it was refreshing to have a friend who could find joy in the simplest of pleasures.

The ghost train didn't appear to be as popular as the dodgems. There was no queue, and the three wagons lined up on the track at the beginning of the ride were all empty except for the one at the back, which had a gory collection of life-sized skeletons, vampires and witch dolls. One of the vampire cats was holding his head under his arm and there was another creature heavily bandaged with its paws crossed across its chest. 'I hope we don't meet anything like those creatures in there,' said Tilly, waving her paw at the entrance to the ride.

'Let's find out,' said Hettie. 'I'll treat you with my winnings.'

The two cats clambered into the first wagon and waited. At this point, a showcat emerged from a brightly painted kiosk to collect the money and Hettie and Tilly wondered if he was another member of the Meakin family. He held his paw out, offered a beaming smile and wished them luck as their train began to move.

The train smashed through a pair of double doors and Hettie and Tilly found themselves in total darkness. It rattled on and suddenly there was an ear-splitting siren, followed by a tangle of something hitting their faces as a giant glowing spider revealed itself right in front of them. Hettie was tempted to scream but Tilly did it for her as the spider receded, only to be replaced by a bandaged cat which sat upright in a coffin, wailing as they went past.

By now, Tilly was clinging to Hettie, allowing her claws to dig into her arm. Hettie winced as a green skull and paws loomed out of the dark, its eyes red and its tongue hanging out of the side of its mouth. Next came another coffin, full of rats seemingly eating a baby kitten, which let out a blood-curdling screech as the train moved on. There was a slight lull in the horror before a giant red devil with horns and bulging yellow eyes loomed out of the darkness and danced in front of them. It seemed to fall under the train and Hettie and Tilly both turned round, expecting to see it flattened on the track, but there was only darkness and no sign of anything behind them. Even Hettie was hoping that the ride would soon be over, but there were a few more tricks still to come.

The walls on either side of the track were suddenly illuminated and seemingly running with blood. Skulls stared out at them on either side, their jaws rattling, their eyes flashing red as the train flew by. Suddenly the vehicle stopped and Hettie and Tilly thought it had broken down. There was absolute silence in the pitch black, which seemed to go on for a very long time until they were aware of a rasping sound getting closer and closer. They could feel a hot breath on their faces but could see nothing until a ghost in a white shroud reared up in front of them, rattling chains that hung around its neck. Hettie nearly revisited her cod balls and Tilly slipped to the floor of the train, bury-ing her head in her paws. The train started to move again, but Tilly refused to sit back on her seat and so missed the final trick. Hettie was just recovering from the ghost when a giant cat dressed in rags swung into view on the end of a noose, the head lolling to one side, the eyes bulging. Fleetingly, it brought back memories of one of their murder cases, but Hettie had no time to dwell on it as the train burst through another set of double doors out into the glare of the fairground.

'How was that?' the showcat asked as Hettie and Tilly clambered out of the train.

Tilly was still in shock and just blinked at him but Hettie was happy to offer her review. 'Actually, it was horribly realistic,' she said. 'How long did it take you to put that lot together?'

The showcat smiled. 'It evolves all the time, depending on what's popular. In my dad's day, it was just white sheets, rattling chains and headless cats. My sister Mary made some scary changes when she ran the ghost train for a bit, but I have to keep up with all the horror movies these days.'

'So you are from the Meakin family?' Hettie asked.

'Yes, of course – only Meakins own the rides. I'm Marty Meakin. Why do you ask?'

'It's just that we're staying at Sandscratchers Villa and Minnie Meakin was telling us all about her family.'

'That's my big sister up at Sandscratchers. There's nothing she doesn't know about the family and she keeps a nice place up there, although give me a wagon any day. Anyway. I best get on. I've got some fares to collect.'

Marty Meakin returned to his kiosk to deal with his latest customers, leaving Hettie and Tilly deciding what to go on next. 'I don't think I can manage another ride just yet,' said Tilly. 'I'm still getting over the ghost train. It was much more frightening than I thought it would be, but we could play some games.

There's hook a duck over there or ball in the bucket next to it.'

'Come on then, let's have a go,' said Hettie, striding across to the stalls. 'Let's do hook a duck first and see if we can win one of those mugs. Betty collects seaside mugs, so we could get her present sorted.'

Tilly paid for a hook on the end of a pole for three goes at the yellow ducks bobbing in the water, which flowed fast in a circular tub. The first two goes failed when the hook turned the ducks on their sides, but she was triumphant with her final go and hooked the duck clean out of the water, allowing it to drip on the head of the cat who was running the stall. He retrieved the pole and the duck from Tilly's paw before passing her a prize mug emblazoned with 'Meakins Mewsments'.

She was delighted with her prize and Hettie set out to win a second mug for Beryl by lobbing balls into buckets but, although her aim was true on all three balls, they hit the bottom of the buckets and bounced out again, causing the young cat running both stalls to shake his head. 'You could have another try,' he suggested, but Hettie was wise to the game and the two friends moved on, with Tilly clutching her prize triumphantly in her paws.

'I fancy a hot dog before we go on anything else,' said Hettie. 'It's been quite some time since Minnie's cod balls.'

'Ooh yes,' said Tilly, 'that would be lovely. There was a hot dog stand near the dodgems.'

'Well, if you're thinking of having another go on them, you can forget it,' said Hettie. 'There's lots of rides we haven't tried yet and it's getting late and a bit rowdy.'

Hettie was right. The atmosphere on the fairground was beginning to change. Families of cats were leaving, replaced by gangs of male cats, all hanging round the rides looking for trouble. Some wore leather jackets with threatening logos like 'Killer Cats' and 'Street Fighters' spelt out in studs. Others swayed to the music from the attractions with bottles of beer in their paws, pouncing on young female cats as they came off the rides and generally making a nuisance of themselves. Hettie also noticed that the music was getting louder and the rides faster.

They made their way towards the hot dog stand and were pleased to see Bruiser in the queue. 'Great minds think alike,' said Hettie. 'How did you get on at the rifle range?'

'Bit of a fiddle,' said Bruiser. 'Them sights on the rifles are way out on purpose – typical fairground trick. I 'ad three goes an' didn't even win a stick of rock. Got lucky on the slots, though, so 'ot dogs is on me.'

The queue moved forward and Bruiser was almost at the front when a gang of cats went to push in ahead of him. Bruiser's hackles rose immediately as two of the cats tried to force him out of the way. He stood his ground, but one of the gang struck out at him. He staggered forward, but regained his balance as another of the cats came at him. This time, Bruiser was ready and sprang at the cat, knocking him to the ground. The others piled in as Hettie and Tilly looked on in horror. Bruiser sidestepped three of the cats and landed a punch squarely on another's jaw. The cat went down and stayed down, but the other three hit back, landing several punches before Marlon Meakin and the cat from the hook-a-duck stall joined the fight, sending two of the thugs spinning into the side of the dodgems ride while Bruiser dealt with the other. The gang lay in the dust, licking their wounds as the cat on the hot dog stand breathed a sigh of relief.

'Nice one,' said Bruiser, patting Marlon on the back and nodding to the other cat. 'Thanks for the extra pairs of paws. Looks like we've sorted 'em out.'

'They've been causing trouble for the last hour,' said Marlon. 'I had to throw them off the dodgems as they were upsetting the other customers. We're used to their sort. My dad taught me to box when I was a kitten and I used to run the boxing booth at the fair to take on all comers, but we don't do that any more. I taught my boy Monty here to handle himself, though – you get some nasty types later in the evening and we have to be ready for them. It's a shame we don't have the boxing booth still. I reckon you'd have been a champion.'

Bruiser grinned at the compliment as Hettie and Tilly joined them. 'Well I never,' said Marlon. 'If it isn't our little Stirling Moss. You're not back for another go, are you?'

Tilly was suddenly shy and tried to hide behind Hettie, but Marlon gently pulled her out. 'Come on – while your friends are getting the hot dogs you can have another spin round on me.'

Tilly giggled and forced her prize mug into Hettie's paw for safekeeping. Hettie and Bruiser watched as Marlon saw her into a bright yellow car. There was no stopping her this time: as soon as the dodgems began to move, she was off like a demon, just as if she were born to it. Hettie and Bruiser watched as she manoeuvred her car around the other drivers, picking up speed as she went. 'Blimey! She'll be wantin' a car next,' said Bruiser. 'At this rate, I'll be losin' me job if I'm not needed to drive you around in Miss Scarlet.'

'I can't see that happening,' said Hettie. 'There's a lot of difference between dodgems and driving on proper roads, and she loves you and Miss Scarlet's sidecar far too much to change anything.'

Bruiser turned to the cat Marlon had called Monty. He was standing over the gang, waiting to spring if they wanted more trouble. 'Perhaps these goons would like a bit of 'elp ta leave the fairground?'

Monty grinned at the prospect. He was bored with hook a duck and balls in a bucket, and had relished the prospect of sorting the gang out. The two cats hauled the thugs to their feet and marched them in a straggly line through the arch and out of the fairground. The leader of the gang hissed back at them, promising vengeance before catching up with the rest of his clan and disappearing into the night.

'I went to school with the one in the torn leathers,' said Monty, as he and Bruiser walked back to the dodgems. 'He was a bully then, but he only picked on kittens half his size. He asked my dad for a job at the fair, but we only have family running the main rides so he turns out to cause trouble instead with his pals, who are all frightened of him. He goes by the name of Killer Quince. At school his name was Brian Dobbs, although only the teachers called him that.'

'I s'pose you get a few odd types in your job,' said Bruiser. 'I 'ad a spell with a travellin' circus a few years back and spent all me time breakin' up fights. Afternoon shows was nice an' peaceful, but the rot set in after dark. Lost a couple of me teeth that summer.'

Monty laughed. 'Trouble is, it goes with the job. One day I'll have to take over running this fair from my dad and one of the biggest problems is keeping things safe for all the cats who come here to have a great time with their families. If it's not safe, they won't come. My dad tears his fur out day after day making sure all the rides are safe and in good order, but you can't account for the thugs who come here to wreck it.'

''Ave you thought about doin' anythin' else?' asked Bruiser.

Monty shook his head. 'Never. Why would I? Being a Meakin Sandscratcher is the best job in the world – making cats happy, seeing the joy we bring to all those kittens on holiday, and down here on the beach isn't a bad place to live, even if it does get a bit rough in the winter. It's all about family, really. We argue like any family and my dad and uncles even have the occasional spat, but it's all about tradition and keeping things going. I'm just proud to be part of it. There's a change coming, though. We're a bit old-fashioned compared to all the new rides springing up around the country and there's attractions like the Wild West show out at Gobbles Point to compete with. They pack them in out there. It's a good show though.'

Hettie and Tilly were waiting with the hot dogs when Bruiser and his new friend Monty returned. Tilly was full of her latest experience on the dodgems, and was keen to have one more ride on something else before they made their way back to the villa. Monty left them to pack away his ducks for the night before joining Marlon on the dodgems, just in case Quince returned with his friends. The hot dogs were dispatched in seconds, although Tilly's T-shirt would carry the memory of them for the rest of the holiday.

'I think I'd like to finish on the waltzer,' she announced. 'Marlon says he thinks I'd like that and we can all go on it together. His brother Maxwell runs it.'

'Well, if Marlon says it, it must be right,' said Hettie, applying a bit of good-humoured sarcasm. 'Come on then – I'm sure I saw the waltzer by the entrance. There's a donut stall next to it so we could get some of those for supper in our room.'

Tilly skipped ahead and Bruiser and Hettie followed on until they came to the waltzer. It was in full swing and they watched as the showcat they assumed was Maxwell Meakin spun the chairs, much to the delight of the customers as the ride gathered speed. 'Not sure if the hot dog was a good idea,' observed Hettie as the ride came to an end and the cats staggered off it, a little unsteady on their feet and somewhat disorientated.

Tilly was undaunted and led them to one of the chairs. 'I'll sit in the middle,' she decided, 'as it's probably safer.' Hettie and Bruiser settled in next to her as the showcat made his way round the ride, collecting the money and pulling the safety bars down on the chairs to lock in the customers, then shouting above the music for them to hold on tight. The ride began slowly, but suddenly gathered pace until Hettie, Tilly and Bruiser were clinging to the bar. The rest of the fairground became a blur as the waltzer pitched them up and down, and Maxwell Meakin added to the thrill by spinning the chairs as they passed him. By the time the ride was over, Tilly was hoarse with screaming, Hettie had broken a couple of claws clinging on to the bar and Bruiser was starting a headache, although he admitted that it was probably from the crack on the head he'd received earlier during the fight. All three were pleased to be back on firm ground, even if it didn't seem like it straight away. Bruiser insisted on buying the donuts, as he'd intended to treat them to the hot dogs but had been thwarted by Quince and his gang.

The donut stand, like the rest of the stalls and rides, was beautifully decorated with brightly painted images in reds, yellows, greens and blues, and the front of the stall proclaimed in bold swirling letters that this was 'Marmalade Meakin's Donuts'. The cat on the stall busied herself pouring batter onto a hot plate, shaping the donuts and tossing them in sugar.

Tilly remembered what Minnie had said about Marmalade painting the bedroom ceiling at the villa and decided to mention it. 'We're staying at Sandscratchers Villa and we love the painting you've done on the ceiling in our room,' she said.

The cat beamed at her. 'That's kind of you to say. Being a fairground artist is a job that gets taken for granted a bit. That ceiling I did for my mother and it was a lovely thing to do. Made a real change from patching up the paintwork on the rides and keeping them bright and cheerful. It's an uphill job, but I'm the only one in the family who does it, so it's nice to be appreciated. Thank you.'

Still smiling, Marmalade Meakin forced the hot donuts into a bag. Bruiser paid up and the three cats wended their way back to the villa, as one by one the lights went out on Meakins Mewsments.

Chapter Eight

The lights were all blazing at the villa and, although it was after ten, the front door was still unlocked. Hettie, Tilly and Bruiser let themselves in and were about to climb the stairs when Minnie popped her head round the lounge door. 'If you fancy a nightcap, we're in here,' she said, 'and can I smell Marmalade's donuts in that bag?'

Bruiser was tempted to hide them behind his back but they'd already been spotted and he didn't want to cause offence. The three friends moved reluctantly towards the lounge, where Wilt Dinsney was sitting on the sofa, twirling his toy gun and shouting 'Ye ha!' at the TV. 'Come in and join us,' said Minnie. 'They're showing an old episode of *Rawhide* with Glint Eastwood. They've moved their wagons into a circle, ready for a dust-up because one of them trespassed on a sacred Indian burial ground in the Haunted Hills. Wilt and I are on the edge of our seats. Even my antimacassars are curling up at the edges.'

It had been a long day and an early start and all Hettie wanted to do was sit up in her bed and eat a donut, but there was no chance of that. Tilly joined Wilt and Minnie on the sofa and Hettie and Bruiser sat in a couple of armchairs. Bruiser felt obliged to share out the donuts as the battle raged on the TV. Once all the enemy had been slaughtered and the titles began to roll, Wilt and Minnie added their voices to the theme tune.

'Well, that was a real treat,' said Minnie. 'I'd better go and check on Mother and make us all a hot chocolate. You three stay here and keep Wilt company.'

Hettie's heart couldn't sink much lower. Her doubts about the merits of staying in a guest house had all come home to roost, but she calculated that a mug of hot chocolate wouldn't take that long to drink and then they would be free to go to their beds. She was wrong, and had completely underestimated Wilt Dinsney's power of conversation. 'So what have you guys been up to since dinner?' he began, sliding his gun back into his holster and producing a large cigar out of the top pocket of his waistcoat.

'We've all been down to the fair,' said Tilly, 'and Bruiser had to fight off a gang of nasty cats. We met lots of Minnie's family running the rides, including the ghost train, which was really scary.'

Wilt made much of lighting his cigar by striking a match on the sole of one of his cowboy boots before giving his opinion on the fairground. 'These little old

English fairgrounds are becoming a thing of the past. Some of those rides down there are over fifty years old, you know. They attract hoodlums as there's no security and it's not really a safe place to be after dark. In the States, we have theme parks with all the latest amusements and patrols to put off the thugs. Kittens of today want real excitement – helter-skelters, roller-coasters, haunted mansions and all that sort of stuff. You need acres of real estate to make it work, not just a tiny space on a seaside beach where no one goes in the winter.'

'But what about your Wild West show,' said Hettie, getting slightly annoyed. 'Isn't that old-fashioned? It's been a long time since the cowboy and American Indian wars and most kittens wouldn't know anything about the Wild West.'

'You're right there, but that's the point – my show is a re-enactment of American history, something folks should know about, and the guys and gals in it are artists and really good at what they do. You don't need talent to run a bunch of bumper cars.'

This time it was Tilly who felt she should say something in Marlon Meakin's defence. 'At least on the dodgems anyone can take part and have a lovely time, and having a fair by the sea makes it extra special. I think Minnie's family has to work really hard.'

'What's that about the family?' said Minnie, barging her way in through the door with a tray full of mugs of hot chocolate.

'Our friends here were singing the praises of Meakins Mewsments,' said Wilt. 'I was just pointing out that little old fairgrounds have had their day.'

'Well don't let Marlon hear you saying that. He'd be most confronted if he thought you were putting his customers off,' said Minnie, passing the mugs of chocolate round. 'It's tradition that keeps the fair alive. Us Meakins were born to it and no one works harder than Marlon to keep it going.'

Wilt could see that his thoughts on English fairgrounds hadn't gone down too well with the assembled company, so he diplomatically changed the subject. 'I want to hear about your murders,' he said, addressing Bruiser directly. 'I bet you've met some pretty bad characters in your work?'

'We 'ave, but Hettie's the boss. I just add a bit of security when it's needed, as there's some nasty types out there and not just in yer fairgrounds,' said Bruiser, keen to bat the subject in Hettie's direction.

'Say, that's a first,' said Wilt. 'A female detective with a guy riding shotgun.'

'Two female detectives actually,' said Hettie, not liking the way the conversation was heading. 'We are a team and Tilly and Bruiser are vital to our operation. Tilly documents all our cases, draws up and works through suspect lists, and is very good at analysing the way that cats behave. Bruiser has put his life at risk on many occasions to save us and innocent victims from harm and he has a world of experience when it comes to life in general. He's also good at driving motorbikes.'

'And what about you?' asked Wilt. 'Are you the Sherlock Bones of the outfit?'

Hettie thought for a moment, taking a sip of her hot chocolate before replying as it wasn't a question that she'd had to answer before. 'Well, I suppose I am in a way. I do sit and think a lot. I like sifting through clues and interviewing suspects, but the best bit is putting things right when terrible things have happened. Oh, and I don't play the violin.'

Everyone laughed, but Wilt was keen to get down to the actual cases. 'So do you go looking for murders?'

'These days, it's true to say that they come looking for us. We used to just take cases in our town, but the national newspapers have run a few of our stories, so now we get calls from all over the country.'

'We even got a commission from Agatha Crispy,' added Tilly, keen to show off. 'We know her quite well, actually, and we've been to her homes in Devon and London.'

'Do you mean *the* Agatha Crispy?' said Wilt, looking really impressed.

Tilly nodded and was about to enlighten Wilt with some of the details of the case when Minnie chimed in. 'Well I never! Fancy that! I've got all her books but I never thought I'd meet someone who actually knew her. *Murder on the Orinoco Express* is my favourite, although I do have a fondness for her

Miss Marble mysteries, too – she reminds me a bit of my mother.'

No one responded to the comparison and Hettie grabbed the opportunity to yawn and get to her feet. 'Well, it's been a very long day,' she said. 'I think it's time for bed. All this sea air has tired me out, but thank you for the hot chocolate.'

Bruiser and Tilly joined Hettie in her bid for freedom and, with only a small protestation from Minnie, the three cats fled the lounge and bounded up the stairs to their room.

'What a bloody nightmare!' said Hettie, shutting the door behind her and sinking down onto one of the twin beds. 'Remind me never to stay in a guest house again. Minnie Meakin is bad enough, but having to put up with her gunslinging boyfriend as well is just too much. We've come here to enjoy ourselves, not to be cross-examined by a cowboy from a cheap end-of-pier show. If he thinks English fairgrounds are old-fashioned, he should look at himself. I mean, who sits watching a cowboy film twirling a toy gun, and at his age? I can only imagine what this show is going to be like tomorrow night and I'm dreading breakfast in the morning. I suppose Wilt will be joining us. I wish we'd never told him we were detectives.'

'I think we'd better share out these savoury lattice tarts that the Butters gave us,' said Tilly, keen to change the subject. 'They've been sitting on this bed in the heat. By tomorrow they'll be nasty.'

There was no argument and the three cats polished off the tarts in record time, followed by the rest of the brownies, enjoying what Tilly described as 'a little taste of home'. When there was nothing left, Hettie lit her catnip pipe and shared it with Bruiser. Tilly, who had never got on with catnip, settled down with her notebook to write a few thoughts on her day, following the advice that Polly Hodge had given in her writer's workshop.

It was still very warm from the heat of the day and it took some time for the three friends to fall asleep, only to be woken by a violent thunderstorm in the early hours. Hettie, still half asleep, staggered to the window to shut it as the rain poured in, making a sizeable puddle on Minnie's floor. Bruiser and Tilly joined her at the window as lightning arced across the sky, followed by deafening claps of thunder. When the lightning came again, the fairground lit up in the distance as if all the lights had been turned on at once, then just as suddenly all was dark. Eventually the storm moved away, reduced to a low rumble. The room was much cooler now, making sleep more possible. Hettie, Tilly and Bruiser knew nothing more until Minnie Meakin hammered on their door the next morning.

Chapter Nine

'Your last chance for breakfast!' Minnie shouted through the door of number seven. 'That's if you want it cooked, as it's Mother's day at the whisker drive and she has to be at the church hall by eleven or she'll miss out on the Danish pastries. If you come down now, I'll just have time to wheel her there.'

Hettie sat up and rubbed her eyes. Tilly shot out of the bed and stumbled to the door. She pulled it open in time to see Minnie scurrying along the corridor and down the stairs. 'I think we'd better get a move on if we want a decent breakfast,' she said, pulling on yesterday's clothes. Bruiser had slept in his so he sprang off his bed and waited at the door for Hettie to make herself presentable.

The three cats bounded downstairs and into the dining room, where Minnie waited to take their orders. 'I've got eggs, poached or fried, bacon, sausages, fried bread or kedgeree, although that has actually stuck to the pan because my non-stick has recently started sticking. I think it's the haddock that's doing it.

I turned my back on it for a second to give Mother her porridge and next time I looked it was a solid lump. Couldn't even shift it with a wooden spoon. That's the kedgeree, not the porridge, although I've had trouble with that from time to time, but Mother insists on it as part of her vagrant diet, although she never sticks to that as she loves her meat too much.'

'I think we'll all have the bacon, fried eggs and sausages,' said Hettie, sliding into a window seat, followed by Tilly and Bruiser, 'and maybe some toast instead of fried bread?'

Minnie shook her head slowly from side to side. 'Don't start me on the toaster saga. It was consecrated by the fire brocade when they came up last time. Chief Fire Officer Mudlark said it was the worst fire hazard he'd ever seen, so he took it away and that was that.'

'Fried bread will be just lovely,' said Tilly, before Minnie had the chance to move on to yet more kitchen disasters.

Satisfied with her order, Minnie returned to her kitchen, leaving Hettie, Tilly and Bruiser patiently waiting for their breakfasts. They were the only cats in the dining room, as the rest of the boarders had been and gone; there was no sign of Wilt Dinsney, much to Hettie's relief. Her fear about sharing a breakfast table with him had not become a reality and when the food arrived they all agreed that it was excellent.

'What shall we do today?' asked Tilly, pushing her empty plate away and scraping some egg yolk off her T-shirt with one of her claws.

'I fancy doing absolutely nothing,' said Hettie. 'After all, we are on holiday. I think we should head for the beach and sit in the sun. We don't want to tire ourselves out – we've got the Wild West show later, heaven help us.'

Tilly agreed that a day on the beach was just what was needed, and Bruiser said he would join them after he'd phoned the Butters and Dolly Scollop to tell them he was staying on for another night. They were about to leave the dining room when Minnie burst through the door to collect the dirty dishes. 'Are you all in for dinner tonight?' she asked. 'I'm doing homemade sardine and pineapple pizza with cold sore salad, followed by jam suet pudding with a choice of custard or cream.'

'Yes please,' said Tilly, trying very hard not to giggle. 'That sounds lovely.'

'So what are you all up to today?' asked Minnie, stacking the plates and clearing the other tables.

'We thought we'd just sit in the sunshine on the beach,' said Hettie. 'It looks like another hot day.'

'Well, take care as that sun can burn before you know it. The cats in number seven before you had to go home early, as they both had a bad case of strickly heat. Covered themselves in columbine lotion, but that didn't help. You'd be better sitting up on the miranda here at the villa, where there's a bit of shade. Anyway, if you'll excuse me I must get on or Mother will miss her pastry and my life won't be worth living.'

Minnie returned to her kitchen and Hettie and Tilly went back up to their room to prepare for their day on the beach, leaving Bruiser to make his phone calls. 'I think I'll take my notebook,' said Tilly. 'Inspiration might strike for a story, and we'd better take the sun cream. Will we be paddling, do you think?'

'I suppose we might be tempted if it gets really hot,' said Hettie, changing into her stained T-shirt from the day before. 'I'm going to wear my jelly sandals, just in case, as I hate walking on pebbles or having sand between my toes.'

'I'll take a towel then,' said Tilly, adding it to the pile of beach items on the bed. 'I've got a crossword book, some fruit pastilles, my notebook and pencil, your binoculars that you got out of that cracker at Christmas, a towel and the rest of my pennies, with some proper money for buying lunch. Can you think of anything else?'

'No, you've got it covered. I think we'd better get down on that beach before all the deckchairs get taken. We'll need a good spot close to the kiosk for ice creams and drinks.'

Tilly rolled up all the things she'd chosen in the towel, changed into her favourite Top Cat T-shirt, pulled on her own jelly sandals and followed Hettie out into the sunshine. The overnight storm had freshened everything, making the white walls of the villa sparkle and stand out against the deep blue sky. In that moment, all was well with the world and so full of expectation.

As Hettie had predicted, the beach was already busy so they headed for the cat who was hiring out the deckchairs. He was sitting under a giant sunshade on the promenade, next to the kiosk, reading a news-paper. Hettie made the approach but it was some time before the cat looked up, as he seemed to be marking up horses on the racing page. 'What can I do yer for?' he said, when he finally noticed her.

'I'd like three deckchairs please,' she said, noticing that there were only four left in a stack next to him.

The cat took a fob watch out of his shirt pocket, checked the time and tutted disapprovingly. 'The thing is,' he began, 'I've three time slots – nine till one, one till five, an' five till dusk. Now, as it's half past eleven, just gone, I feel obliged ta charge yer fer two sessions unless you only want them chairs till one – in which case I'll 'ave ta charge yer for a full session from nine till one. But if you wants them till five, that'll be two ses-sions, but if you bring 'em back before five there won't be no refund. I should also point out that these chairs is not transferable, which means you can't pass 'em on.'

Tilly sensed that Hettie might be tempted to take a swipe at the deckchair cat if the one-sided conver-sation continued. It was really hot and she felt that the sooner they settled for their day on the beach the better, so she stepped forward. 'We'll take three deck-chairs until five o'clock, please.'

'That'll be two sessions times three,' said the cat, 'so that's thruppence a chair times two times three, so that's one shillin' and sixpence in old money, or seven and a half pence in the newfangled money. I don't mind which, as the slots take the old coins and I'm fee-lin' lucky. But mark my words, there's trouble brewin'. My hackles is up an' that can only mean one thing.'

'What's that?' asked Tilly, counting out the correct money into the cat's paw.

'Death,' the cat replied, 'and not just one.'

Hettie had had enough of the deckchair cat. Even though Tilly was keen to find out more about his prophecy, she grabbed the three deckchairs they'd paid for and bumped them down onto the sand. Tilly followed, feeling a little uneasy about what she'd just been told, but she forgot about it completely when Bruiser joined them with news from home. 'Dolly says Lavender Stamp 'as taken on a new postcat – Elsie 'addock's niece frum the fish shop. She says she's really nice an' 'er name is Squeak an' she's doin' two deliveries a day, which is more than Lavender 'as man-aged since 'er last postcat got murdered.' Hettie, Tilly and Bruiser shared a sad moment as they remembered the tragic death of Teezle Makepiece during one of their earlier cases. 'The litrey festival 'as 'ad ta be called off completely,' Bruiser continued. 'Betty says the out-door barbecue got too close fer comfort to the main marquee. The whole thing went up in a giant fireball, an' the St Kippers pawbell ringers 'ad ta be treated fer minor burns. Good job Cherry Fudge was there with 'er ambulance – 'arf of Sheba Terrace 'ad to be evacuated cause of the smoke.'

'Why does none of that surprise me?' said Hettie, settling into her deckchair. 'Putting Turner Page in charge of a literary festival is like giving a kitten a razor blade to suck. He should stick to running that library instead of branching out into events, which is the kindest way to describe them.'

'I think it's just a bit of bad luck,' insisted Tilly, who had a soft spot for Turner and his library. 'At least no one got murdered this time – and the death of Downton Tabby really put our detective agency on the map at his first festival.'

'Along with several other victims,' Hettie pointed out. 'I seem to remember having more corpses than paying customers by the end of it.'

There was nothing more that Tilly could think of saying in Turner's defence, and the whole conversation was suddenly hijacked by a family with three noisy kittens setting up next to them. Hettie stared in disbelief as the adult cat, whom she assumed was the mother, proceeded to blow up two lilos and several rubber rings. The kittens pulled out their buckets and spades from a large bag and set to digging in the sand, pitching it high into the sky and covering Hettie, Tilly and Bruiser in the process. The mother seemed oblivious to the impact that her little darlings were having on the surrounding sunbathers; Hettie even offered several of her deadliest looks, but nothing seemed to dampen the kittens' enthusiasm for excavating the beach. A short time later, one of them took off, dragging a lilo towards the sea, but the other two preferred to take it in turns to bury each other in the sand.

The final straw came shortly after the mother cat pulled a transistor radio from one of her many bags. The sound of gentle waves, excited kitten squeals and the occasional squawking seagull was instantly eclipsed by the latest pop tunes blaring out across the beach.

'That's it!' said Hettie, struggling out of her deckchair. 'Would you mind turning that down?' she demanded. 'Some of us are here for a bit of peace and quiet.'

The mother cat blinked back at Hettie before offering her thoughts. 'If you wants peace and quiet, there's a graveyard in the town. Or you could go and sit in one of them colonnade things up on the prom with a blanket over you like the rest of God's waitin' room. I likes me music and me kittens love the beach. If you don't like it, you know what you can do.'

Hettie was furious, but Tilly thought the mother cat had a point and was wondering how to defuse the situation when all attention suddenly turned towards the sea. Several cats were standing up and pointing at the water. Hettie scrabbled in the towel for her binoculars and was horrified to see the mother cat's kitten being carried out to sea on the lilo. She shot a look at Bruiser, who responded immediately by bounding towards the shoreline and splashing into the sea.

The mother shut off her radio, tossing it into the sand, and stood sobbing with her paws over her eyes, too scared to watch as one of her kittens was carried away from her. 'Don't worry,' said Tilly, doing her best to console the cat. 'Bruiser will save him. He's really good in an emergency.' There was nothing more that could be said as the horror unfolded.

Bruiser was a strong swimmer but the current was against him and the sun and the stinging salt water were in his eyes. It was hard to see the lilo, but he could hear the kitten's screams so he knew he was getting closer.

By now, all the cats on the beach were on their feet, watching the attempted rescue and willing Bruiser on. Even the deckchair cat had deserted his sunshade to come down to the sand. Tilly glanced at him nervously, remembering his doom-laden prediction and hoping that he would be wrong.

The atmosphere on the beach had changed dramatically and so had the sky: giant black clouds had appeared from nowhere, smothering the sun and making the sea look as black as ink. The lilo and the kitten were fast becoming a dot on the horizon as Bruiser swam on, getting more and more exhausted.

It was the storm that saved the day. As the thunderclouds rolled in, the wind began to blow in Bruiser's favour, pushing the lilo towards him. Soon it was in reach, and he used his last ounce of strength to haul himself out of the water and onto the air bed. A cheer went up from the spectators on the beach as he lay down on his stomach with the kitten clinging to his back and paddled towards the shore with his paws.

Hettie and Tilly rushed to greet him, taking the mother cat with them. The kitten rushed into his mother's arms, but Bruiser lay exhausted on the pebbles as the heavens opened and the rain poured down. The beach became chaotic as cats scrambled to collect their belongings and round up their families. Windbreaks were ripped out of the sand and buckets and spades hurriedly tossed into bags along with sandwiches and picnic rugs as the moving army of sunbathers headed to the promenade in search of shelter.

It was as if the mother cat hadn't noticed the rain: she hugged her kitten to her, now joined by its brother and sister, who clung to her legs. 'I just don't know how I can ever repay you for saving Freddy,' she said, staring down at Bruiser who was starting to get his breath back. 'Raising three kittens on my own is hard work and I need eyes in the back of my head, but I will never forget this day for as long as I live. Is there anything I can do for you or your friends to say thank you?'

Bruiser sat up and coughed, before finding his voice. 'I think getting rid of them lilos would 'elp.'

'And maybe the transistor radio,' Hettie suggested, in an attempt to lighten the mood.

The mother cat smiled, taking both comments on board before offering exactly the right reward for Bruiser's fearless bravery. 'My sister runs a café on the pier – perhaps I could treat you all to lunch?'

'Sounds good,' said Bruiser, as Hettie helped him to his feet. 'I'll 'ave ta find some dry clothes first though.'

'I think we all will,' said Hettie. 'Shall we meet you there in an hour? And I'm sorry but we don't even know your name.'

'It's Maisie, and these three are Freddy, Frankie and Lizzy.'

Hettie introduced herself, Tilly and Bruiser, then they made their way back to their abandoned deck-chairs. Tilly was pleased to see that her notepad had found shelter under her deckchair, but the towel, crossword book and fruit pastilles had become a soggy mess.

Maisie gathered up all her bags and her kittens and headed off along the promenade, arranging to meet them on the pier when everyone had dried out. It was noticeable that she chose to abandon the lilos and the rubber rings on the beach, not wishing to be reminded of the horror that could have been.

The deckchair cat, who had made a dash for his beach umbrella as soon as the rain started, approached Hettie as the three cats made their way towards the path leading up to the villa. ''Scuse me,' he said, but

Hettie was in no mood to talk about deckchairs and walked on. The cat quickened his pace and overtook her. ''Ang on a minute – I just needs ta give you this.' He forced a collection of coins into Hettie's paw. 'That's the first time I've ever given a refund,' he said, 'but you and your friends deserve a medal for what you done today.' He patted Bruiser on the back and made him cough. ''An' as fer you, fella, you're just a bloody hero. Any other cat would 'ave turned back when that storm struck. I thought for a minute you were a gonner. Anyway you an' yer mates can 'ave yer deckchairs on me from now on, no charge.'

'Excuse me,' said Tilly, 'you said there were going to be some deaths when we hired our deckchairs but everyone was all right after all. Did you make a mistake and get it wrong?'

'Me, get it wrong?' said the cat. 'Not likely! I knows things and I stand by me words. There are deaths comin' very soon and I reckon you'll be up to your neck in 'em. They don't call me Premo Pete fer nothin'.'

'But why do you think we'll be involved?' Hettie asked.

'Ah, I knew as soon as your friend 'ere paid for your deckchairs. Touch of a paw's enough ta set me knowin's off.'

'So who's going to die?' pressed Hettie, thinking to call the cat out.

'Well, if I knew that I wouldn't be stackin' deckchairs for me livin', would I? All I knows is cats is goin' ta die around you – an' soon!'

Chapter Ten

Hettie, Tilly and Bruiser changed out of their wet things in their room. Bruiser borrowed one of Hettie's T-shirts and Tilly took the soggy bundle of clothes downstairs in search of a washing line. She found the kitchen, but there was no sign of Minnie or her mother, much to her disappointment; she wanted to meet Minnie's mother, particularly after what Bruiser had had to say about her.

There was a back door leading out of the kitchen into a small yard. Tilly was pleased to see a washing line, and even more pleased that the sun had emerged from the black clouds that had brought the storm. She pegged the clothes out, leaving them to dry in the sunshine, and caught up with Hettie and Bruiser as they came down the stairs.

'I've brought your bag of pennies in case you want to have a go on the fruit machines after lunch,' said Hettie. 'Minnie said that her sister ran the slots on the pier where the café is. I think we've probably had enough of the beach for one day.'

Bruiser nodded his head in agreement, feeling just a little sorry for himself. Having been roughed up by thugs at the fair and nearly drowned at sea, he was beginning to think that Felixtoe wasn't the safest of holiday destinations.

The sun was warm again and they gave Premo Pete's deckchair hire a wide berth on their way to the pier, just in case he had any further premonitions to add to his doom-laden comments. The pier, which jutted out some distance into the sea, was a very old-fashioned affair, full of small shops, a substantial amusement arcade and the café that Maisie had told them about. The various businesses were flanked on either side by glass-fronted sitting-out areas, where cats could enjoy a picnic away from the strong winds that came in off the North Sea.

The café was fairly busy, but Maisie had saved a table in a pool of sunshine by the window. Her kittens were contentedly sucking milkshakes through striped straws, looking as angelic as any small kittens could. Maisie waved at Hettie, Tilly and Bruiser and they made their way across the café to join her. 'I hoped you'd come,' she said. 'I was worried that Mr Bruiser might feel bad after his ordeal.'

'Nothin' that a nice pie an' chips won't fix,' said Bruiser, eyeing up a meal on the table next to them as Hettie and Tilly settled in their seats.

'Have anything you want from the menu,' said Maisie, wiping milkshake from Freddy's whiskers with her handkerchief. 'My sister will be over in a minute to take your orders. She said she was rushed off her feet when the storm broke but it's a bit quieter now the sun's out again.'

Hettie gave the menu a quick scan, deciding almost immediately on the fish and chips. Bruiser stuck with his first choice of a pie, but Tilly – true to form – looked at the menu in much more detail, reading out the list of foods on offer to the amusement of Freddy, Frankie and Lizzy, who thought they were getting an early bedtime story. Eventually she settled on a fish finger sandwich with a side order of chips, just in time as the waitress came across to them.

'This is my big sister Monica,' said Maisie, 'and this is Bruiser, who saved Freddy from the sea.'

Monica threw her order pad on the table and hugged Bruiser, causing him to have a bout of coughing and spluttering. 'We can never thank you enough for what you did today – you and your friends here,' said Monica. 'Order anything you like from the menu and there'll be no charge. We owe you a huge debt of gratitude, and if you're staying the week then make sure you come here for your lunches. We won't take a penny off you.'

Hettie was secretly beginning to enjoy her holi-day of free deckchairs and free food, not forgetting three tickets to the Wild West show. Bruiser was prov-ing to be a real asset and there was the prospect of even more complimentary amusements still to come. When Monica returned to the table with the lunches, she passed a piece of paper to Bruiser. 'I'm married to Marlon Meakin,' she said. 'He runs everything round here as the family business and that piece of paper entitles you and your friends to free rides on anything on the fairground.'

'We've met Marlon,' said Tilly. 'He taught me to drive a dodgem and Bruiser fought off some nasty cats with him at the fair last night.'

'Well, I never!' said Monica. 'So you must be the detectives staying up at the villa? News travels fast in our family, especially if Minnie has anything to do with it.'

'Felixtoe seems to be a very small world full of Meakins,' said Hettie, cutting into her fish.

'Maisie's a Meakin too,' said Monica, nodding to her sister. 'Anyway, enjoy your meals. I'd better get on as I have scones in the oven for the afternoon teas, but thank you again for saving Freddy's life.'

Monica returned to her kitchen and Hettie, Tilly and Bruiser turned to Maisie hoping she might explain her connection with the Meakins.

'I was married to Micky Meakin, Marlon's twin brother,' Maisie said, wiping a tear from her eye with one of the kittens' bibs. Micky missed out by two minutes on inheriting the family business, as Marlon was born first. Micky had a terrible accident on the fairground at the beginning of the season. He ran the Moon Rockets ride, which is almost as popular as Marlon's dodgems. A bunch of cowboys came over to the fairground from the Wild West show late one night and started a fight with some local cats, and Micky got caught in the middle of it. The cowboys got into the moon rockets just as they were starting up. The local gang followed them and Micky tried to break up the fighting, but he was thrown clean off the ride and crashed into a picket fence. They brought him back to our wagon, but he died in the night. The next day I had my three kittens.'

'That's a terrible tragedy,' said Hettie. 'I'm surprised that Minnie didn't mention it when she was telling us about the family.'

'None of the Meakins mention it. If word gets out that the fairground isn't safe, no one will come and the whole family will be out of work. It's a hard living, but it's all about family. They've been very good to me and the kittens since it happened. We've wanted for nothing and we've been allowed to keep our wagon, but it's hard raising a family on your own. Minnie used to be my best friend, but I can't look her in the face since Micky died because she's walking out with Wilt Dinsney. He's a nice enough cat, but I can't bear the thought of any of those cowboys since the accident.'

'All the Meakins have names beginning with "M",' said Hettie, 'but your kittens don't. Didn't you want to follow the family tradition.'

'No and I don't want them to, either. That fairground killed their father and the last thing I want them to do is be part of that when they grow up. I want them to have a proper life, with choices. I don't even let them go to the fair and I can't go anywhere near it as it makes me so sad. I find it hard being a Meakin; it's like I'm part of a strange commune sometimes.

Monica manages because she loves her café and she loves Marlon and her son Monty, who will inherit everything one day, but now Micky's gone I feel like an outsider. There's times when I could strike a match and burn the whole fairground down.'

'It must be hard having it all on your doorstep as a constant reminder,' said Hettie. 'Have you thought of moving away with your kittens?'

'I'd love to start somewhere new, but I have no money of my own. I'm totally dependent on the family and I would hate to be parted from Monica. For Micky's sake, I need to bring Freddy, Frankie and Lizzy up in a safe place and that's what the family gives us. I'm sorry – I don't know why I'm telling you all this. I think the floodgates seem to have opened at the thought of losing Freddy in the sea. You surely must want to get on with your holiday. I bet you're keen to get back on the beach now the sun's out again.'

'Actually,' said Tilly, wiping the excess tomato sauce off her paws, 'we're going to have a go on the fruit machines here on the pier. We've decided that we've had enough of the beach for today.'

'I'm not surprised after what I've put you through,' said Maisie, 'and I'm sorry for being so rude to you on the beach, but I'm afraid there are holidaymakers who come here for a week and think they own the place with no consideration for us who live here. They bring in money during the season, but then we have to spend the whole of the winter cleaning up their mess and making the town look respectable for their return the following year. The cats who run the guest houses are in despair by the end of the season, clearing up the damage to their rooms, redecorating and making everything look lovely again. I used to help Minnie get the villa ready for the season and it was hard work.'

The kittens were now starting to fidget. Their milk-shakes were long gone and the adult conversation was of no interest to them. Freddy began to sing 'Twinkle, Twinkle Little Star' and Frankie and Lizzy joined in, filling the café with their high-pitched little voices. Even Hettie found their sudden foray into song admirable as it was actually in tune, but Maisie saw it as a sign that she should be moving on before the singing was replaced by naughtiness and devilment. 'It's been really nice to meet you all properly rather than leaving things unsaid on the beach. I'm here most days at lunchtime, so I hope we'll meet again. I've spent the whole of my time talking about my troubles and I know nothing about you all except that you're detectives, which sounds much more exciting than my life.'

'Not at all,' said Hettie, pushing her chair back to let the three kittens out from the table. 'It makes a refreshing change to talk to someone who isn't a potential victim or a murderer – as long as you don't burn the fairground down.'

The comment was meant as a joke, but before long Maisie Meakin would be included on Tilly's list of suspects in a real murder case.

Chapter Eleven

Bruiser decided to give the amusement arcade on the pier a miss after his lunch. The rescue of Freddy Meakin had taken its toll and, although he was looking forward to the Wild West show, he needed a rest and made his way back to the villa. Hettie and Tilly were keen to try their luck on the one-arm bandits and out of curiosity they hoped to bump in to Mary Queen of Slots, as Minnie had called her.

Mary was very easy to spot when they entered the arcade. Her throne room was a heavily decorated kiosk where she sat counting pennies and putting them into bank bags. Swirling around her was a cacophony of sound – jingling money, clunking fruit machines, sirens, maniacal laughter from dummies in glass cases, and the strains of a fully preserved Wurlitzer fairground organ with pipes and ornate panels depicting cats of yesteryear.

Mary indulged herself by wearing a small crown on her head, set at a jaunty angle to endorse her nickname. 'Fancy yer chances?' she said, as Hettie and

Tilly approached. 'Me fruits are payin' out well today, or you could try yer skills on the pinball? If you needs any change, just shout – all me slots only take old money.'

It hadn't occurred to Hettie and Tilly that the recent decimalisation of currency had had a profound effect on the slot machine industry, and it was a well-known fact that there was growing resistance across the country to the new pennies that had come into circulation. Tilly took her bag of coins to Mary's kiosk and offered them up for exchange into the old dark brown pennies, thrupenny bits and silver sixpences. Mary clawed the new pennies into a bank bag and cast them aside, lovingly counting out the old coins into Tilly's paw. 'There you go,' she said, 'and be lucky, my dear. I'll change yer winnin's back into the nasty stuff when yer leave. If yer wants to play the token slots, you'll 'ave to come back to me and buy some – five tokens for an old shillin'.'

Tilly had to agree that the old coinage felt so much more substantial as she slipped it into the pocket of her shorts. Hettie decided to wait and see how Tilly got on before changing any of her own money. The fruit machines stood in a row on a long table along one wall, and a few cats were trying their luck. Tilly chose one to start her winning campaign, based on Mary's advice. Hettie watched as the machine gobbled up the old pennies refusing to return any of them. 'I think I'll move on while I still have some pennies left,' said

Tilly, feeling a little disheartened, but the sound of a machine further down the line pouring pennies into the paws of an elderly cat gave her reason to believe. She chose a Bonanza Bank slot next, as it boasted a glass-panelled box full of pennies waiting to be won. The first penny she invested gave her three out of four sevens; excitedly, she pressed the hold buttons, hoping to hit the jackpot by turning up the final seven, but the machine was in no mood to empty its treasure into Tilly's paws. She moved on again and again, getting more frustrated and lighter in her pocket.

Hettie saw with interest how addictive the machines were, and how there were so few wins and a lot of disappointed players. Cats arrived with their expectations high and their pockets jingling with coins, and left dejected, possibly having spent their dinner money on a row of fruit that didn't match. Tilly enjoyed playing the slots but, being a sensible cat, she knew when to stop. 'Aren't you going to have a go?' she asked, offering Hettie her last old penny. 'I think it's time for an ice cream and a sit in the sun.'

Hettie took the penny and chose a machine at random. The machine promised a ten pound payout super jackpot for four bells in a row. She put the penny in the slot and yanked the arm on the machine to spin the symbols. The first was a bell, and the second and third; the two cats held their breath, waiting for the fourth symbol to stop spinning; it lodged between a cherry and a bell, and Hettie looked to her left and right before nudging the machine and jolting the bell into place. There followed a gurgling sound as it spewed pennies all over the floor, and Hettie and Tilly tried to catch as many as they could in their paws.

Such was the excitement that Mary Queen of Slots left her kiosk to congratulate them. 'That's the first time that old slot 'as paid out in years,' she said. 'You must 'ave the Midas touch. Are you goin' to play on or shall I change them pennies for you?'

'I think we'll quit while we're winning,' said Tilly, 'or our luck might run out.'

'Sensible,' said Mary, helping to gather the pennies off the floor. 'Cats like you could see me out of business, but I'm pleased for you. Better this way than not knowin' when to stop.'

'I suppose you get some real gamblers in here,' said Hettie, following Mary back to her kiosk. 'It must be hard sometimes, watching cats throw their money away.'

'It's like anythin' in life – the thrill of the chase, you win some, you lose some, but in the end there's no real winners. I 'ave cats who come in 'ere day after day, waitin' for the big win, tryin' to calculate which slots are due for a payout. I've even been accused of fixin' the reels on the machines, but fact is I wouldn't know how. All I do is polish 'em up and make 'em shine. Now my sister Minnie knew the inside of the slots like the back of her paw. She could fix the reels soon as look at 'em, not that I should be tellin' you that.

Anyway, how would you like your winnin's? I could give it to you in pounds if that's easier?'

Hettie would have loved to learn more about Minnie Meakin's nefarious practices, but an ice cream and a sit in the sun beckoned. 'Pounds would be lovely,' she said.

Mary counted out ten one pound notes into Hettie's paw and the two cats left the arcade considerably richer than when they had arrived, while Mary counted the mountain of old pennies that the slot machine had surrendered. The beach was busy when they reached it and Hettie decided that they should take Minnie's advice and sit on one of the villa's verandas rather than join the seaside throng. They queued for the ice creams, getting one for Bruiser as well, and made their way up to Sandscratchers.

All was quiet when they arrived. The ice creams were in grave danger of melting on Minnie's carpets, so Hettie pushed on up the stairs to their room where Bruiser was waking up from a deep sleep. Tilly lingered on the landing, trying several doors until she found one that led out onto a veranda. Hettie and Bruiser joined her and the three cats sat in basket chairs, enjoying their ice creams and watching the comings and goings on the beach.

'I can't believe that we came up on the slot machines,' said Hettie, cleaning her whiskers. 'We'll be going home with more money than we came with at this rate.'

'Especially as we don't have to pay for lunches or fairground rides,' Tilly pointed out.

'Them slots in the fairground are easy too if yer give 'em a nudge,' said Bruiser. 'I won a couple of quid on them last night.'

'Speaking of nudges, it seems you both know how to cheat those machines,' said Tilly. 'I spent nearly all my pennies and got nowhere.'

'Well, you've got five pounds for a penny stake,' Hettie pointed out. 'I'm very happy to share my "winnin's", as Mary called them. After all, it was your penny that won.'

Tilly was pleased with Hettie's generosity but puzzled about what Mary had said on the subject of Minnie. 'I wouldn't have expected Minnie to fix the slot machines. She seems too nice to do anything like that.'

'That's fair cats for yer,' said Bruiser. 'They got ta make a livin' and fixin' slots is no different from bendin' sights on rifles or gluein' coconuts so you can't knock 'em down. If everyone won, they'd be broke in no time.'

Their attention was suddenly drawn to a blue Cadillac climbing the hill to the villa's car park. 'Blimey!' said Bruiser. 'That's one of them flash American cars and Wilt Dinsney's drivin' it. That must 'ave set 'im back a dollar or two.'

'You know what that means,' groaned Hettie. 'Looks like we'll have company at the dinner table again. He gives me indigestion.'

Tilly giggled. 'It's a lovely car, though. I think Minnie has landed on her paws with Wilt.'

'Try telling that to Maisie Meakin,' said Hettie. 'You'd think he'd keep his cowboys under control. They sound no better than that Killer Quince character and his band of thugs.'

'Billy the Kit seemed nice when we met him,' said Tilly, getting up from her chair. 'I'd better go and rescue our washing off the line so that Bruiser can have his clothes back ready for the show tonight.'

Tilly made her way into the kitchen, where there was a hive of activity. Wilt was settling himself down at the table with a large slice of chocolate cake. Minnie was busy stretching dough into pizza shapes and was covered in flour from head to toe, and there was an elderly cat sitting in a chair next to the Aga, eating cherries and spitting the stones out into a coal bucket. Tilly noticed that most of the cherry stones had missed the bucket but no one seemed to mind.

'I hope it's all right,' said Tilly, 'but I've put some washing on your line. We got caught in the storm and Bruiser had to rescue a kitten from the sea.'

'That'll be my little nephew Freddy,' Minnie said, plastering one of the pizza bases with chopped tomato. 'Mr Bruiser has become a real hero – the whole family is singing his praises, although Maisie needs to keep a better eye on those kittens.'

Tilly felt that Minnie's response regarding Maisie was a little unfair and decided to stick up for her. 'But she's been through a terrible time and looking after three kittens on her own must be really difficult.'

'Difficult, you say? It's Maisie being difficult, not wanting those kittens to be part of the family business, especially as we've all looked after her. All families need fresh blood and those three kittens should be our future, but she just doesn't see it that way.'

Tilly realised she'd touched a nerve with Minnie and didn't want to make things worse. She was about to rescue her washing when Wilt offered some pearls of wisdom. 'I reckon Maisie's got a point. The fairground is a dying tradition. By the time those kittens have grown, there'll be nothing left for them to inherit. She's right to want them to make their own way in the world.'

'Any more comments like that, Wilt, and I'll have to call our enragement off,' said Minnie, taking her anger out on a ball of dough. 'You don't know what it's like to be part of a proper family, surrounded by all those young cowboys. We do things differently in this country and we have traditions we're proud of.'

Tilly was beginning to feel she was caught in the middle of one of Wilt's gunfights and moved towards the back door, but the elderly cat by the Aga was keen to join in the conversation. 'I want to know why Micky never comes to see me any more,' she said. 'I hope he's keeping them moon rockets nice. They was the first ride we bought when we settled down as Sandscratchers.'

The silence could easily have been sliced with Minnie's pizza cutter. Tilly scuttled out to the yard as if she hadn't heard the old cat's comments, pulling the door shut behind her. As she unpegged the washing off the line, she remembered what Maisie had said about the family never talking about Micky's death and wondered if that extended to his mother. Did she really not know that he was dead, or had her great age made her forget?

Keen to avoid going through the kitchen again, Tilly spied a gate in the yard which led to a narrow path running round the front of the villa and into the car park. Relieved not to have to re-enter the war zone, she skipped briskly across the front of the building, in through the main entrance and up the stairs to their room. She left the clothes on Bruiser's bed and returned to the veranda, where Hettie and Bruiser had both fallen asleep in the sun.

Tilly crept back into her basket chair and closed her eyes for a moment. The sun was warm and the gentle sound of the waves in the distance, punctuated by the occasional cry of a seagull, lulled her into a pleasant and peaceful doze.

It was Hettie who woke first, and with a start that made her heart pound. She hadn't meant to fall asleep and felt totally disorientated for a few moments, trying to work out why nothing seemed familiar to her. She was relieved to see Tilly and Bruiser either side of her, sleeping in their chairs, but she was also aware of a bell ringing somewhere in the villa.

She popped her head out into the hallway and witnessed a stampede as the family with the kittens tumbled down the stairs, followed at a more sedate pace by the elderly couple they'd seen at dinner the night before. It was clear now that the bell she'd heard was a signal that dinner was being served. She returned to the veranda and woke Tilly and Bruiser with some urgency. 'Come on or we'll miss out on the pizzas,' she said, as Bruiser and Tilly staggered into their room, still half asleep.

Bruiser was pleased to see his T-shirt dry again and relinquished the one that Hettie had lent him. Tilly changed into the one she'd already worn for dinner and Hettie stayed as she was, keen to get to the dining room as quickly as possible. The table they'd shared the night before was laid up ready for them so they slid into their places as Minnie arrived with the first tray of pizzas. She served them to the family in the window and returned minutes later with the elderly couple's dinner. The four female cats arrived late, looking sunburnt and a little fractious, but soon cheered up after Minnie had put their dinners in front of them.

'I hate to tempt fate, but there doesn't seem to be any sign of Wilt joining us,' Hettie whispered. 'We just might be able to have our dinner in peace.'

'I think he might have gone off to his show early,' said Tilly. 'He's not exactly in Minnie's good books at the moment.'

She went on to explain the spat she'd witnessed in the kitchen and the odd comment from Minnie's mother, but the conversation was brought to an abrupt end as Minnie arrived with their dinners. 'Mind you don't burn your mouths on that pineapple,' she warned. 'I've been keeping them hot in the arbour. That extra big pizza is for our hero, Mr Bruiser, who saved a kitten from drowning this morning.'

The rest of the diners stopped eating and offered a round of applause, and the four female cats added a lager-fuelled cheer before getting back to their food. Bruiser looked extremely embarrassed and shyly acknowledged their praise.

'Did you get your washing in all right?' Minnie continued. 'Only I didn't see you come back with it. Me and Wilt were having a bit of a tiff at the time.'

'Yes, thank you,' said Tilly. 'I hope you and Mr Dinsney have made it up?'

'Bless you,' said Minnie. 'Me and Wilt are as different as chalk and peas when it comes to families and fairgrounds. Those American cowboys don't have the proper history that we do. It's all guns and cattle rustling, but he's a fine cat and he makes me happy most of the time. He's gone off in a huff to his show and next he'll be sulking, but I'm making him a steak pie for his dinner tomorrow so he'll soon come round. Don't forget to eat up that cold sore – Mother shredded the cabbage and carrot and she'll be upfronted if there's any left.'

Minnie bustled back to her kitchen, leaving Hettie, Tilly and Bruiser to eat their dinner. There was no further conversation as they devoured their pizzas, but Bruiser was forced to eat the lion's share of the coleslaw as Hettie and Tilly couldn't stand it. The jam suet pudding followed, with a jug of custard on each table, and once again Minnie's guests showed their appreciation with empty plates and bowls.

'We'd better make a move if we're to get to Gobbles Point by seven,' said Hettie. 'We wouldn't want to miss the start of the show.'

The three friends stood to leave the dining room as Minnie arrived to clear the tables. 'Before you all disappear,' she said, 'I'm giving my steak pie, dolphin was potatoes and petty pot peas for tomorrow's dinner, with a lattice plum tart and ice cream for pudding.'

In spite of the pronunciations, a hum of enthusiastic approval came from the diners – but tragedy would strike before the pies were pushed into the Aga.

Chapter Twelve

With Hettie and Tilly in the sidecar, Bruiser negotiated the coastal road to Gobbles Point, giving Miss Scarlet full throttle. The road took them through the middle of a golf course, past a yacht club and on out to a marina, where a host of old boats stood in dry dock. Some were inhabited by cats and others had been left to rot as the harsh North Sea winters had damaged them beyond repair.

Just beyond the graveyard of boats was a giant big top and a signboard announcing that this was 'The Wilt Dinsney Wild West Show'. A line of cats snaked their way towards the entrance, and Hettie, Tilly and Bruiser joined them, after leaving Miss Scarlet parked next to a row of motorbikes and cars. Hettie showed their tickets at the door to an American Indian Chief. The costume was impressive and the cat wore a headdress of feathers that reached the ground. 'Sit wherever you like,' he said in a northern accent, breaking the spell of authenticity. 'Don't forget your souvenir programme – fifty pence and you're all set.'

As the seats were free, Hettie paid up for the pro-gramme and passed it to Tilly for safekeeping. The seats were tiered and followed the line of the big top, leaving a huge circular space in the middle covered in sand. There were giant plastic cacti dotted around the arena and, in the centre, a row of buildings mounted on a run of wooden decking. The Dinsney Saloon was flanked by Marshall Wyatt Twerp's jail and Buffalo Lill's general stores. The set-up was impressive, and Hettie, Tilly and Bruiser managed to find three seats on the front row, facing the buildings where they assumed the action would take place.

'This looks really exciting,' said Tilly, opening the programme. 'That Indian Chief's costume was just like on the TV. I always want them to win when the cowboys fight them, but they never do.'

'We all loves a cowboy film,' said Bruiser, 'but fact is them American Indians was driven out of their lands and made to live on reservations. Them cowboys did terrible things to 'em.'

'Probably not the time or place to have that conver-sation,' Hettie pointed out. 'I'd put money on the cowboys coming out on top in this show if Wilt Dinsney has anything to do with the script. The fact that he's got an American Indian Chief selling programmes says it all, even if he does come from Yorkshire.'

The seats were filling up with cats of all ages. A band of musicians, dressed as Mexicans in wild colourful outfits with puffed sleeves and sombreros, began to march around the arena, playing trumpets and guitars. The audience joined in by clapping their paws and swaying in their seats. Then came the parade. Wilt Dinsney led the way on a beautiful white stallion that lifted its hooves and pranced in time to the music, followed by a line of cowboys doffing their Stetsons to the crowd as they passed by. Next came an open wagon pulled by two horses. The wagon was driven by a buxom female cat, dressed as a Wild West saloon bar hostess in a bright red, low-cut costume and wearing a band around her head stuffed with ostrich feathers.

'Ooh look!' said Tilly. 'Do you think that's Buffalo Lill?'

'I wouldn't be at all surprised,' said Hettie, 'although she's a bit done up for the general stores. I think the cat behind might be her. She looks more like a cowgirl who runs a shop and she's carrying a rifle.'

'I love her fringed jacket,' said Tilly. 'I wonder if you can get fringed cardigans? I wouldn't mind one of those.'

''Ere comes the American Indians,' said Bruiser. 'I wonder which one of them is Crazy Paws, the cat descended from Sittin' Bill? I reckon 'e's the one with the tomahawk – nasty things, but good fer choppin' wood.'

'I'm looking forward to the spirit and fire dance,' said Tilly, studying her programme. 'Look – there's a picture of it.'

Hettie leaned across to look. 'I just hope they've checked the fire extinguishers. It wouldn't take much for this tent to go up in smoke. Look what happened to Turner Page's marquee, although I think that was a blessing.'

Gradually the cats taking part in the parade disappeared into a backstage area and Wilt Dinsney's voice boomed out across the arena from a commentary box, where he'd installed himself ready for the action to begin. 'OK, folks – hang on to your hats,' he said. 'Please put your paws together for Wild Bill Hiccup and Billy the Kit.'

The audience cheered as the two cowboys burst through the saloon doors in a rolling cat fight which went on for some time. The cats were well matched, and surprisingly rather fine acrobats as they tossed each other in the air and landed punches that looked incredibly realistic. The crowd responded by shouting for the cat they wanted to win, their allegiances well matched between the two fighters. The saloon doors burst open again and out came the female cat in the red dress from the parade.

'According to the programme, she's Bessie Saddlebow,' said Tilly. 'I hope she's not going to try joining in the fighting in that dress.'

Tilly's fears were unfounded as the cat pulled up her dress and drew a gun out of a garter, firing it first at Billy the Kit and then at Wild Bill Hiccup. The two cowboys obliged her by falling into the dirt and the audience went wild. The cowboys were soon on their feet again and the three performers took a bow before leaving the arena.

Next came a daring display of bareback riding from two of the American Indians. Tilly was particularly taken with the way they sprang onto each other's horses, crossing over in mid-air. One of the cats stood up on his horse and juggled three tomahawks, catching one by its handle in his teeth. Not to be outdone. the other performer leapt from his horse and turned three somersaults before making a perfect landing on his horse's back. The audience was well and truly energised by the display and even Hettie was on the edge of her seat by the time the performers left the arena. Wilt Dinsney's voice boomed out again as the stage was set for a lasso demonstration. 'Please welcome back Billy the Kit!'

A row of horned bulls was wheeled on, their nostrils smoking and their eyes glowing red for effect. Billy stood quite some distance away from them and twirled a rope above his head before securing the first bull and pulling it over. The crowd willed him on and he completed his task by roping all the bulls without a fault, treating the audience to an encore by roping a young kitten in the front row, much to the delight of his parents as Billy and the kitten took a bow.

Next came Buffalo Lill out of her general stores. She set up a row of bottles right along the decking, stood back and aimed her rifle at them, firing and loading in quick succession until all the bottles were smashed to pieces and not missing any of them. It was an amazing display of shooting and it reminded Bruiser of his lacklustre performance on the fairground's rifle range. Lill took a bow and moved towards the audience, looking for a victim. Before he had time to protest, she'd dragged Bruiser from his seat. The crowd watched as she placed a tin of beans on his head. She stepped back and took aim with her rifle. Bruiser closed his eyes and Hettie and Tilly held their breath. The bullet found its mark and knocked the beans clean off. A cheer went up as Buffalo Lill took Bruiser's paw and kissed it. Bruiser grinned from ear to ear and went back to his seat.

The Mexican band returned to play some more tunes as Wilt announced the interval, directing the audience to the various food and drink stalls outside. 'Come on,' said Hettie. 'Those pizzas of Minnie's went nowhere. I'm starving and I bet there'll be queues.'

'I'm with yer there,' said Bruiser. 'I might 'ave ta stay another day as she's doin' steak pies tomorrow, but I shan't be wantin' beans for a while.'

'I wish you would stay another day,' said Tilly. 'It's lovely having you with us and I'm so pleased that Buffalo Lill didn't shoot your head off.'

The three friends made their way out of the big top and followed the sign to refreshments and stalls. There was so much on offer as they wandered through the crowds. Wilt Dinsney had set up a whole street market, selling hamburgers, hog roast and even a substantial barbecue with ribeye steaks almost as big as Tilly. There was a drinks bar selling root beer, coca cola and a wide selection of alcoholic bottled beers. 'What shall we have?' said Hettie. 'My treat from my slot winnings.'

'I'll 'ave one of them burgers with everythin',' said Bruiser.

'Me too,' said Tilly.

'Right, that's three burgers with everything,' said Hettie, getting in the queue. 'One of you should queue for drinks, as I'm not sure how long the interval is.'

'Righto,' said Bruiser. 'I fancy one of them root beers – what are you two 'avin'?'

'I'll have a coca cola,' said Hettie. 'I don't trust those American beers.'

'I'll come with you and choose,' said Tilly, 'although I like the sound of a root beer, but it might be too grown up for me.'

Tilly and Bruiser left Hettie in the hamburger queue and made their way to the bar. It was busy and much rowdier than the burger van. 'Oh look,' said Tilly. 'There's those horrible cats who started the fight in the fairground last night. They're at the front buying beer. I hope they don't start any trouble here.'

Bruiser's hackles rose as the queue for drinks shuffled forward. Killer Quince and his gang lingered at the bar after they'd been served, laughing and joking with each other and getting in everyone's way. The cat serving the drinks was dressed as a saloon bar host and was looking nervous as Quince and his followers started poking fun at other cats in the queue. 'I think you'd better go back an' 'elp with them burgers,' said Bruiser, keen to get Tilly out of the way of the thugs, but the danger was suddenly removed by Wilt Dinsney himself, who made his way to the front of the queue and had a short conversation with Quince. Wilt led the gang away from the bar and took them to the side of the big top, where he had a longer conversation with them. 'Looks like Wilt's warnin' 'em off,' said Bruiser. ''E don't want the likes of them wreckin' 'is show, not with all these families 'ere.'

Tilly was relieved that Wilt had come to the rescue and decided on the root beer. Hettie was having trouble carrying the burgers when they returned to her. 'Why is everything American so big?' she said. 'There's no such thing as small anything and look at the stuff they've crammed into these burgers. It puts Greasy Tom's van back in the town to shame.'

The three cats sat on hay bales that had been strategically placed around the food area and enjoyed their burgers and drinks. By the time they'd finished, Tilly's T-shirt looked like it had been part of a Wild West massacre; undaunted, she decided to brave the crowds again to look at some of the stalls that were selling other things besides food.

As they wandered along, Bruiser kept a watchful eye out for Quince and his gang but there was no sign of them, only happy families enjoying their evening. Tilly was keen to take a souvenir or two home with her, as the five pounds that Hettie had given her was burning a hole in the pocket of her shorts. She stopped to admire some American Indian beadwork, choosing a necklace in blue, red and purple with splashes of white. To even things up, she bought a sheriff star badge from a cowboy stall and was tempted by a colourful foldaway wigwam, which she thought would provide a perfect bit of shade on the Butters' lawn, but decided against it in favour of a bow and a set of arrows with suckers on the ends. She loved watching *The Adventures of Robin Hood* on TV and had always fancied a go at archery.

Bruiser chose a fine leather waistcoat from the cowhide stall and Hettie treated herself to an ornate peace pipe for smoking her catnip. The Mexican band struck up again in the big top, heralding the start of the second half of the show. The audience resumed their seats, now overburdened with food and shopping, as Wilt Dinsney's voice rang out across the arena once again.

'Guys and gals, all the way from the Sacred Mountains of Montana, please give a Wild West welcome for the one and only Crazy Paws, directly descended from Chief Sitting Bill himself and accompanied by the Black Foot Spirit Dancers.'

The crowd went wild as the arena filled with the extraordinary sight of over twenty American Indian cats in full regalia. They shuffled and hopped to the beat of a drum in perfect formation, singing out their war cries as they circled a cat wearing a full headdress. 'That must be Crazy Paws,' said Tilly excitedly, 'and look – he's blowing fire out of his mouth and lighting those torches.'

It was a true spectacle as Crazy Paws passed the lit torches to the Black Foot Dancers. The lights in the big top were suddenly switched off and the fire dance began. The cats had painted their faces and feet with a fluorescent substance and as soon as the lights went down the effect was truly magical. The bodiless dancers threw their torches high up into the big top like giant rockets, letting them fall almost to the ground before catching them and tossing them back up into the air once more. Tilly was beside herself and Hettie sat open mouthed. Bruiser clutched his new waistcoat, delighted that he'd stayed another night to come to the show.

The grand finale was a little less pleasing. Once the spirit and fire dance was over, there was a rush of mounted cowboys into the arena, firing their guns into the air as they rounded up the American Indians and herded them in front of the sheriff's office. There was a roar from the crowd as Marshall Wyatt Twerp stepped out of the building and systematically shot all the Black Foot Dancers dead before twirling his guns and forcing them back into their holsters.

With only Crazy Paws left standing, Billy the Kit rode forward and lassoed him, dragging him to a beam that jutted out from the front of the Marshall's building. The mock hanging went down well with the audience but Tilly was distraught and covered her eyes with her paws.

The Mexican band struck up again as all the Black Foot Dancers came back to life and stood up. Crazy Paws, fresh from his hanging, removed the rope from around his neck and, with perfect timing, jumped onto the back of a horse and rode bareback around the arena, much to the delight of the crowd and Tilly's great relief.

The Wild West show finished as it had begun, with all those taking part parading around the big top and taking their final bows as the audience stood to show their appreciation.

'That's all folks,' said the voice of Wilt Dinsney. 'Safe journey home now and goodnight.'

Chapter Thirteen

The road from Gobbles Point was a little more treacherous in the dark, made problematic by the cars and motorbikes heading back into town after the Wild West experience and Bruiser was glad Hettie was riding pillion as an extra pair of eyes.

As well as the audience, many of the performers appearing in the show were now heading for the late night bars and clubs in Felixtoe, keen to relax after their triumphant endeavours under the big top.

Bruiser congratulated himself on being ahead of most of the traffic and he was making quick work of the road that ran through the golf course when a squadron of motorbikes appeared from the direction of the town and roared towards Miss Scarlet. Assuming they would slow down, Bruiser continued at a steady pace but the motorbikes approaching him showed no sign of reducing their speed. The crash, when it came, felt like everything was in slow motion. Bruiser's instinct was to swerve into a bunker just off the road, but not before he'd come face to face with Killer

Quince, who was steering his bike straight at them. Hettie, riding pillion, was thrown clear and the sand from the bunker cushioned her landing, but Miss Scarlet was turned upside down with Tilly trapped in the sidecar and the motorbike on top of Bruiser's legs. Quince and his gang roared on across the golf course without a backward glance, set on creating more havoc with the oncoming cars.

The bunker obscured the crash from the road and traffic passed by oblivious to what had just happened. Hettie lay dazed, seeing stars for several minutes, but eventually she managed to haul herself up onto her feet, desperate to get to Miss Scarlet. 'Are you all right?' she shouted, seeing that Bruiser was struggling to get free of the motorbike.

'It's on me legs and it's too 'evvy ta lift, but it's Tilly I'm worried about,' said Bruiser. 'Yer need ta get some 'elp.'

Hettie scrambled up the side of the bunker and onto the road, hoping to flag down someone to help, and she was relieved to see the blue Cadillac coming into view. She stood in the middle of the road and waved her arms and Wilt Dinsney slowed down and pulled over. 'Please help us!' Hettie said, as Wilt got out of his car. 'We've been driven off the road and Bruiser and Tilly are trapped.'

Wilt reacted immediately and slid down into the bunker, followed by Hettie. 'Don't you worry,' he said, assessing the situation, 'we'll have them out of this in no time. The first thing we need to do is get this bike off Bruiser.' He made several attempts to pull the motorbike away from Bruiser's legs, but with the added weight of the sidecar it was just too heavy. 'I'll have to get my jack from the boot of the car. It won't take a minute.'

Wilt clambered his way back to the road and returned minutes later with the jack, wasting no time in forcing it under the motorbike. Inserting the handle, he wound it up until the bike began to lift and Hettie waited until it was high enough for her to pull her friend out. Bruiser struggled to his feet, looking reasonably unscathed except for some cuts to his legs, but all eyes now turned to the sidecar that was upside down and partially buried in the sand. 'I think we need ta disconnect the bike,' said Bruiser, 'but I can't get at me tools 'cos they're in the boot.'

'I got a whole bunch of tools in my car,' said Wilt, scrambling up to the road again.

Hettie and Bruiser circled the sidecar, desperately looking for any sign of life, but it was impossible to see anything and there were no sounds coming from it either. Wilt slid a large toolbox down into the bunker and Bruiser pounced on it, searching for something he could use to separate the bike from the sidecar. He found what he was looking for and set about the task with an adjustable spanner. Within no time, the bolts were undone and Wilt helped him to pull the bike free. The three cats rocked the sidecar until it freed itself from the sand and with a huge effort they forced it back onto its wheels the right way up. It was hard to see through the windscreen, which was covered in sand, but Bruiser wasted no time in sliding it back to reveal Tilly sitting up as bright as a button, clutching her bow and arrows. 'Thank goodness everyone is all right!' she said, looking at Hettie and Bruiser. 'I felt like one of Beryl's upside-down cakes for a minute there. I hope Miss Scarlet will be OK. She seems to have lost her motorbike.'

Hettie and Bruiser laughed from sheer relief and Wilt lifted Tilly out of the sidecar. 'There you go little lady,' he said. 'I think you'd all better ride with me back to the villa and sort your bike out in the morning when it gets light.'

Bruiser had a quick look at Miss Scarlet to assess the damage. The paintwork would need some touching up and a mudguard on the sidecar might have to be replaced, but he was satisfied that he could get her back on the road in the morning. Not wanting to leave his tools behind, he grabbed the box from Miss Scarlet's boot and Hettie carried the things they'd bought from the stalls at the show, including Tilly's bow and arrows. Tilly wrapped herself in her tartan blanket, suddenly beginning to feel the shock of her accident.

The three friends scrambled out of the bunker and into the Cadillac, all sharing the back seat, where there was plenty of room. Wilt followed them back onto the road and put his toolbox and jack in the boot before driving home to the villa. It was late and the fairground was in darkness when they passed it, but – as Wilt turned the car onto the hill – a dark shape stepped out in front of them. Wilt swerved to miss it, but Hettie recognised him straight away. 'That was Premo Pete,' she said. 'It's a bit late for hiring deck-chairs so I wonder what he's up to?'

'That guy's a real nuisance,' said Wilt, turning into the car park. 'He's always skulking around late at night. I don't reckon he has a home to go to.'

Minnie greeted them at the door. 'I was wondering where you'd got to,' she said. 'It's nearly midnight and just look at the state of you. Looks like you three have been dragged through a fridge backwards, and where's your lovely motorbike?'

Wilt explained briefly what had happened as Hettie and Bruiser helped Tilly up the stairs to their room. By now, she was shaking, starting a headache and barely able to put one foot in front of the other. They put her to bed and Minnie arrived with a hot water bottle and a tray of hot chocolates and shortbread. Wilt followed her into the room with a box of plasters and a tube of antiseptic cream for Bruiser's legs.

'What an awful thing to happen,' Minnie said, put-ting the drinks down on the other bed. 'That road out to Gobbles Point is a nightmare and the bikers who squat on the old boats in the marina use it as a racetrack. Mind you, living out there, at least they don't bother the holidaymakers so much in the town, that's why no one has tried to invent them.'

'Trouble is, they meant ta get us,' said Bruiser, applying the cream to his cuts. 'That was Killer Quince an' 'is mob – ran us off the road, 'e did. They was spoilin' fer a fight at the Wild West show, too, but Wilt 'ere sorted 'em.'

'It's a shame that no one has run them out of town,' said Hettie, munching absent-mindedly on a shortbread finger. 'They seem hell-bent on ruining anything good about Felixtoe. First the fairground and now the Wild West show, not to mention a spot of hit and run on the golf course.'

Minnie nodded. 'And then there was the fire on the pier a couple of weeks ago. My sister Mary put that out before it took hold. It started in Monica's café when Mary was in there having a marmite and cheese roll. She said it was bikers who started it in an ashtray. She got it under control by pouring a banana and chocolate milkshake over it, but it melted the Fablon table top.'

'Come on, Minnie,' said Wilt. 'Let's leave these guys to get some sleep. If you need a lift back to your motorbike in the morning, though, just let me know at breakfast and I'll run you out there.'

'That's kind of you,' said Hettie, 'and thank you for coming to our rescue.'

'Pleasure's all mine,' said Wilt. 'Glad to help you out.'

Wilt and Minnie left them to enjoy their bedtime drinks. Tilly sipped her hot chocolate, but refused a piece of shortbread. She was beginning to feel a little better, comforted by the hot water bottle, and soon drifted off to sleep.

Bruiser and Hettie finished the shortbread and took to their beds. Bruiser fell asleep as soon as his head hit the pillow but Hettie lay awake, mulling over the day's events. She was troubled by how close they'd come to being killed on the golf course, but there was something else bothering her which she couldn't quite put her claw on.

Chapter Fourteen

The day started well: Tilly woke feeling much better after a good night's sleep; Bruiser was none the worse for a few cuts and a sore foot; and Hettie was unscathed except for a broken claw, although she had hardly slept. Refreshed from his rest, Bruiser was keen to rescue Miss Scarlet from the bunker. 'If I can get 'er runnin' OK, I'd better take 'er back to the town an' sort the paintwork out,' he said. 'I reckon Lazarus will be able ta fix me up with a mudguard from 'is spares department if I can't fix the old one.'

Lazarus Hambone and his aged mother, Meridian, ran the hardware store in the town where Hettie, Tilly and Bruiser lived. There was nothing Lazarus couldn't lay his paws on and his passion was motorbikes. Hettie had bought Miss Scarlet from him when she and Tilly had started their detective agency, and Bruiser spent many a happy hour in his yard at the back of the hardware store, chewing over the merits of Royal Enfields, Triumphs and Nortons.

'It's a shame you're going home,' said Tilly. 'It's been lovely having you with us.'

'I'll be back at the end of the week ta pick you up,' Bruiser promised. 'I might even bring Dolly fer a day out.'

'Maybe we could all go back to the fair?' suggested Tilly. 'I'd love another go on Marlon's dodgems.'

'I bet you would,' said Hettie, 'but one crash a week is enough.'

Tilly giggled but realised that her head still hurt. She investigated it with her paw and discovered a walnut-sized bump between her ears which was very sore. 'I suppose you're right,' she said, 'but I'm much more experienced now on the dodgems, and I've also been in a real crash. Not many cats have been turned upside down in a sidecar.'

'Well, maybe your friend Marlon could introduce it to the fairground as a new ride,' suggested Hettie, 'although I've had enough thrills and spills to last me a lifetime on this holiday.'

The smell of bacon drifted under their door, reminding them that breakfast was being served. Tilly slid out of bed and pulled on a clean T-shirt, casting the one she'd eaten the hamburger in at the Wild West show into her tartan shopper. Hettie and Bruiser stuck with their clothes from the day before and the three cats made their way down to the dining room. Breakfast was in full swing when they got there. The kittens belonging to the two cats in the window were banging their spoons on boiled eggs; the four female cats were drinking orange juice and looking nauseous after frequenting the Sailor's Sloop cocktail bar the night before; and the elderly couple tucked into scrambled eggs and bacon.

Minnie bustled through from the kitchen, followed by Wilt, who joined Hettie, Tilly and Bruiser at their table. Since he had rescued them from the crash, Hettie felt much more affable towards him, especially as Bruiser was about to take up his kind offer of running them out to Miss Scarlet.

'I'm doing scrambled eggs, bacon and sausage this morning, on account of Mother knocking the eggs off the kitchen table,' said Minnie. 'Luckily they were still in their box, so I managed to salvage most of them. I can do a boiled egg at a pinch, if I can find some that aren't cracked, but I've given the best ones to the kittens. The good news is I can now do toast, as Chief Fire Officer Mudlark returned my toaster yesterday. He said he'd had to rewire it but he was satisfied that it was no longer a fire hazard.'

'If it's not too much trouble, I'd like my eggs scrumbled,' said Tilly, 'with bacon and toast.'

'Scrumbled it is,' said Minnie. 'It's years since I scrumbled eggs, leaving the white bits in.'

Tilly was delighted that Minnie knew about scrumbled eggs, as she usually got a strange look when she ordered them in other places. 'I'll 'ave the same as Tilly, but with a sausage as well,' said Bruiser, 'an' some toast.'

'That will be lovely for me, too,' said Hettie. 'We have to go and rescue our motorbike this morning and Bruiser is supposed to be going home today.'

'Well that's a shame,' said Minnie. 'You can move into number six later, when these ladies have left.' She pointed in the direction of the four female cats, who looked a bit less green. 'Full sea view in there and four beds. I like to call it my combination suite for lounging or sleeping, and there's an occasional table in there, too – all mob coms.'

Wilt, who had been quieter than usual, added his breakfast order and Minnie returned to her kitchen.

'Thank you again for what you did to help us last night,' said Hettie. 'We could all still be lying undiscovered in that bunker.'

'Glad I could help,' said Wilt. 'Someone needs to talk to those guys before they kill someone. You three had a narrow escape.'

'If yer' sure yer don't mind, a lift out to the golf course would be great,' said Bruiser.

'And we'll come too,' said Tilly. 'I'd love another ride in your Catalack. It's a lovely blue and the back seat is nearly as big as our room back at home.'

Wilt laughed. 'Well, we have to have big cars back in the US because of all the long drives from state to state. You need to be comfortable going across those prairies. In the old days, they did it by horse or wagon, often driving cattle at the same time. It took them months.'

'I don't think I would have liked to live in the Wild West,' said Tilly. 'The trouble is, I wouldn't want to be a cowboy. I'd much rather be an American Indian, as they have nicer clothes and perform magic, but the cowboys always seem to want to kill the Indians, which doesn't seem very fair.'

Wilt laughed again at Tilly's logic. 'It's true that there was big trouble out there in those days, but cowboys spent a lot of their time killing other cowboys too. In those early pioneering days, life was hard and you had to live by the gun or get cut down yourself. Anyway, many of those cowboys came across from little old England as settlers, looking for gold in them there hills.'

Wilt's history of America was brought to an abrupt halt by Minnie's arrival with the breakfasts. 'Help yourselves to the plates,' she said, banging the tray down on the table. 'Marlon has just turned up in a terrible state, so I'll have to go and see what's amiss. He's got Mother all aggravated and that's the last thing I need with the breakfast dishes and numbers six and seven to change over.'

Minnie disappeared back into her kitchen, leaving Hettie, Tilly, Bruiser and Wilt to get on with their breakfasts. When their plates were licked clean, they left the dining room. Wilt went out to his car, saying that he would wait in the car park, and the others returned to their room to pack up for the move to number six. They'd only been there a few minutes when there was a knock at the door. Tilly opened it to Minnie, who forced her way in with some urgency. 'I'm sorry to ask,' she said, 'as I know you're all on holiday, but could one of you come and have a word with Marlon? He's in a real state and I can't get a sensible word out of him. He keeps saying that the whole family has disappeared, which is ridiculous.'

'I'll come and talk to him,' said Hettie. 'Why don't you two go with Wilt to fetch Miss Scarlet? We don't want anyone stealing her and it may take some time to get her back on the road.'

Tilly was torn between wanting to know what was wrong with Marlon and having a ride in Wilt's car. She decided that her priority was Miss Scarlet and reluctantly followed Bruiser and his toolbox out to the car park as Hettie and Minnie headed for the kitchen.

The scene downstairs was not a happy one. There were stacks of unwashed breakfast dishes piled up in the sink, a baking tray full of empty pastry cases waiting to be filled on the kitchen table, and a pot of stewing steak and onions bubbling away on top of the Aga. In the middle of this promise of dinner sat Marlon Meakin with his head in his paws, while his mother knitted furiously and talked to herself in some sort of unintelligible language.

'Don't pay any attention to Mother,' Minnie said. 'She's in a world of her own. She always turns to her knitting when she's anxious and starts talking nonsense – old fairground speak is what that is. I think you've met my brother, Marlon? Marlon, this is one of my guests who's a detective. Why don't you tell her what's bothering you while I put the kettle on and get these pies sorted?'

Marlon looked up at Hettie. 'Oh yes,' he said, 'you were at the dodgems with your friends the other night. You helped Monty get rid of Quince and his gang.'

'That's right,' said Hettie, sitting on one of the kitchen chairs, 'although it was Bruiser who helped Monty, but you taught my friend Tilly to drive a dodgem. Minnie says that you think your family has disappeared – would you like me to try and help?'

'I'm not sure you can,' said Marlon, looking utterly miserable. 'I just don't understand what could have happened to them.'

'Why don't you start at the beginning. Who exactly is missing?'

'My son Monty, my brothers Maxwell, Matty and Marty, and my sister Marmalade, as far as I can see. I haven't checked the pier yet to see if Mary is running her slots.'

'And what makes you think they're missing?' asked Hettie. 'Maybe they've gone off on a family jaunt or something?'

'Not without telling me. They all have responsibilities and they should have been at work this morning, checking the rides, but there's no sign of any of them. I even checked their wagons before I came up here. Monty's is next to mine and Monica's. She tidies up after him but she says his bed hasn't been slept in.'

'So when did you last see them all?'

'Last night, around six. Monica and me were having a night off to celebrate our anniversary. I booked a table at the Sailor's Sloop, as they have dancing there. Monica loves to dance. I took the float round to all the rides before we left and put Monty in charge of the dodgems. He was really pleased as it was the first time I've trusted him to handle them on his own.'

'So what time did you get home?' asked Hettie.

'Close to midnight, I suppose. Monica was keen to dance the night away and we'd had such a lovely time.'

'So the fair was closed by the time you got home?'

'Oh yes – we always close at ten in the week. We wouldn't want to be open when the pubs turn out.'

'You said that no one turned up to check the rides this morning,' said Hettie. 'Why aren't the rides checked at night before everyone goes back to their wagons?'

'Because someone might tamper with them over-night. If we check them in the morning, we've got time to fix anything that needs fixing before we open again.'

'Have you checked the rides today?'

Marlon shook his head. 'No. All I've done is look for everyone. I came up here thinking they might be visiting Minnie at the villa. It was the only place I hadn't looked.'

'As you went round the fair this morning, looking for your family, how had the rides been left?'

'Same as usual,' said Marlon. 'All packed away and cashed up, but there was no sign of the takings in Monty's wagon. I left him in charge of collecting the cash.'

'Could he have run away with the money?'

'Not in a million years. He's a good boy and the fairground means everything to him.'

'What about the others who are missing? Was there any bad feeling between them?'

'Not that I know of. There's rows from time to time, like in any family, and Maxwell and Marty don't always hit it off, but none of them would steal the takings and run away.'

'Why don't you go back down to the fairground with Hettie here?' said Minnie. 'It's not good for Mother to hear all this and I bet they've turned up while you've been gone. I wouldn't be at all surprised if Maxwell hasn't booked an all-night fishing trip for them on that boat of his, although I can't see Marmalade getting her feet wet or reeling in a fish. She's got lots of admirers, though – she could have gone off with any one of them. She told me she had a fancy for that Billy the Kit from Wilt's show, but I'm not sure it came to anything.'

'I agree with Minnie,' said Hettie. 'I think we should go down to the fair and see if anyone has turned up before we start getting worried. I'm sure there's a simple explanation.'

'OK,' said Marlon. 'You're probably right. It was just really strange for the fair to be so deserted this morning, especially as Monty was a no-show. He's always so reliable.'

Marlon and Hettie stood up to go. 'Bruiser and Tilly have gone off with Wilt to retrieve our motorbike,' said Hettie. 'If they come back here before me, could you let them know where I've gone? Bruiser is supposed to be going home today and I wouldn't want to miss him. You could ask them to meet me in Monica's café on the pier for lunch.'

'Don't worry, I'll let them know,' said Minnie, 'and when I've filled these pastry cases, I'll move your things from number seven to number six. If Bruiser decides to stay on, there's plenty of room for him in there.'

Hettie and Marlon left the villa and walked across to the fairground. The beach was virtually empty, as the weather had changed. There was a slight drizzle in the air and it had grown much colder. The sea looked dark and uninviting and Hettie noticed that Premo Pete was huddled under his umbrella by the kiosk with a stack of unwanted deckchairs next to him.

'The pier will be busy today,' said Marlon, as they crossed the sand. 'Monica and Mary will be rushed off their feet, that's if Mary has turned up. The slots are only popular on days like this, and they all go in the café afterwards. Poor Monica needs a bigger café, really, and with this decimalisation the slot machines are completely out of date. It would cost us a fortune to convert them. The whole of the pier needs a revamp. There are days like today when I wish me and Monica could run away to one of those islands out there and never see a slot machine or a dodgem car again.'

'It's a big responsibility that your father put on you and I don't suppose there's much money in it with such a big family to support,' said Hettie.

'You're right there, especially as the work is seasonal – a bad summer could finish us, and days like today don't help. There's a storm brewing out there on the horizon, and if it comes in it'll scupper the weekend takings. The trouble here is that we flood easily. That's why my dad built the rides high off the ground. Thinking about it, the sensible thing to do is to sell up to Wilt Dinsney. He offers me good money at the beginning of every season for our pitch on the beach, but I just can't do it to the rest of the family.'

'So is Wilt wanting to move his Wild West show to the beach?'

'Not just the show. He's got plans to build a whole Wild West town, with cafés and bars and re-enactments – a theme park, basically. According to him it's the next big thing and he's probably right – it would bring the holidaymakers in from miles around, that's for sure.'

'Is it just the family that's stopping you taking him up on his offer?'

'That and the tradition. We're one of the oldest Sandscratcher families in the country. If I did sell to him, we'd all be homeless as he wants the wagon park as well.'

'Couldn't you all go back to living at the villa?' suggested Hettie.

Marlon laughed. 'I don't think Minnie would be very happy about that. She's the only one of us who makes a decent living all year round with her guest house, and she gets to keep her money because she looks after my mother.'

The discussions about the family and Wilt's desire to build a town full of cowboys were curtailed as Hettie and Marlon walked through the arch of Meakins Mewsments. The fairground was a very different place to the one that Hettie had visited the night before last. It was a ghost town. The rides stood motionless, the stalls were closed up and the slot machines had been covered over, making them look like a faceless canvas army. The only sign that there had been life was the litter on the ground: discarded wrappers from hot dogs; half-eaten toffee apples; and the odd bag of candyfloss, blowing like tumbleweed down the avenues that led to the rides. The drizzle had now become a fine sea fret, covering everything in a salty moisture, and the visibility was becoming poorer as Hettie and Marlon made for the dodgems, where he kept a small office.

'It doesn't look like anyone has turned up,' said Hettie. 'Maybe the weather has put them off. Do you still open when it's bad?'

'We only close if it's really bad. These sea frets lift as soon as they arrive, so we could be looking at blue sky in half an hour – but that's not the point. Even if we have no customers, there's still work to be done, supplies to fetch and general maintenance of the rides. I've got a couple of dodgems at the back of my office that need some repairs, and on a day like today that's what I should be doing. That goes for the rest of the family – there's always plenty to do on a fairground. I just don't understand where they've all got to.'

'Would you mind if I take a look around?' asked Hettie, feeling as defeated as Marlon and not really having a clue what she might be looking for.

'Be my guest,' he said, slumping down behind his desk. 'I've got some paperwork to catch up on and some ordering to do for Monica's café. Go where you like – you might spot something I've missed.'

Hettie left Marlon's office and wandered down the main avenue of the fairground. A thick fog had descended, transforming the colourful rides into solid blocks of giant machinery that loomed out in front of her as she progressed through the fair. She passed the gallopers, the joyful horses now presenting themselves as grotesque figureheads bathed in swirling mists. The fog had deadened all sound and Hettie was hardly aware of her own footsteps. She felt disorientated and tried to work out where she was. Ahead of her was a ride she hadn't noticed when she'd visited with Tilly. Unlike the other attractions, this one seemed out of use; as she drew closer, she could see that it was the moon rocket ride. The moon rockets themselves were covered over and she realised that this must be the place where Micky Meakin had had his accident; she could just make out the picket fence that Maisie had described, and by it lay a bunch of dead flowers. So Micky hadn't entirely been forgotten, she thought, as she moved on.

She turned left at the end of the avenue and walked by a parade of rifle ranges, coconut shies and hoopla stalls, all shuttered like abandoned lock-ups. A little further along, she could just make out the ghost train and allowed herself a small shudder at the memory. Since becoming a detective, she had attended some horrific murder scenes, but her experience in Marty Meakin's ghost train had made a lasting impression on her and had terrified Tilly. It was strange, she thought, that cats would want to pay good money to be frightened in such a way.

The ghost train, when she reached it, appeared to be locked up. The kiosk was shuttered and there was a bar across the double doors where the train began its journey into the horrors that Marty had prepared for his customers. The carriages stood empty on the tracks and Hettie climbed into the one at the front, confident that this time it was going nowhere. The fog showed no sign of lifting and she sat contemplating what to do next. As Marlon had said, the fairground was deserted and it was moving towards the time when it should be open for the day. Then she remembered what Premo Pete had said. Could it be possible that the missing Meakins were all dead?

Chapter Fifteen

As predicted, Monica Meakin's café was busy when Hettie arrived. The weather had gone from bad to worse and she'd left Marlon pondering over his paperwork and getting more and more anxious about his son and brothers and sister, who still seemed to be missing. As luck would have it, Maisie was just finishing her lunch at her usual table by the window, this time without her kittens. She waved to Hettie to come across and join her. 'I'm nearly done,' she said, 'so you can have my table. I'll have to be off in a minute as I've left Freddy, Frankie and Lizzy at one of those holiday playgroups at the Spa Pavilion on the seafront. Goodness knows what state they'll be in. They're doing potato prints, which means more paint than kitten when I collect them, but it does give me a break. I can't wait for school to start, although as soon as they go I'll miss them. Monica has promised me a few hours here at the café when the new term begins, which will bring in a few extra pennies.'

'You said that you lived in a wagon with the rest of the Meakins?' Hettie said, keeping a watchful eye out for Tilly and Bruiser. 'I don't suppose you saw any of them this morning or late last night?'

'No,' said Maisie, 'why do you ask?'

'Well, it seems that several of them have gone missing.'

'Missing?' Maisie repeated. 'I know that young Monty has gone off somewhere, as Monica is in a bit of a flap about it, but I didn't realise there was a problem with any of the others. They should all be down at the fair by now.'

'That's the problem,' said Hettie, 'none of them showed up for work this morning and Marlon is beside himself. That's why I wondered if you'd seen any of them around the wagons?'

Maisie thought for a moment before replying. 'I saw Marmalade yesterday morning when she was painting one of the horses from the gallopers outside her wagon. My kittens were trying to join in and that's why I took them to the beach – they were being a bit of a nuisance. But I don't think I saw any of the others. They'd be at the fairground, I suppose.'

'And late last night?' Hettie continued. 'Did you hear or see anything out of the ordinary around the time the fair closed?'

'Not really. I was listening to the radio until late, but I think Mary might have had a visitor. She has the wagon next to mine and I heard her door slam around ten, although I couldn't be certain as there's a lot of comings and goings at that time of night. I shouldn't tell you this, but she's been walking out with Premo Pete recently. She thinks it's a secret but I've seen him come and go from her wagon. If the family found out they wouldn't be happy about it as he's an outsider.'

'What's wrong with being an outsider?' asked Hettie.

'Well, it's bad enough marrying into the family if you're female – it takes years to be accepted – but bringing a male cat into the family is unheard of. That's why Marmalade and Mary are still single, although Marmalade has been seen out with Billy the Kit from the Wild West show. She's got lots of admirers.'

'So what about Minnie?' said Hettie. 'Isn't she going to marry Wilt Dinsney?'

Maisie laughed. 'That engagement has lasted years. Every summer she announces that there's going to be an autumn wedding and by the end of the season it's all off. Although if she did want to marry him, I don't think the family would mind as there's no danger of Wilt taking over the fair and the pier, and Minnie is fairly self-contained up at the villa.'

Hettie was tempted to repeat what Marlon had told her about Wilt's bid to build his Wild West town on the site of the fairground, but decided against it as her attention was drawn to the door, where Tilly and Bruiser had just arrived. She waved her paw at them and they made their way over to the table.

'I'd better be off,' said Maisie, 'or I'll be late to pick up the kittens. I hope I'll see you again before you go home. Sorry I couldn't be more help about your missing Meakins but I'm sure they'll turn up.'

She nodded to Bruiser and Tilly, and made her way out of the café as they sat down at the table. 'So how is Miss Scarlet?' asked Hettie. 'Did you get her back all right?'

'Yep,' said Bruiser. 'No bother with 'er mechanics an' the sidecar bolted on OK, but she's goin' ta need a bit of a respray 'ere an' there and two new mudguards. Lazarus will sort me out with them.'

'We had to come back in the fog,' added Tilly, 'and that was a bit scary across the golf course. Bruiser thinks he might stay another night because of the weather.'

'I think that's an excellent idea,' said Hettie. 'The weather is pretty bad and Marlon thinks there might be a storm coming. You don't want to be biking in that. Also, we may have a case on our paws.'

'How did you get on with Marlon?' asked Tilly.

Hettie was about to explain the situation regarding the disappearing Meakins when Monica arrived with her order pad. 'I don't suppose you've any news on Monty?' she said, looking anxious. 'Marlon's just phoned me to say that you were kind enough to go down to the fairground this morning. I really don't understand where Monty has got to. He's not the kind of cat to take off and let his father down, and as for the rest of them, it just doesn't make any sense.'

'I'm sorry to say there's no sign of any of them,' said Hettie, 'but we do intend to get to the bottom of it, I promise you.'

'That's kind,' said Monica. 'What can I get you for lunch? At least being busy helps while I wait for news.'

'I'd like scampi and some red sauce to dip them in please,' said Tilly.

'I'd like a cheese omelette an' chips,' said Bruiser. Hettie scanned the menu but decided to have the same as Bruiser, and Monica returned to her kitchen.

While they were waiting for their food, Hettie brought Tilly and Bruiser up to speed on her conversations with Marlon and Maisie. 'The trouble is, they do all seem to have disappeared into thin air,' she said. 'It was hard to see anything down at the fairground this morning in this fog, but the whole place was deserted. No sign of life anywhere. It's like they packed up last night and just walked away.'

'Bit like the *Mary Celeste* then,' said Bruiser.

'Did she work on a fairground?' asked Tilly.

Bruiser laughed. 'She was a ship,' he explained, 'back in the eighteen 'undreds, cast adrift with all 'er crew missin', but on board everythin' was as normal, with provisions and personal effects. No sign of any trouble but the crew was never seen again. Some say a giant squid got 'em, others that it was one of them paranormal 'appenin's, but I don't s'pose we'll ever know what 'appened to them cats.'

'Another nugget from the Bruiser thesaurus,' said Hettie. 'I bet that didn't come from *Bikers' Monthly*?'

'No,' said Bruiser. 'I learnt that at the Cat an' Fiddle pub quiz.'

'What does thesaurus mean?' asked Tilly. 'It sounds like a sort of dinosaur.'

Hettie was about to explain but Monica arrived with the lunches and any further conversation was put on hold as the three cats tucked into their food.

The fog seemed to be clearing, although the sky was full of dark clouds and there was no sign of the sun putting in an appearance. As Hettie, Tilly and Bruiser left Monica's café, Mary Meakin rushed past them, snatching a late lunch break while her slot machines were quiet. Hettie stared after her, tempted to see if she could shed any light on the current situation, but thought better of it.

'One thing's clear,' said Hettie as they walked along the pier and past the slot machine arcade, 'only the fairground workers seem to be missing. Mary, Minnie, Marlon and Monica seem to have escaped whatever happened last night.'

'I can't believe that Mary Queen of Slots is going out with Peter King of Deckchairs,' said Tilly. 'I can see why she wants to keep it a secret – they don't seem very well matched.'

'It was a revelation to me,' said Hettie, 'but look at Wilt and Minnie – they make an odd pair too, and it seems with all this family stuff the female cats don't have a lot of choice in who they get close to.'

'So what shall we do now?'

'I think we'd better go down to the fairground and see if anyone has turned up for work. Now the fog is lifting, we can have a proper look round to see if there's any sign of a fight or an accident that would explain these disappearances.'

'Quince an' 'is mob were comin' from the town when they ran us off the road last night,' said Bruiser. 'Maybe they'd been ta the fair, causin' trouble after Wilt 'ad seen 'em off from 'is Wild West show.'

'That was my first thought,' said Hettie, 'which is why we need to take a closer look at the fairground. It's possible that the Meakins were attacked and locked up somewhere, or even worse. Quince and his thugs are clearly capable of anything. They could have killed us last night and there's definitely some animosity between Quince and the fairground workers.'

'Minnie told us that Quince and his gang live on some old boats out by the marina,' said Tilly. 'She said they were squatters, but nobody wanted to get rid of them because they didn't want them in the town to frighten the holidaymakers away.'

'She's got a point,' said Hettie. 'If the missing Meakins don't turn up, we may have to pay them a visit out there.'

The fairground was still deserted when they reached it. There were a number of families with disappointed kittens coming away from the entrance, where Marlon had put up a sign saying closed until further notice. 'That answers my question,' said Hettie. 'Clearly no one has turned up for work. I think we should split up and search every ride. There must be some clues somewhere. Cats don't just disappear without a trace.'

'Unless it's the *Mary Celeste*,' Tilly pointed out. 'What are we looking for in the way of clues?'

'Anything out of the ordinary: signs of a fight, blood, anything broken, drag marks on the ground,' said Hettie. 'I'll go and see if Marlon is still on site.'

The three cats set off in different directions. Hettie found Marlon round the back of his office, attending to one of his dodgems. 'I don't suppose you've heard from anyone?' she said.

Marlon shook his head. 'No, nothing, and I'm getting really worried. I've had to close the fair as there's no one to run the rides, and I'll have to keep it closed until I get some news. At least Mary is OK. Monica says she's having lunch in the café so whatever has happened it's just to the family working the fairground.'

'My friends are searching all the rides at the moment,' said Hettie. 'It would be helpful if you could unlock the stalls that have shutters so we can check them too.'

'Of course,' said Marlon. 'I'll just get the keys.'

Marlon collected the keys from his office and walked down the avenue with Hettie to where the rifle range and other games were. He unlocked the shutters and threw them open one by one, but there was nothing out of the ordinary to be seen. 'I noticed that the ghost train was locked when I was here earlier,' said Hettie. 'I'd like to take a look in there if possible, just in case someone has got trapped or had an accident.'

Marlon slipped a key off the bunch he was holding in his paw. 'This unlocks the kiosk and the bar on the double doors. I'm going back to ring some of our extended family who have a fairground in Devon on the off-chance that Monty has gone there. I lent him to them for a bit last year and he made some friends. It's a long shot but I've got to try everything for Monica's sake.'

Marlon walked away and Hettie watched him go. She was beginning to believe that something terrible had happened on the fairground the night before, but even Hettie could not have predicted how terrible.

Chapter Sixteen

Hettie walked back towards the ghost train and met Tilly climbing down from the waltzer. 'I've checked all the chairs on here and the swing boats,' she said, 'and Bruiser is looking at the moon rocket ride. The only place we haven't been is the ghost train, but that's all locked up.'

'We're going there now,' said Hettie, showing Tilly the key, 'although I'm still getting over our last experience in there.'

'It was horrid, but at least this time we know what to expect.'

The two cats made their way towards the ghost train just as the sun forced its way through the thick cloud. Instantly it became humid and squadrons of sand flies emerged. Shafts of sunlight brought the rides to life in Marmalade's kaleidoscopic colours, giving an air of hope to the situation. Before unlocking the kiosk, Hettie looked back at the entrance arch expecting the missing Meakins to come marching through to take up their places, but all she saw were a couple of disappointed families reading Marlon's closure note.

'Come on,' she said, 'let's get this over with, then I suppose we'd better take a look at the wagons to see if there's any traces there.' Hettie opened the kiosk and stepped inside. 'There's a load of switches and a lever in here,' she said. 'I suppose that's what makes the train move and the switches must be for the effects so I'm switching them all on. If you take the key and open the padlocks on both sets of double doors, I'll start the train and we'll have to jump in quickly.'

Tilly undid the padlock to free the doors and got into the first carriage. Hettie pulled the lever down in the kiosk and jumped on board as the train began to move. As before, it crashed through the doors into the darkness and the giant spider swung into view. Next came the cat sitting up in a coffin and wailing, but this time it wasn't swathed in bandages. Instead, the dead eyes of Marmalade Meakin stared back at them. The train rattled on past the green skull and paws to the second coffin, which had been full of rats eating kittens. Now the rats and kittens were piled up at the side, and the coffin had a new occupant. Hettie was ready to spring out to investigate but the surrounding darkness and the speed of the train made it impossible. The red devil with horns and bulging eyes came next, followed by the walls running with blood and staring skulls – but there was something very odd about the shrouded ghost in chains, which seemed much more stationary than before. Its shape suggested that it was headless. The final trick made it tragically obvious to Hettie and Tilly that they had found most of the missing Meakins: just before the ride concluded, Monty Meakin's body swung into view with a noose around his neck. Then the train burst out into the sunlight.

Hettie rubbed her eyes with her paws, blinded for a second by the dazzling light. Tilly jumped out of the train and pulled the lever back in the kiosk, not wanting to repeat the ride they'd just had. It was a while before either of them could speak. 'We'd better go and find Marlon,' said Hettie eventually. 'There's no easy way to break the news, and we need to get some light in there. It's a multiple murder scene and there could be evidence everywhere. Whoever did this has a real sadistic streak, but they must have been busy setting it all up so hopefully they've made some mistakes.'

They were about to make their way to Marlon's office when Bruiser turned up to report that he'd found nothing on the moon rocket ride. Hettie explained what she and Tilly had discovered and they left him guarding the site.

Marlon was on the phone to Monica when they arrived and Hettie listened as the cat assured her that all would be well and that Monty would turn up very soon. He turned and saw Hettie's face and immediately put the phone back on the receiver without saying goodbye. 'What is it?' he asked, suddenly looking desperate. 'What have you found?'

'It's the worst news I'm afraid,' said Hettie, her mind racing to find words that would bring some comfort to the cat in front of her, but there were none. 'I think we've found most of your missing family. They're in the ghost train.'

Marlon misunderstood for a moment. 'Whatever are they doing in there?' he said. 'I suppose someone was playing a prank and locked them in?'

Hettie shook her head. 'I'm afraid not. As far as we can see, they're all dead.'

'Dead!' screamed Marlon. 'They can't be dead! Monty can't be dead! Please tell me he isn't?' Hettie and Tilly watched as the realisation hit and Marlon crumpled back into his chair and sobbed. 'What am I going to tell Monica?' he cried. 'And my brothers and sister as well? I just don't believe it. What happened to them? Was there an accident? Was it a trick that went wrong?'

'We need to get some light in there to look properly,' said Hettie, 'but there's no doubt that they were murdered.'

'Murdered?!' said Marlon. 'You mean someone has wiped out nearly all my family? Why would they do that?' He rose to his feet. 'I must see this for myself. I must go to Monty.'

In his haste he pushed past Hettie and nearly knocked Tilly over as he made his way out of his office and down the avenue towards the ghost train. Hettie and Tilly gave chase and caught up with him at the kiosk.

Marlon reached in and pulled on a switch Hettie hadn't seen behind the desk, then pushed his way through the double doors with Hettie, Tilly and Bruiser following. The ghost train was flooded with light and suddenly looked very ordinary. It was one big room full of nooks and crannies where various skulls and figures had been set up as tableaux of horror. The giant spider was far less threatening and obviously plastic. The rails that the train ran on were crossed occasionally by sensors that triggered the effects. Now that the lights were on and the mechanics of the ghost train were all visible, the whole ride had suddenly become industrial.

Marmalade Meakin sat up in the first coffin, her body posed as if she'd just sat down for a rest, but her blood-soaked T-shirt told a different story. The dummy of the bandaged cat had been dragged out of its coffin to make way for her and lay in a crumpled heap. Hettie, Tilly and Bruiser stayed back, not wanting to disturb the scene any more than they had to, while Marlon moved on. He stopped at the next coffin where his brother Marty lay, his paws crossed over his bloodstained white shirt, his throat cut from ear to ear. The ghost in rattling chains gave no hint that Maxwell Meakin was wearing its blood-spattered shroud as the head was missing. Marlon didn't stay to investigate, drawn instead to the pitiful sight of his son Monty dangling from a rope, a noose around his neck, the blood from the stab wounds to his chest in a pool on the floor.

Marlon was inconsolable. He moved to try and take the body down but Bruiser intercepted him and led him out into the fairground through the exit doors. 'Leave all that to us,' said Bruiser. 'We'll look after everythin' in there, but we 'ave ta look fer anythin' that might 'elp us find who's done this.'

Hettie and Tilly joined them in the sunshine, which offered no comfort to the butchery they'd just observed. Marlon was in shock but Hettie needed to ask a question before she set to work on the murder scene. 'We promise you we will find out who did this to your family,' she said, 'but I need to understand what happens when the fair shuts down at night. You said it closes at ten but how long before everyone leaves the site?'

'Well, we switch everything off at ten, then one of us goes round and checks that there aren't any customers hanging about – that's usually Maxwell. The rest of them close up or lock up and bring the cash to me at the dodgems. I suppose we're off back to our wagons by about half ten, although Monty often goes into town to meet up with friends in the late night bars. The cowboys are in town by then after their show and Monty gets on really well with them.' Marlon's voice cracked at this point and Hettie could see that the mention of his son was just too much for him.

'I think you'd better go and see Monica,' she suggested, 'and tell Mary and Minnie what's happened. We'll stay here and take care of things. I hate to ask but is there an undertaker we could call who could look after Monty and your brothers and sister?'

'Davy Button – he looked after dad and Micky. You can use my office to call him. I'd better go and find Monica. I just don't know how I'm going to tell her that Monty isn't coming home.'

'Before you go, is there only one key to the ghost train?' asked Hettie.

'The one I gave you is a spare,' said Marlon. 'Marty had his own key to the kiosk and the doors.'

Hettie, Tilly and Bruiser watched as Marlon left the fairground. The spring in his step was gone, replaced by a slow, deliberate need to put one foot in front of the other while the world that he and his family had created lay in shreds around him. 'Poor Marlon,' said Tilly, allowing a tear to escape from her eye and roll down her face. 'He'll never get over this and I just can't imagine how Monica's going to take this awful news.'

'Well, it's up to us to catch who's done this and we should waste no time in getting on with it,' said Hettie, going into detective mode. 'The first thing we need to do is take a closer look at those bodies now that we can see them properly and work out how they got there. I'm not sure it was a one-cat job. Bruiser and I will go back in there and you can go to Marlon's office and call the undertaker. If he could be here in about an hour, that should give us time to have a good look round before the bodies are taken away. I just wish we had the benefit of Morbid Balm's input on this one, but Davy Button will have to do.'

Morbid Balm worked for Shroud and Trestle, the town undertakers, and was often called in to help on Hettie and Tilly's cases. The mortician had been extremely helpful on many occasions and was regarded as an important part of The No. 2 Feline Detective Agency, but Felixtoe was too far out of her area for Hettie to call on her services this time.

Tilly wasted no time in heading for Marlon's office. She had often found the murder scenes they encountered difficult to deal with, and Hettie and Bruiser always tried to protect her from the worst aspects of their work. She believed that kindness kept the world turning and – wherever possible – found it important to think the best of the cats she came into contact with, but there were limits and she was also aware of how easy it was to find evil in plain sight.

'I suppose we need to try and establish where the Meakins were actually killed first,' said Hettie. 'There doesn't seem to be any sign of blood out here, so the question is were they all killed inside the ghost train and posed in the positions we found them in, or were they killed somewhere else? If the fair was closed at ten, I assume they were all killed quite soon after that but the killer – or killers – would have had all night to put the bodies in place once they were out of sight behind those doors. Let's take a closer look at the scene.'

Hettie and Bruiser pushed through the double doors, stopping at Marmalade's body. On closer inspection she'd been stabbed through the heart but there was no blood around her. 'I think she must have been killed somewhere else,' said Hettie. 'There's a lot of blood on her T-shirt but nothing in the coffin except for a few smudges that must have happened when the killer sat her up.'

'She looks quite peaceful,' said Bruiser, 'like she wasn't expectin' it, so maybe she knew the killer?'

'That's a good point, and whoever did this was quick and efficient. Let's move on to Marty.'

Hettie took in the scene around the second coffin, noting that once again there was no blood surrounding it. Due to the nature of Marty's injuries, there was plenty of blood on his shirt from the stab wound and slit throat, but – like Marmalade – it was clear that he had been killed somewhere else. 'We need to search his pockets if we can to see if he has a key on him,' said Hettie.

Bruiser obliged by lifting the body up so that Hettie could get at Marty's pockets. The body was stiff and not easy to deal with, but she managed eventually to search the side and back pockets of the cat's trousers. There was no key. All she could find was some loose change, half a tube of polo mints and a penknife.

'That's something positive, I suppose,' she said. 'The killer must have taken the key, which explains why everything was locked up this morning. But that's interesting – look, there's sand under the body. I wonder what that means? Although thinking about it there's sand everywhere.'

Bruiser gently lowered Marty back into the coffin and they moved on to the ghost in the shroud. The body stood upright, supported by a stand at the back and anchored by the chains that were draped across it, but on removing the shroud it was painfully obvious that the corpse had been stabbed through the heart before his head was cut off.

'I wonder where the rest of him is?' said Hettie, looking around the walls where lifelike papier-mâché skulls stared back at her. The skulls were quite disturbing, but one of them was more realistic than the others. 'Here it is,' she said. 'It's just about recognisable as Maxwell. Our killer obviously has a really warped sense of humour, but I'm beginning to wonder who this particular horror show is aimed at, and why.'

'Smacks of Quince an' 'is gang,' said Bruiser. 'They 'ad it in fer the Meakins. Monty told me Marlon 'ad refused Quince a job on the fair and 'is thugs was involved in Micky Meakin's death with them cowboys too.'

'They've certainly got to be our number one suspects and the timing is about right for the actual murders, but they ran us off the road at ten-thirty so they wouldn't have had time to do all this in here.'

'Maybe they did the murders an' came back later ta set this all up?'

Hettie agreed that it was a possibility and moved on to the final body. 'This is completely different from the rest of the corpses,' she said. 'Monty has bled out on this floor and he has multiple stab wounds. There's so much blood, which suggests that he was killed here or died here as the killer strung him up. In any event, he was still alive when he was brought in to the ghost train because of the bleeding, or maybe he disturbed the killer whilst they were setting up the bodies?'

'Shall I cut 'im down?'

'Yes, I think we'd better, and it would be a good idea to reunite Maxwell with his head. I don't know if Davy Button is used to scenes like this particular chamber of horrors.'

'There's another door over there,' said Bruiser. 'Maybe that's 'ow the bodies was brought in.'

While Bruiser was cutting Monty down, Hettie went over to investigate the other entrance. It was a fire door and she pushed on the bar to open it. The door led out to the back of the ghost train, where a generator stood next to a wheelbarrow. 'Looks like we've solved the mystery of how the bodies were transported,' she said. 'This wheelbarrow is covered in bloodstains.'

Hettie looked around and noticed a row of wagons parked in close proximity to where she stood. It was clear to her that the Meakins had only a short distance to travel from the fair to their homes, but the big question was where were they murdered? Had they got back to their wagons or were they still on the fairground when they were attacked? The lack of blood in the ghost train meant that the murders had happened somewhere else, possibly with the exception of Monty. Had the killer lured the family en masse or were they killed one by one? And why was Monty's murder different from the rest of his family? It was as if he were being made an example of, and she wondered if he had been made to witness the murders of his family before the killer finished him off. All these questions were running through Hettie's head, but what she really needed was some answers.

Chapter Seventeen

Davy Button proved to be efficient in collecting the bodies. Discretion and sympathy were both evident, and the cat hardly raised an eyebrow as he took the dead Meakins into his care. It was the first family massacre he'd attended and the first murder scene, but Hettie watched with great admiration as the undertaker went about his business, focused only on what was best for his dead clients.

'I'll leave things for a day or two before I get in touch with Mr Meakin to make the arrangements,' he said, 'but if any of the family would like to pay their respects, they just need to let me know. There's some work to do on the bodies to make them presentable and I'll need to know what sort of funeral the family would like – but all that can wait.'

'That's really kind,' said Hettie, 'and thank you for all that you've done so far.'

Davy got into his van and drove away from the fairground, leaving Hettie, Tilly and Bruiser to get to the bottom of what had happened there. 'I think we should go back to the villa,' said Hettie. 'It's getting late and we need to draw up a suspects list and a list of cats we need to talk to. Anyway, it's nearly dinner time, although that's going to be a sombre affair if Marlon has told Minnie about the murders.'

'I'd better give the Butters a call an' tell 'em that I'll be stayin' on,' said Bruiser. 'They can let Dolly know. I don't s'pose we'll be goin' 'ome till we've got these murders sorted.'

'At least we had a couple of nice holiday days,' said Tilly. 'I feel really sad about the fair. I suppose it will close for good now.'

'Maybe that's the point,' said Hettie. 'It's a really strong motive. If our killer wanted to put the Meakins out of business, then it's job done. I can't see Marlon recovering from this.'

She locked up the ghost train and the kiosk and the three friends walked slowly back up to the villa, enjoying some early evening sunshine after the horrors of the day. The terraced gardens that sloped down from Sandscratchers were alive with cats sitting on benches or strolling through the flower beds, enjoying their holidays in peaceful contentment. Hettie took in the scene with more than a little resentment and asked herself why it was that murder seemed to follow her wherever she went.

The villa looked welcoming from the outside but offered a very different mood as Hettie, Tilly and Bruiser crossed its threshold. They were instantly aware of some high-pitched wailing coming from the kitchen and Hettie felt obliged to go and investigate. 'I'll see who's here,' she said, 'and find out if there's any prospect of dinner. I think Minnie might have moved us to number six. If you two go and check that out, I'll come up after seeing where the land lies.'

'And I'd better write up my notes on the murders so far,' said Tilly. 'Bruiser can help with the nastier details.'

Tilly and Bruiser left Hettie in the hallway, plucking up courage before heading for the kitchen. They were pleased to see that all their things had been moved to number six, which was a much bigger room and offered two sunny bay windows with commanding views of the promenade, pier and sea. There were four beds, a sofa and a table in the room; under the circumstances, it was ideal as a base for their investigations. Tilly was particularly pleased to see that there was a TV as well, but saddened when she saw that the ceiling was plain white and didn't have Marmalade's wonderful artwork.

The kitchen was nowhere near as peaceful as number six. When Hettie opened the door she was met by what was left of the Meakin family. The scene before her resembled a Boz cartoon that she'd seen in one of Tilly's Dickens books. Marlon, Monica, Mary and Minnie were all dressed in Sunday best black, and old Mrs Meakin sat by the Aga wearing black bombazine and wailing as she rocked backwards and forwards on her chair. The whole family looked as if they'd just returned from a funeral and, in spite of the sombre nature of the vision before her, Hettie found the whole situation quite bizarre. She felt as if she'd walked on stage in the middle of a Victorian melodrama.

'I'm so sorry to disturb you all at this time,' she said, not really knowing who to address her remarks to, 'but I thought I should let you know that Davy Button has now taken your family into his care.'

Old Mrs Meakin let out a deafening wail and Minnie ran to her, doing her best to calm her down. Hettie detected a smell of cooked pastry on the air and treated it as a positive sign that there would be dinner of some sort, but Marlon stepped forward to pick up on the subject of the undertaker. 'I hope there's no rush as far as the funerals are concerned,' he said. 'I'll need time to get our families together. They come from all over the country and they'll want to be here.'

'I'm sure that won't be a problem,' said Hettie. 'Davy Button is happy for you to see him when you're ready.'

'I want to see my boy,' said Monica, suddenly getting to her feet. 'I don't want him lying in an undertaker's all alone. I want him home in his wagon where I can look after him.'

It was Mary who responded this time, taking hold of one of Monica's paws. ''E's best where 'e is, my dear,' she said, 'and 'e's not alone – 'e's with 'is aunt and uncles. 'E couldn't be in safer paws and yer don't needs any more stress. You should let Marlon take you 'ome so you can get some rest.'

Monica shook off Mary's paw and tore into her. 'You just don't understand, do you?' she hissed. 'I've put up with this family for years – lived from paw to mouth in wagons all round the country and raised my boy in the middle of your fairground politics. I've watched him trying desperately to live up to his father's expectations, having the burden of taking on the responsibilities of family and fairground while the rest of you queue up once a week with your paw out for a cut of the takings. All I have to show for those years is Monty lying dead in a funeral parlour and a husband who's more interested in turning his funeral into a giant family occasion. You sit there all day long changing pounds into old pennies, wearing that stupid crown like some cheap circus act, and you're proud to say that's a family tradition. I might remind you that you're not part of this branch of the family. Well, to hell with you and the family because now your precious traditions are dead in the water.'

Hettie was tempted to applaud Monica as she swept out of the kitchen with Marlon hot on her heels. It had been an impressive speech, which had stunned Mary; even Mrs Meakin had stopped wailing, but Hettie felt awkward in the silence and couldn't think of anything to say.

Minnie came to her rescue by changing the subject to something much closer to Hettie's heart, or more especially her stomach. 'You'll have to forgive me for not putting on a proper dinner tonight,' she said, 'on account of the situation. I can offer you and your friends a couple of pies each for your suppers and some of me lattice plum tart with ice cream. I won't be doing veg, as it doesn't seem decent.'

Hettie was a little bemused as to why vegetables should be regarded as indecent but was grateful that dinner hadn't been cancelled. 'Thank you,' she said. 'That will be very nice, as long as it's not too much trouble.'

'No trouble at all after all you're doing to help the family,' said Minnie, 'and I won't be charging you and your friends for board and lodgings either. You stay as long as you like in number six while you're detecting. I just hope you catch who's done this to our family.'

Mary, who was recovering from Monica's scolding, added her thanks in a back-pawed sort of way. 'If yer wants distracting from yer investigations, yer very welcome to play me slots.'

'That's very kind of you, but I think we're going to be busy with interviews over the next couple of days,' Hettie pointed out. 'Perhaps we could come and see you at the arcade tomorrow? I just have a few questions. The more cats we can eliminate from our enquiries, the closer we'll get to the killer or killers.'

'You surely don't think I 'ad anythin' to do with it?' said Mary, looking horrified.

'Don't be silly Mary,' said Minnie. 'We all have to be illuminated, just like on the TV in those Miss Marble films with Margaret Rutherfur. Did I mention that Hettie and her friend Tilly know Agatha Crispy personally?'

Mary looked a little bewildered by her sister's last remark and Hettie felt it was time to go and find Tilly and Bruiser, leaving Minnie and Mary to discuss the finer points of crime fiction. 'Shall we come down to the dining room?' she asked before leaving the kitchen.

Minnie shook her head. 'No, I'll bring it up to number six on trays. You're the only ones in tonight and I've cancelled the rest of my guests, as we'll probably need the rooms for some of the family coming to the funerals. I suppose I'd better start planning some sort of wake. I don't expect Monica will want it in her café.'

After what Hettie had just witnessed she was inclined to agree, but left the kitchen to Mary, Minnie and their mother and went to announce the glad tidings that supper would soon be on its way. She popped her head round the door of number seven, noting that Minnie had been good to her word: the room was empty and she moved along the landing to number six, where she found Bruiser and Tilly watching the evening news.

'Wilt's just been on,' said Tilly, as Hettie joined her on the sofa. 'He seemed to be speaking on behalf of the family.'

'I bet he was,' said Hettie. 'What did he say?'

'That four members of the Meakin family had been murdered in the ghost train at Meakins Mewsments and that the remaining members were devastated as they'd had to close the fairground and it was the end of an era.'

'How convenient,' said Hettie. 'I suppose he went on to give his Wild West show a plug?'

'Not exactly, but he did say that his show out at Gobbles Point was cancelled this evening out of respect and that anyone who had tickets could exchange them for another night. I thought that was really nice of him.'

'You would,' said Hettie. 'You always like to see the best in cats, but Marlon told me that Wilt had tried several times to buy out the fairground and build a Wild West town down on the beach, so he must be thinking that all his Christmases have come at once.'

'I'm sure he doesn't feel like that,' said Tilly. 'He seemed very sad on the TV.'

'Did they say anything else about the murders?'

'The best bit was the reporter saying that The No. 2 Feline Detective Agency had been called in to investigate. They showed a film of the fairground in better days, then a clip of Davy Button's van driving away with the bodies.'

'That's very comprehensive coverage. I wonder who put them onto it?'

'Maybe Davy Button told 'em,' suggested Bruiser. ''E would know when 'e was goin' ta be there.'

'Possibly,' said Hettie, 'but he didn't seem the type to broadcast other cats' misfortunes. Anyway, the good news is that Minnie has offered room service and will be bringing pies and lattice tart up very soon.'

'That is good news,' said Bruiser. 'I'd better go down an' tell the Butters that we've got a big murder investigation on our paws.'

'Be sure to wear a tin hat if you go anywhere near the kitchen,' Hettie warned. 'Civil war broke out while I was down there. I wouldn't trust any of the remaining Meakins with a kitchen knife at the moment.'

Bruiser went down to make his phone call and Hettie told Tilly all about Monica's outburst. 'I suppose she's a bit like Maisie,' said Tilly, 'and if it wasn't for the fairground, then Monty might still be alive. It must be really difficult being part of the Meakin family and having to put up with all their traditions and history.'

'I think you're right, but we have to decide which path to go down in this investigation. Do we go for an outsider with a reason for having the fair closed down, like Wilt Dinsney or Quince and his gang, or do we look closer to home at Maisie, Mary or even Minnie. After dinner we'll draw up a list of suspects and tomorrow we'd better get out there and check out some alibis.'

'While you were in the kitchen, I jotted down a few notes on the bodies in the ghost train,' said Tilly. 'I'm pleased I didn't see them close up, judging by what Bruiser told me. It was beginning to sound like our Downton Tabby case.'

Hettie laughed. 'I see what you mean, but I get the feeling that this case is much more complicated than a spate of murders at a literary festival, although the motives may be similar. Monica said an interesting thing during her rage at Mary, though – she said that Mary wasn't part of the family, which was a bit odd, and as I came back upstairs I suddenly realised that there was another member of the Meakins missing.'

'Who?' asked Tilly.

'Matty Meakin. If you remember, Minnie told us that he was her odd job cat and that Marlon had borrowed him to run the gallopers, but we haven't met him and he wasn't with the family just now.'

'Oh dear,' said Tilly. 'Do you think he's dead and lying somewhere hidden in the ghost train?'

Hettie shook her head. 'No, I don't. When the lights came on it was obvious where everything was, but he's certainly conspicuous by his absence.'

'And what about Mary? Minnie said she was her sister so how come she's not part of the family?'

'I think that's a question for Minnie,' said Hettie, staring out to sea. 'I'm enjoying this new room, but look at that band of black across the horizon. Marlon said there was going to be a storm and it's just sitting there out at sea.'

Hettie's concerns about the weather were interrupted by Bruiser returning from his phone call with a tray laden with pies, followed by Minnie with another tray of lattice tart, bowls and three small tubs of ice cream. They put the food down on the table. Minnie looked around the room and, without warning, slumped down on one of the beds.

'Forgive me,' she said, 'but everything feels normal in here, as if nothing terrible has happened. My kitchen has just become a place where my family shout and scream at each other and my mother hasn't stopped wailing for three hours. Normally it's my sanctuary, and I love cooking and keeping an eye on Mother. I haven't had a minute to ingest what's happened down at the fair and I can't believe that I'll never see Marmalade again.'

Minnie's voice broke into a sob at the mention of her sister and Hettie, Tilly and Bruiser watched as the cat cried her heart out. When there were no tears left, she wiped her face on her apron and stood up to go. 'I'm so sorry,' she said. 'I don't know what came over me. Us Meakins aren't ones for showing our feelings.'

'We completely understand,' said Hettie. 'Can we make you a cup of tea or something?'

'I shouldn't, as I've left Mary with Mother,' said Minnie, 'but that would be lovely. I can't remember the last time anyone made me a cup of tea.'

Tilly sprang to the kettle and Minnie sat down again, this time on the sofa.

'Do you feel up to answering a few questions for us?' said Hettie, seizing her opportunity to start the investigation.

'I'll try,' said Minnie, 'but I'm not sure that I can be much help. I don't have much to do with the fairground and yesterday was the first time Marlon had been up here since Micky's funeral at the start of the season. We keep our businesses quite separate – it works better that way.'

'It's not really about the fairground, more about the family,' Hettie explained. 'Monica mentioned that Mary wasn't really part of the family but I thought she was your sister?'

'She is my sister, but not in the same way that Marmalade was,' said Minnie accepting a cup of sweet milky tea from Tilly. 'You see Mary came from the

London Meakins. She was my uncle's daughter, but he died in a fight with one of the Devon Meakins over a pitch they both had their eye on. Bad business, it was – they stabbed each other, but Uncle Milchip came off worse. My father adopted Mary after it happened and said we were all to treat her as our sister – and whatever my father said went. There's a lot of that sort of thing in our family – mothers turn out to be sisters and sisters turn out to be mothers and everyone seems to be a cousin to someone else. It's all about keeping the family name going. Mary tries hard to be part of the family, but she's different – brought up as a cockney, working the travelling fairs – and it took her a while to settle down to being a Sandscratcher. There's no love lost between her and Monica.'

'That seems obvious,' said Hettie, 'but is there any reason why Monica doesn't get on with her?'

'Monica wants to expand her café on the pier and that would mean taking over the space where the slots are, so Mary is in her way. Marlon tries to keep the peace but I know he agrees with Monica – he thinks the slots have had their day and he's probably right.'

'So what would Mary do if Marlon decides to let Monica expand the café?'

'Marlon would find a place for her on the fairground, if it survives. She's run several of the big rides in her time. She's very paws on and inflatable.'

'I noticed that there was no sign of your youngest brother Matty today,' said Hettie, suppressing the giggle rising in her throat. 'Does anyone know where he is?'

'Matty blows in and out with the weather,' said Minnie. 'Being the youngest, he's at that age where he can't settle. Marlon tries to give him some responsibility, but he's got a wandering eye. If he had his way, he'd join up with Wilt's Wild West show. He gets on well with the performers out at Gobbles Point and he's got a fancy for Buffalo Lill, but he's punching way above his weight with that one. He does a bit of work for me for some extra money but he's not reliable. He'll turn up eventually, I'm sure, as soon as he hears what's happened.'

'And what about Maisie?' asked Hettie. 'What can you tell me about her? I believe you were close once?'

Minnie looked down at her slippers, as if Hettie's question was one too many, before giving an honest answer. 'Maisie blames Wilt for Micky's death because his cowboys were involved in a fight on the moon rockets the night that Micky had his accident. Because I'm with Wilt, she blames me as well. She was my best friend and I miss her, but unlike her my loyalty is to the family.'

Minnie drained her tea mug and stood up to go. 'There's one last thing I have to ask you,' said Hettie. 'Where were you between ten and midnight last night?'

Minnie blinked, realising that Hettie required an alibi and that Tilly was poised to write her reply in her notebook. 'I was here with Mother until you all came back with Wilt after your accident,' she said.

'And after midnight? Did you or Wilt go out again?'

'No,' said Minnie, moving to the door. 'Now if you'll excuse me, I really must get back to Mother.'

Minnie made her way back to the kitchen, leaving Hettie, Tilly and Bruiser to eat their supper. All thoughts on the day's events were suspended briefly as the three cats enjoyed their pies and pudding and watched an episode of *The Waltons*, a TV show about a family of cats living in the wilds of Virginia. 'I love the way they all say goodnight to each other,' said Tilly, posting the final piece of lattice tart into her mouth.

'It's certainly more harmonious than it would be if the Meakins all lived in that house on the prairie,' Hettie pointed out, reaching for the new catnip pipe that she'd bought from the Wild West show. 'It's time for us to draw up a list of suspects and look for some motives.'

Bruiser settled himself on one of the beds and Tilly sat down next to Hettie on the sofa with her notebook. She turned to a clean page and wrote 'Suspects'. 'Shall I put Killer Quince and his gang at the top, as they're the nastiest cats and ruined Miss Scarlet's mudguards?'

'Good idea,' agreed Hettie. 'They were also around at the time the fair closed last night and could easily have returned later to put the bodies in the ghost train.'

'And they 'ad issues with Monty and Marlon and was fightin' them cowboys when Micky died,' added Bruiser.

'I think we should put Wilt Dinsney next,' Hettie suggested. 'I know he has an alibi as he was getting us out of that bunker, but he may have paid Quince and his gang to do the killings – we know that he had hopes of building a Wild West town where the fairground is. There's no doubt that whoever did this has put paid to Meakins Mewsments, whether they set out to or not.'

'I suppose we should put the cowboys down as well,' said Tilly. 'They were all leaving the show at the same time as us and they could have made it to the fairground before everyone left the site. Several of them overtook us on the golf course.'

'Good point,' said Hettie, blowing a perfect smoke ring and passing the pipe to Bruiser, 'although Minnie said she thought Marmalade was more than a little interested in Billy the Kit.'

'Maybe she refused 'im and 'e got angry?'

'Fairly radical to go on and kill three more of the Meakins,' Hettie pointed out, 'but it's possible. I think we should put Mary Meakin next, especially after what Minnie has just told us. She could have killed out of spite if she thought her slots arcade was in danger of being closed. We'll need to ask Marlon about that tomorrow to see if he was really considering it.'

'What about Premo Pete?' suggested Tilly. 'He said there were going to be deaths and that we were involved, and we saw him near the villa late last night.'

'Yes, he should definitely be on the list. According to Maisie, Mary was seeing him in secret and she told me she thought that Mary had had a visitor to her wagon around ten – that could have been Pete, although if it was him that would give them both an alibi. He could have been coming back from Mary's wagon when we saw him just before midnight.'

'I'll put Maisie next shall I?' said Tilly. 'She doesn't seem happy with the Meakins and would pack up her kittens and leave if she could afford it.'

'Yes, and the way they seem to have swept Micky's death under the carpet hasn't made things any easier for her. Even Minnie seems to disapprove of her attitude to the family.'

'So what about Minnie – do you think I should put her down on the list?'

'I do,' said Hettie. 'Using her mother as an alibi isn't as safe as she may think. The old cat could have been tucked up in bed early, leaving Minnie with no alibi at all until we got back just before midnight. The question is – why would she wipe out half of her family? Unlike the other suspects, she has no axe to grind – unless she did it for Wilt, so he could fulfil his dreams of a Wild West town.'

'I suppose we should put Matty Meakin on the list, as he seems to have gone missing?'

''E could 'ave 'ooked off somewhere after killin' 'em,' added Bruiser.

'Yes, he's a bit of a wild card,' said Hettie, 'and from what Minnie says he doesn't seem like a cat who's happy to toe the family line. Alternatively, he may be lying dead somewhere and we haven't discovered him yet.'

'Well, that's about it I think,' said Tilly, 'unless you want me to put Marlon and Monica down?'

Hettie thought for a moment before replying, 'We've had cast-iron alibis in the past that have crumbled. I don't think Marlon or Monica would have set out to kill their own son, but his death was different from the others. He died in the ghost train, which suggests that he might have disturbed the killer when he or she was setting up the bodies. We should check out this Sailor's Sloop place to see if anyone remembers them being there and what time they left.'

'I'll do that if yer like,' offered Bruiser.

'Excellent,' said Hettie, 'and Tilly and I will start with Marlon in the morning and see how many of the suspects we can get through. Tomorrow afternoon we'll pay a visit to Quince and his gang out at Gobbles Point, and maybe catch some of the cats from the Wild West show before their evening performance. It's going to be a very long day.'

The three cats settled into their beds and it was Tilly who had the last words of the day, 'Goodnight Hettie. Goodnight Bruiser.'

Chapter Eighteen

Much to Hettie's dismay, breakfast proved to be a scant affair. There was no smell of bacon as the three friends made their way down the stairs and it was obvious on reaching the dining room that there was very little on offer: a box of cornflakes; a jug of milk; and a selection of rather dry Danish pastries that the Butters wouldn't have given house room to.

The villa was very quiet and when Hettie popped her head into the kitchen she found it empty. There was no sign of Minnie or her mother; even more disturbingly, there were no signs of any preparations for dinner.

They ate what had been left for them and set off to find and interview the suspects on their list. Bruiser struck out into the town to find the Sailor's Sloop, arranging to meet up with Hettie and Tilly on the pier for lunch.

'Let's go and find Marlon first,' said Hettie leading the way down the path. 'Hopefully he'll be in his office at the fairground. Then we need to speak to Mary and Monica if they're at work on the pier.'

The sun was pleasantly warm as they made their way across the beach, disappearing occasionally behind fluffy white clouds, much to the annoyance of cats keen on a day of sunbathing. The sea was several shades of green and didn't look that inviting with the persistent black band of cloud across the horizon, making the giant passing cargo ships look quite threatening.

It was, however, a good day for Premo Pete, who sat under his beach umbrella next to the kiosk reading a book. He occasionally lifted his head to survey his empire of colourful striped deckchairs, all hired out to customers keen to get the most out of the good weather. Hettie was tempted to stop and have a conversation with him, but decided that the Meakins were a higher priority.

The fairground looked sad when they reached it, in spite of the sunshine; it was as if the colour had been drained from all the rides. They stood motionless, now more like exhibits in a seaside museum, a physical history of long-gone glory days. Hettie and Tilly passed the ghost train, remembering the horror of the day before and struck by the contrast between that and the joy of the days when the fair was vibrant and alive to visiting families.

Marlon Meakin was on the phone when they arrived at his office. As they stood in the doorway listening, it was clear that he was talking to Davy Button the undertaker. Marlon sounded very matter-of-fact and almost devoid of emotion as he made arrangements for his son Monty to be brought back to his wagon, as Monica had insisted. He went on to point out that there would be many family members who would want to view the bodies and that Davy should prepare for more than two hundred Meakins and extended family to attend their funerals. He looked up as Hettie and Tilly entered his office and brought the phone call to an end. 'Any news?' he asked, looking hopeful.

'I'm afraid not,' said Hettie, pulling up a couple of chairs for her and Tilly. 'We've drawn up a list of cats we'd like to talk to and we'll be going out to see Quince at Gobbles Point this afternoon.'

'Good luck with him,' said Marlon. 'I've no doubt that he was involved – he's had it in for the family for some time, but he and his gang seem to get away with murder.'

Marlon suddenly realised what he'd said and a darkness passed across his face. Hettie could see that he was doing his best to remain detached from the horror of the situation; his handling of the undertaker had seemed rather impersonal but inside she felt that he was hurting just like the rest of his family. 'I'd like to ask you some questions about the family,' she said. 'Before we talk to them it would be helpful to know a bit more about them – and maybe the victims, too.'

'Shouldn't you be concentrating on who did this to us?' Marlon objected. 'I doubt that any of the relatives I have left can help. We're a proud and loyal family and I don't think any of us would welcome you digging about when there's a killer out there and one of us could be next.'

'That's exactly why I need to understand the family dynamics,' said Hettie, feeling a little frustrated at Marlon's attitude. 'After witnessing the exchange between Mary and Monica up at the villa last night, it's clear to me that there are grudges and family rivalries that we need to be across. As you're the head of the family, you're in the best position to help us.'

'We're just like any family,' said Marlon, 'and all being in the same business is bound to create the odd tiff here and there, but if you're thinking that one of us could do what I saw in the ghost train yesterday, you might as well give up now.'

'We don't intend to give up,' said Hettie. 'I don't think I've seen a more malicious and staged murder scene since we started our detective business. Whoever is responsible has to be caught – and quickly.'

'All right,' said Marlon, 'you've got half an hour and then I have to go to the undertaker's to start making the arrangements. They're bringing Monty back to his wagon later so I'll have to arrange a vigil with the family.'

'What sort of vigil?' asked Hettie.

'In our tradition, out of respect, a corpse is never left on his own until the burial, so I'll have to draw up a rota to sit with Monty.'

'What about the other victims?'

'We'll have to visit them at the funeral home. Minnie suggested we lay them out at the villa, but we'll need her rooms and the other empty wagons for the family to stay in. The Devon Meakins are on their way and the Londoners arrive tomorrow. I'm trying to get messages to the travelling family, as they've got fairs all over the country. The funerals can't take place until everyone has been told.'

Hettie was beginning to realise the complexities of the traditions linked to a fairground family and the enormous burden that had been put on Marlon's shoulders, but still there were questions that needed to be answered. 'I'd like to begin with you telling us a bit about the victims,' she said. 'Could we start with Marmalade?'

Tilly pulled her notebook and pencil from her shorts pocket and turned to a clean page, writing 'Victims' at the top.

'Marmalade was my favourite sister,' said Marlon. 'She was a really talented artist and I suppose we held her back.'

'Why do you say that?'

'Well, when she was younger all she ever wanted to do was to go to art school but my father insisted that she channel her talent through the family business. She loved painting the rides and keeping them nice, but I always felt that she wanted more in her life than being a Sandscratcher. She never complained, though, and she was a lovely cat who would do anything for anybody.'

'Minnie said she had lots of admirers – was there a cat who was special to her?'

'She was a beautiful girl and attracted the boys, but she knew that she'd have to choose from the family and she chose not to.'

'I gather she liked Billy the Kit from the Wild West show. Was that serious?'

Marlon shook his head. 'No, she'd have never gone off with him or any of those cowboys. They'd all meet up occasionally with Monty and Matty but there was no romance.'

'Has anyone seen Matty or is he still missing?'

'No sign of him as yet,' said Marlon. 'I checked his wagon this morning but it's not strange for him to take off for days on end. A Sandscratcher's life doesn't really suit him. He'd rather be out on the road with a travelling fair or even a circus.'

'What about Maxwell?' asked Hettie. 'We only met him briefly but he seemed a nice cat.'

'He had an eye for the girls,' said Marlon, 'but there were two things he loved more than anything – the waltzer and his old fishing boat. When Father first brought us here, we all had trouble settling down as Sandscratchers – we were used to travelling – but Maxwell settled straight away. He loved the sea and when he wasn't working the waltzer he was out on his boat. He was good on security, as well, and kept his eye open for any troublemakers. He was very close to my other brother Micky and took it hard when Micky died.'

'And Marty? You mentioned that Maxwell didn't get on with him?'

'Just sibling rivalry really,' said Marlon, shrugging his shoulders. 'There's a lot of jealousy over the rides. I think Marty was hoping for the waltzer, but when we had to move Mary from the ghost train to the slots on the pier Marty was her obvious replacement.'

'Why did Mary have to be moved?' asked Hettie.

'Because Minnie, who'd been running the slots, took over the villa and the care of my mother after Father died. I inherited the fair, the pier and the dodgems.'

'Why couldn't Mary have looked after the villa and your mother?'

'Because she's not suited to that kind of work and she has the gift of the gab, which is perfect for the customers who play the slots.'

'I suppose her being a cockney cat helped?'

Marlon looked a little taken aback. 'What do you mean?' he asked.

'Minnie told us that Mary was adopted from the London Meakins and was the daughter of your Uncle Milchip, who was killed in a fight.'

'Did she now?' said Marlon, scowling. 'My sister Minnie has no business digging up old wounds. My father would turn in his grave if he knew she was broadcasting those details to strangers. As far as we are concerned, Mary is one of us and that's all that matters. Milchip was a bad lot and best forgotten.'

'But not by Monica, it would seem,' said Hettie. 'She seemed happy enough to remind Mary that she was adopted last night.'

Marlon looked uncomfortable and Hettie decided that this would be a good time to raise the issue of the pier. 'Minnie told us that you've been thinking of expanding Monica's café and closing down the amusement arcade. Obviously that would have affected Mary and she might have seen it as a threat to her livelihood. How definite were those plans?'

'Before all this happened it would have been a good idea,' said Marlon. 'Monica has made a real go of her café and it's full to bursting all year round. The slots only get busy in bad weather – the rest of the time it's the same old cats spending their pensions on trying to get lucky. It just isn't viable any more to have all that space taken up by out-of-date fruit machines.'

'And have you spoken to Mary about all of this?'

'I've tried over and over again, and I even offered her the ghost train back as she made a good job of that, but she just ignores me. That's why her and Monica don't get on – they tolerate each other, but that's about all.'

'Tell me about Marty and his role in the family,' said Hettie. 'If Mary had returned to the ghost train, what would have happened to him?'

'Marty was like Marmalade – loyal and easy to get on with and great with the customers. If Mary had agreed to move back to the ghost train, I had it in my mind to offer him Micky's old ride. The moon rockets is one of our oldest rides and my mother used to run it before she retired and passed it on to Micky.

After Micky died, I decided to rest it out of respect, but Marty would have made a real success of it next season if my plan for the pier had gone ahead.'

'Did Marty know you were thinking of changing things?'

'No. I didn't think I could mention it until Mary had agreed to give up the slots, but now all my plans have gone for nothing.'

'It's probably too soon to ask but what will you do about the fair now there are so few of you to run it?' asked Hettie.

'It'll have to stay closed,' said Marlon. 'When the family arrive for the funerals I'll have to see if any of them want to buy the rides. The Devon Meakins might take some of them off my paws, as they have a big site down there. As for the pitch, I'll have to see if Wilt Dinsney's offer still stands – unless I can find a buyer for the whole fairground and all the rides.'

'Couldn't you get some of your extended family to run the rides for you?' suggested Tilly. 'It's such a shame that the fairground will have to close.'

'I'm afraid my heart is no longer in it,' said Marlon. 'The thing that kept me going was knowing that one day I would pass it all on to Monty, just like my father passed it on to me. Even though the work was hard there was a reason for it all; now that reason is lying in an undertaker's and my hopes and dreams have died with him. If you'll both excuse me, I need to bring him home.'

Chapter Nineteen

Marlon Meakin made his way to the undertaker's to oversee the transfer of Monty's body to his wagon, and Hettie and Tilly headed for the pier in hopes of having a conversation with Mary and Monica. The amusement arcade was virtually empty when they got there and Mary sat in her kiosk, staring into space like a waxwork dummy. Her crown was nowhere to be seen and the smile that greeted Hettie and Tilly as they approached her was as mechanical as her slot machines.

'I wondered if we could have a word with you while things are quiet?' Hettie asked. 'I promise we won't keep you long.'

'I've got all the time in the world as long as you don't intend to win another of me jackpots,' said Mary.

Hettie got straight to the point. 'I'm asking all the family where they were the night before last at around ten o'clock. We're keen to eliminate as many cats as possible from our investigations.'

'I was in the ghost train murderin' 'alf me family if that's what yer wants to hear,' said Mary. 'Everyone round 'ere thinks I done it, so I may as well own up an' be done with it.'

'Are you actually confessing to the murders?'

Mary threw her head back and cackled like the jolly sailor in the glass box next to her. 'Course I'm not,' she said, 'but it's no better than any of 'em deserve. You can pick yer friends but family – well, that's a life sentence.'

'Why do the family think you did the murders?'

''Cause it suits 'em,' said Mary, 'especially Monica. You 'eard what she said to me up at the villa. She thinks she's special 'cause she's married to Marlon and she wants me out of 'ere so she can expand 'erself across the pier. When Milo Meakin brought me home to the villa all them years ago after me dad was murdered, I felt like I'd found a proper family, but when Monica came along all that changed. There was never a day went by when she didn't remind me that I didn't belong and now she's pointin' 'er painted claw at me for the murders.'

'So where were you the night before last at around ten?' repeated Hettie, trying to avoid any further conversation about Monica.

'I left me wagon about ten-ish an' went down the beach, where I made a fire and grilled some sausages. I likes ta sit under the pier late at night an' 'ave a bit of supper. When the fair closes it's lovely an' peaceful down there.'

'And were you on your own?'

'I'm not sure what you're getting at, but I likes ta keep things private about who I spends me time with.'

Hettie was in two minds as to whether to mention Premo Pete at this point but decided not to as Maisie had told her in confidence. 'I just wanted to establish your alibi,' she pointed out instead. 'Obviously if you were with someone then they could confirm where you were and you could confirm where they were.'

'What I can confirm is that I didn't kill no one the night before last, an' I don't see that I 'ave to say any more than that. You might think this family is all sweetness an' light, but it's built on dark dealin's an' jealousies that go back years. None of 'em is what they seem.'

'Would you like to enlighten me about those dark dealings?' asked Hettie, intrigued by what Mary had just said.

Mary threw her head back and cackled again. 'You're the detectives – you just needs ta ask the right questions ta the right cats. I'm not tellin' tales or pointin' me claw.'

Hettie could see that she was getting no further with Mary and a hunger pang due to the derisory breakfast had just struck her. 'We may need to talk to you again,' she said, 'but now we have to go and find Monica.'

'Good luck with that one,' said Mary, 'but she's not in 'er precious café. She's down the wagon park, prettying up Monty's place for 'is vigil.'

Hettie and Tilly left Mary to her slot machines and noticed that in spite of what she'd said the café on the pier was open. They arrived in time to get a table for lunch and were pleased to see that Maisie was running it. They settled at what had now become their usual table by the window and Maisie made her way over to them. 'What a terrible business,' she said, passing them both a menu. 'I just can't believe that all four of them have been murdered, and in the ghost train – how awful is that? Poor Monica. She's devastated. They're bringing Monty back to his wagon this afternoon.'

'Yes, we know,' said Hettie. 'We were hoping to speak to her, but it's going to have to wait under the circumstances so we thought we might get some lunch before going out to Gobbles Point.'

'Well, I hope you manage to catch up with Quince and his gang,' said Maisie. 'Their paw prints are all over these murders. They got away with killing my Micky and those cowboys are just as bad. If Marlon had stood up to them at the time, Monty, Marmalade and her brothers would still be alive. He couldn't wait to brush it all under the carpet to save his precious fairground and now look where it's got him. He's lost his only son and his business. I can't see the fair opening again and I suppose we'll all be turned out of our wagons if he has to sell up.'

'It is a terrible situation,' agreed Hettie, 'but just now we need to find out who has done this before they kill again. Whoever it is is extremely dangerous and I suspect that they will do anything to cover their tracks. We're asking all the family where they were at around ten o'clock the night before last. You told us you were in your wagon listening to the radio – can anyone confirm that?'

Maisie looked taken aback at Hettie's question and waited a moment before replying. 'I was on my own – except for the kittens, of course, but they were tucked up in their bed. Since they were born I haven't been out at night as there's no one to look after them, but you surely don't think I had anything to do with the murders, do you?'

'Sadly, in an investigation like this, we have to keep an open mind about everyone until we get some solid evidence that points in a definite direction. It's plain to see that there are issues within the Meakin family that could make them all suspects, and that unfortunately includes you.'

'I didn't and couldn't kill anybody,' said Maisie, 'but I can see what you mean about the family and things will be even worse now they've started accusing each other. I feel sorry for poor Mary. Monica thinks she's done it out of spite because Marlon is thinking of closing the slots down.'

'And what do you think?'

'Me?' said Maisie. 'I think it's Quince and his gang or the cowboys – they're always causing trouble and I should know better than anyone about that.'

Hettie had to agree that Maisie had every good reason to suspect the cats who had brought about Micky

Meakin's death. She decided to focus on the menu in front of her, as interviewing Quince was becoming more and more of a priority. 'What do you recommend for lunch?' she asked, gently changing the subject.

'The fish pie is very good, freshly made by Monica this morning, or we've got a cottage pie. The minute steaks are lovely with chips, or there's a cheese and potato pie – my kittens love that with baked beans.'

'I'll go for the fish pie then,' said Hettie, looking at Tilly, who was still trying to make her mind up.

'I'm torn between the minute steak and chips and the cheese pie and beans,' said Tilly, 'so I'll have the cottage pie instead with small peas.'

There was never any logic to Tilly's food choices, but Maisie dutifully jotted down the orders and was about to return to the kitchen to prepare them when Bruiser arrived looking a little flustered. Hettie pushed the menu at him and Maisie lingered to complete the order. 'I'll 'ave the minute steak an' chips,' he said, not wishing to hold things up, 'an' jam roly poly fer pudding – with custard, please.'

'Ooh, make that two jam roly polies,' said Tilly, not wanting to miss out on her sweet course.

'In fact you can make that three jam roly polies,' chimed in Hettie, thinking ahead to the possibility that there might be very little dinner available later at the villa.

Maisie returned to the kitchen and Bruiser slid into the seat next to Tilly. 'How did you get on at the

Sailor's Sloop?' Hettie asked, keen to catch up with his morning.

'Well, the cat 'oo runs it told me they 'ad a spot of bother the night before last,' said Bruiser, as Tilly pulled her notebook out ready to jot any bits of important information down. ''E said some of the cowboys turned up around eleven an' disrupted the dancin'. 'E said they'd been fightin' an' was covered in blood, and they was the worse fer drink. It upset all 'is customers an' most of 'em left early. 'E sent the cowboys packin' an' they all 'eaded off for the beach.'

'What about Marlon and Monica?' asked Hettie. 'Did they leave early? Marlon said they were back at their wagon around midnight.'

'That's the interestin' bit,' said Bruiser. 'I asked 'im if 'e remembered them an' 'e said they was 'ard ta forget as they 'ad a terrible row at their dinner table an' Marlon stormed out, leavin' Monica ta finish 'er dinner on 'er own. 'E said 'e didn't take much notice after that as 'e was busy and then later 'e 'ad ta deal with the cowboys.'

'Well, well, well,' said Hettie. 'So are we to assume that Marlon has lied to us about being at the Sailor's Sloop, dancing the night away?'

'From what the cat 'oo runs it said, there was 'ardly any dancin' that night as everyone was upset by the cowboys.'

'And you say the cowboys were covered in blood when they arrived?' said Hettie, working through the information that Bruiser had brought them. 'That means they could easily have done the murders. Who-ever is responsible must have been covered in blood and the timing is about right, although they would have had to go back later to put the bodies in the ghost train.'

'And what about Marlon and Monica?' asked Tilly. 'All this means they probably don't have an alibi either, but surely they wouldn't kill their own son?'

'Who can say?' said Hettie. 'The more we delve, the thicker the plot becomes. Just remember what Mary said about none of the family being what they seem – and it's now clear that even Marlon can't be trusted.'

'But he seems such a nice cat,' Tilly protested, 'and he taught me to drive a dodgem.'

'We've solved enough cases by now to know that murderers can be charming, even loveable, but thoughts like that aren't going to help us to get to the bottom of these murders.'

Their conversation was interrupted by Maisie deliv-ering their lunches and all thoughts of murder were brushed to one side as Hettie, Tilly and Bruiser took on the serious business of eating. Tilly managed her cottage pie without incident or damage to her T-shirt, Hettie had a brief tussle with a fish bone before clear-ing her plate, and Bruiser disposed of his steak and chips in record time. The puddings went the same way and the three cats made their way back up to the villa to collect Miss Scarlet before heading out to Gobbles Point.

Chapter Twenty

The car park at the villa had descended into chaos when Hettie, Tilly and Bruiser reached it and Minnie Meakin didn't seem to be helping. Her attempts at being a parking attendant were not going down too well with the Devon Meakins, who had arrived en masse in three showcat wagons. The drivers were doing their best to avoid Minnie's instructions and the rest of the cats stood in their funeral clothes, tired and irritable after their long journey.

'Blimey!' said Bruiser, fearful that Miss Scarlet would be crushed during the manoeuvres. 'I'd better give 'em some 'elp if you can get Minnie out the way.'

Hettie responded by taking Minnie to one side on the pretence of discussing whether she would be able to offer dinner that evening. Bruiser took control of the parking and received an understated round of applause from the onlookers before Minnie marched them all into the villa, with a promise that there would be some sort of supper later.

After a bright morning, the sun had been replaced by a bank of cloud offering a fine drizzle as Bruiser drove Miss Scarlet across the golf course towards Gobbles Point. There were clutches of golfers in plus fours and harlequin-patterned socks, braving the weather to fulfil the eighteen holes that the course provided. Hettie stared in dismay from the comfort of the sidecar at what she regarded as a pointless pursuit by cats who had nothing better to do than wear ridiculous clothes and churn up the countryside, hacking away at tufts of grass with an alarming array of sticks in all weathers.

Bruiser slowed down and stopped to allow a party of golfers to cross the road, keen to get on to the next hole, and Tilly was grateful that the lid was firmly shut on the sidecar, suppressing the colourful collection of expletives that Hettie uttered as the golfaholics passed in front of them. Bruiser wasted no time in picking up speed again and headed towards the dry dock of the marina. He parked the motorbike at a safe distance, not wanting to incur any further damage to Miss Scarlet, and the three cats made their way on foot towards the boats.

Once in the marina it was clear that the boats were of mixed fortunes. Those close to the estuary leading out to sea were respectable craft, well maintained and obviously loved by their owners. The older boats that had seen better days formed more of a shanty town, their hulls free of the water as if the sea had abandoned them to a life of static decay. There was a network of gangplanks linking many of them together and it was on one of these that Quince sat watching as Hettie, Tilly and Bruiser approached. 'So you survived the crash then?' he said to Bruiser as more cats joined him on his plank, emerging from some of the derelict boats.

Surrounded by his gang he looked intimidating, but Hettie was having none of it. 'It's Brian Dobbs, isn't it?' she began, remembering what Bruiser had told her and guessing that Quince's real name would be a source of amusement to his followers. She was right: Quince was noticeably stung by her opening gambit and his gang reinforced his discomfort by sniggering.

'What's it to you?' he said, doing his best to reassert his authority.

'We've come to talk to you about the fairground murders,' said Hettie, getting straight to the point.

'And what murders might they be, and who might you be?'

'I am Hettie Bagshot from The No. 2 Feline Detective Agency and this is Tilly Jenkins and Bruiser. We are investigating the murders of four cats from the Meakin family whose bodies we discovered yesterday. We believe they were murdered the night before.'

Quince leapt down from his gangplank followed by his entourage and moved so close to Hettie that she could smell his breath as he hissed at her. Bruiser stepped closer to Hettie and Tilly stepped back behind

Bruiser, fearing that Quince would spring on them at any moment. The stand-off only lasted seconds as Hettie stood her ground and Quince backed away. The situation became slightly less confrontational. 'Why would you want to ask me about killing Meakins?' said Quince. 'There's plenty of them to go around, so losing a few shouldn't make much difference, but you're barking up the wrong tree there. We like to fight Meakins and killing them would spoil the fun.'

'We saw you at the Wild West show on the night they were killed,' said Hettie. 'What did you do after Wilt Dinsney asked you to leave?'

'Proper little detective, aren't you?' said Quince, employing some playground sarcasm. 'For your information, Wilt didn't ask us to leave – he was paying up for a few jobs we'd done for him and then we were on our way into town.'

'What sort of jobs?'

'I don't see that's any of your business,' said Quince. 'You need to stick to your murders and we can't help with them.'

'So what did you do when you got into town?' pressed Hettie.

'What we always do. We had a bit of fun with some of the prettier cats coming away from the fair, then we had a few drinks down on the beach and roughed up a few of the cowboys when they arrived after their show. Come to think of it, one of them was a Meakin who'd defected. I had fun giving him a bloody nose.'

'Do you mean Matty Meakin?'

'Probably,' said Quince. 'One Meakin is the same as another when you're thumping the living daylights out of him. He's often hanging out with the cowboys though. He's not one of your dead ones, is he, because I didn't hit him that hard?'

'No, he just hasn't been seen for a couple of days,' said Hettie, 'but at least you've helped to solve that mystery.'

'Oh I do like to be helpful,' said Quince. 'Maybe you should be pointing your claw at him if he's done a bunk. He obviously wasn't happy working the fairground so perhaps he decided to do some of his family in.'

'You say that you went onto the beach – did you notice anything out of the ordinary while you were there?'

Quince shook his head. 'Not that I remember. That cat from the slots was down there under the pier, lighting a fire, but she does that quite a lot. Oh, and Marlon Meakin was giving Monty a dressing-down at the entrance to the fairground.'

'What time was this?' asked Hettie, feeling that at last there was some sort of breakthrough.

'It was after ten, I suppose. Monty was putting up the closed sign and we were on our way back to our bikes.'

'Before running us off the road?' Hettie couldn't resist reminding him. 'Did you hear any of the conversation between Marlon and Monty?'

'We didn't hang about but Monty was saying something like "It's all been a lie". He was really shouting.'

'You've been very helpful,' said Hettie, 'but I don't understand why you spend your time fighting and running cats off the road.'

'Because there's nothing else in this godforsaken town for us to do. It's all about buckets and bloody spades and seaside rock. For those of us born here, there's nowhere to live and no jobs, as the Meakins stick with family, and no hope of a future. We have our bikes, these old boats and each other, and that for us is survival.'

Hettie was pleased that her conversation with Quince had borne fruit and – although she could never condone the sort of violence that he and his followers meted out – she was beginning to see that there were two sides to life in a seaside town like Felixtoe: the flourishing holiday trade for those spending a happy week with their families; and the dead-end cul-de-sac that Quince and his gang inhabited.

Her mind was racing as they returned to Miss Scarlet. The case had suddenly gathered speed with the revelation that Marlon had had a heated conversation with Monty on the night he was murdered. She was tempted to get Bruiser to run them back into Felixtoe to have it out with Marlon, but as they were so close to the Wild West showground it made sense to talk to some of the cowboys and to check out Quince's story.

By the time they'd reached the showground car park, the drizzle had stopped and the sun was gradually burning off the cloud to reveal a deep blue sky. They walked towards the big top. Inside Billy the Kit was treating himself to some lasso practice on one of the giant plastic cacti that stood in the arena, three times taller than he was. Seated on the front row of the audience area were Buffalo Lill, Wild Bill Hiccup, Wyatt Twerp and a cat Hettie didn't recognise from the show, although the resemblance to the Meakins was clear. 'Looks like we've found Matty Meakin,' she said, as Buffalo Lill got up from her seat and came towards them.

'Show doesn't start until seven,' Lill said. 'The ticket office opens at six if you'd like to come back then, although it's nearly a sell-out – we had to cancel last night's show.'

'Actually, we've come to talk to some of the cowboys,' said Hettie. 'We're investigating the fairground murders.'

'Oh dear,' said Lill. 'Well, you'd better come in and sit down. Who do you want to speak to? Maybe you should start with Mr Dinsney – he's in his office round the back of the arena.'

'We would like to see him, but first we'd like to speak with any of the cowboys who went into the town after the show the night before last.'

'That'll be Billy, Bill and Wyatt, then,' said Lill. 'I hope they're not in any trouble.'

Hettie decided not to answer and followed Lill to the front row with Tilly. Bruiser lingered by the entrance in case they needed back-up. 'These cats are investigating the murders,' Lill said, pointing to two seats next to Wild Bill Hiccup. 'If you'll excuse me I need to practise some knife throwing.' Lill stepped into the arena and proceeded to spin a rather lethal collection of long knives through the air at a target placed several yards away. Her aim was deadly and true and Hettie's mind couldn't help but conjure up the recent vision of the stabbed bodies in the ghost train.

She sat down with Tilly and Bill smiled at them. 'Bad business,' he said, 'and not what you'd expect in a little ol' seaside town. We have shootings in the States every day but you don't expect it here.'

Hettie decided not to allow Bill to run through the gun laws of America and their impact and wasted no time on niceties. 'I believe that you and some of the other cats from the show had a fight with Quince and his gang in Felixtoe the night before last?'

'Yep, we certainly did, and I've got a loose tooth to show for it.'

'What was the fight about?'

'Nothing really,' said Bill. 'We take it in turns to ambush each other – it's a way of letting off steam after the shows. Those biker cats are our punch buddies, really, and they were waiting for us this time, but we'll settle up when they least expect it.'

'Tell me what you did after the show that night?'

'Hang on to your horses a minute,' said Bill. 'I'm just wonderin' where this is all going? You don't think we had anything to do with those murders that Wilt told us about, do you?'

'I'm sure you didn't,' said Hettie, 'but we're trying to establish where everyone was that night. As you were in the town shortly after ten, I need to ask the question.'

By now, Wyatt was taking an interest in the conversation and Billy had wound up his rope and come over to sit down with them. The other cat, whom Hettie was sure was Matty Meakin, took no interest at all and stared straight ahead of him. He appeared to be watching Lill intently.

Bill decided to be helpful and answer Hettie's question. 'We headed out to go drinking at the Sailor's Sloop,' he said. 'Billy drove us in his pick-up and we parked by the fairground and started walking across the beach into the town when Quince and the others jumped us outside the Spa Pavilion. It was a good fight but we came off worse than them. They left us in a heap on the sand and took off on their bikes. We were in a pretty bad way so we cleaned up a bit on the shoreline and headed for the Sailor's Sloop for a drink. The cat who runs it wasn't very keen to let us in and I can't really blame him, but we had a drink and then headed back here in the pick-up to lick our wounds.'

Hettie looked across at Billy and Wyatt. 'Do you two have anything to add?'

Billy shook his head. 'No, I guess not,' he said, 'but I wish I'd been able to see Marmalade. Maybe if I had she'd still be here.'

'So you were seeing her?' Hettie asked.

'Not really,' said Billy. 'Her family didn't approve but we were going to meet up that night, then she cancelled as she said she had too much to do at the fair. She was repainting all the horses on the gallopers. She was a really talented artist and a lovely cat.'

'What about you, Wyatt?' asked Hettie.

'Me?' said Wyatt. 'I just go with the flow created by these guys. We didn't know a damn thing about these murders until Wilt told us the show for last night was cancelled.'

'When did he tell you that?'

'I guess it was late afternoon yesterday. He had a TV crew up here doing something on the murders and that's when we knew something terrible had happened. He doesn't cancel shows that easily, as it hurts his pocket.'

Hettie was very conscious of the quiet cat who had continued to stare straight ahead throughout her questions to the other three. She was about to challenge his silence when Bill, Billy and Wyatt got up to go. 'If there's nothing else, we need to get on with setting up tonight's show,' said Bill. 'Lill here will show you to Wilt's office when you're ready.'

Hettie now turned her full attention on the cat who was left. 'You must be Matty Meakin?' she said, as Tilly turned to a clean page in her notebook. 'Shouldn't you be with your family at a time like this?'

'What family?' he said, refusing to look in Hettie's direction. 'If you mean that collection of spiteful, power-crazed liars with their jealousies, rules and regulations, put in place by my father to glue us all together, then why would I want to be with them? The shame is that they didn't all die.'

Hettie was a little surprised at how succinctly Matty had described his feelings. 'That's quite some statement,' she said. 'I'd be interested to know why you feel like that.'

'I've been denied everything I've ever wanted because I'm part of that family. I'm the youngest son, the runt of the litter if you like, made to accept the crumbs off my brothers' and sisters' tables, forced to be an odd job cat and a spare part on the fairground with nothing to look forward to except more of the same. There's a whole world out there and I want some of it. When the season's over, Lill and me will be off on our adventures and no one is going to stop us.'

Matty had hardly taken his eyes off Lill, who continued throwing knives at the target. Hettie remembered what Minnie had said about him punching above his weight, but – from the looks that passed between them – Lill seemed to be as keen as Matty. 'I have to ask you where you were at around ten o'clock the night before last?' she said. 'Were you with the other cats in the town?'

Matty nodded. 'Yes, I went into town with them and after Quince had beaten us up I decided to walk back. The others were going on to the Sloop and I didn't feel like drinking. I got back here just after eleven, then I was with Lill in her caravan with Crazy Paws, another of the performers. We played cards and had some supper. Crazy Paws went back to his caravan at around midnight and I stayed with Lill.'

'Did you pass by the fairground on your way back here?'

'No, I stuck to the main road – it's the quickest way to Gobbles Point.'

'And finally,' said Hettie, 'who do you think might have done this to your family?'

'All of them or any of them,' said Matty. 'They're all capable of murder. It runs in the family.'

'What do you mean?'

'Ask Marlon,' said Matty, bringing the conversation to an abrupt end as he got up and walked away to join Lill in the arena.

Chapter Twenty-One

Wilt Dinsney's office was exactly what Hettie had expected it to be: the biggest and shiniest caravan in the park, situated behind the big top and dwarfing all the other accommodation that his performers lived in. She sent Bruiser to find Crazy Paws to check out the time that Matty had arrived back from the town, then she and Tilly headed for Wilt's office with much to discuss.

Wilt sat behind a substantial desk, smoking a cigar and pawing over some paperwork. He seemed more than a little surprised when Hettie and Tilly burst through the door of his sanctum. 'Well,' he said, getting to his feet, 'this is an unexpected pleasure. What brings you guys out here? Aren't you supposed to be catching a murderer?'

'That's why we're here,' said Hettie. 'We're talking to all the cats connected to the Meakins and the fairground and some of your cowboys were in Felixtoe around the time of the murders.'

'Hey, what are you saying? That one of my boys did this terrible thing?'

'No, we're not saying that at all,' said Hettie, 'but we had to come out to talk to Quince and he told us that he and his gang had beaten some of your cowboys up in the town the night the Meakins died. We're just checking alibis so we can eliminate cats from our enquiries.'

'So are you satisfied that none of my boys were involved?'

'Yes, I think we are, but there are a few questions we'd like to ask you before we go back into Felixtoe.'

'Well I've got the perfect alibi, as you know – I was digging you guys out of a bunker that night,' said Wilt. 'I really don't see what else I can tell you.'

'It's the family we'd like to discuss, more than the murders, and we'd value your opinion,' said Hettie, applying a less threatening, more conspiratorial approach. 'You know the family much better than we do.'

'That sounds like a thirsty conversation,' said Wilt. 'Sit yourselves down and I'll go and rustle up some tea from our chuck wagon.'

Wilt left, giving Hettie and Tilly an opportunity to give his office a closer inspection. The caravan was arranged for domestic and business use and the office area boasted a stack of filing cabinets; the desk that took up most of the space; a large safe; and a noticeboard with photos from his shows pinned to it. The desk was littered with paperwork and rolled-up charts. Tilly, who loved a map, unrolled one of them and it was a moment or two before she realised what she was looking at. 'This looks like the beach where the fairground is,' she said. 'There's the pier and these buildings must be his Wild West town.'

'Looks like he's jumped the gun, if you'll pardon the pun,' said Hettie. 'I wonder if Marlon has seen this?'

Tilly allowed the chart to roll itself up again while Hettie cast her eye across the other end of the caravan. Wilt's living quarters were much more comfortable, with a good-sized bed, a dazzling array of cowboy boots and costumes on a clothes rail, and a motley collection of guns and holsters. The walls were lined with black-and-white cowhides and the one on the floor had a bull's head with giant horns which made quite a statement.

They took their seats again just before Wilt returned, carrying a tea tray which he put down on his desk. 'I know you English cats love your tea, but there are some real American cookies to go with it. Lill makes them to sell on one of the stalls from my own ma's recipe.'

Tilly poured out three cups while Wilt settled himself behind his desk. The cookies proved to be moreish and there was very little conversation until they had all been eaten. 'Now then,' said Wilt, relighting his cigar and sitting back in his chair, 'you had some questions about Minnie's family?'

'Yes,' said Hettie. 'Marlon told me you were interested in buying the fairground – are you serious about it?'

'I sure am. In fact, take a look here.' Wilt unfurled the chart that Tilly had been looking at and spread it out on his desk, holding it down with a couple of paperweights. 'This is my plan. I want to build a whole Wild West town based on Dodge City in Kansas, where the famous cats Doc Holiday and Wyatt Twerp came from. Every year since I've been bringing my show here, I've offered Marlon a stack of dollars for that site on the beach, but he's always said no – although I guess there's a good chance that he'll change his mind now.'

'And what about the rest of the Meakins? Do any of them know what your plans are?'

'I've discussed it with Minnie but she gets upset at the thought of anything changing. She loves her villa and I think she enjoys being independent from the rest of them, but I don't think she'd like to see the end of the fairground.'

'How do you get on with the Meakins?'

'I used to get on just fine with them until Micky died at the start of this season. My boys got into a fight with Quince and his gang, and Micky tried to break it up and fell off the ride at the fairground. It was a terrible accident but I got the blame for it, which made things difficult for me and Minnie. That family don't take prisoners and they don't like any of their females taking a liking to cats outside the family. I find that all a bit sinister, really, and a waste of some great female cats.'

'Sinister in what way?' asked Hettie.

'Well, take Marmalade for instance. She was a great girl and sweet on Billy the Kit, but as soon as Marlon got wind of it he put his foot down. It's like he's frightened that a male cat will come in and take over the precious fairground that he waited so long to inherit.'

'Did you meet old Mr Meakin before he died?'

'Yup. Milo Meakin was the king of the fairground and he ruled that family with a rod of iron. He was a cat of very few words, but he only needed to look at you and you felt he was giving you the evil eye. He seemed to disapprove of everything and every-one, but none of that family dared to step out of line while he was alive. You meet some cats and feel you've known them for years, but Milo Meakin was a one-off. To be honest, I think they all breathed a sigh of relief when he died. Marlon has tried really hard to follow in his paw prints but Monica wears the trousers these days.'

'How do you know all this?' asked Hettie.

'Because of young Matty,' said Wilt. 'He spends a lot of time here because he hates his family and he's poured his heart out to me now and again. He wants out of the family altogether because he says that they're all really unpleasant cats – except for Minnie, who sticks up for him when Marlon is having a go at him. I give him some jobs round here and I know he's very close to Lill, and he gets on with the rest of the performers in the show.'

'You haven't been around the villa since we discovered the murders,' said Hettie, 'is there a reason for that?'

'I'm not one for walking into a gunfight,' said Wilt. 'I'm holed up here keeping my head down. Minnie has family coming from all over and they won't take kindly to a Yankie cowboy being in the middle of them.'

Hettie could see that Wilt's presence in the middle of the cats who'd just arrived at the villa would not be welcome and moved on to her next question. 'When we spoke to Quince, he told us that you employed him and his gang to do odd jobs for you occasionally. He seems a strange choice of worker, given his reputation as a troublemaker – what does he do for you?'

'Nothing wrong with hiring a few outlaws now and then,' said Wilt. 'Quince takes no prisoners and he acts as a bit of insurance against the real threats to my shows. We get some pretty unpleasant holidaymakers from time to time, hell-bent on destroying what we do here, and having Quince and his guys about the place is like calling on the cavalry when we need them. Those guys get a lot of bad press, but I think I help out a bit by paying them to stay out of bad trouble.'

'And what about the fights they start on the fairground? That doesn't help Marlon and his business.'

'Well, that's Marlon's shout. He leaves himself wide open to trouble, thinking that he and his brothers can handle it, but a fairground like his attracts troublemakers. He doesn't have enough cats running it and he alienates the locals when he could be giving them jobs. To be brutally honest, he just doesn't cut it. Milo Meakin put a lot on his young shoulders, but Milo was a very different cat from his son. Marlon is soft and lets Monica walk all over him. It's really sad that Monty is dead. That boy had a spark about him and if he'd been allowed to, he would have modernised that business or maybe come into partnership with me, but Marlon is stuck in the mud that his father created and he's not strong enough to dig himself out.'

'What about old Mrs Meakin?' asked Hettie. 'What's your opinion of her?'

Wilt laughed. 'Now you're talking! She wields more power than that nuclear plant out in the North Sea. She sits there in Minnie's kitchen all day long, looking totally gaga, but she has a razor-sharp memory and was the only member of that family to talk back at Milo. From what Minnie has told me, it was her mother's side of the family that had the money to buy the villa and the land from Gervaise Smith. It was her decision that they came off the road and settled as Sandscratchers.'

The more Hettie delved into the Meakin family, the more interesting they became, but she and Tilly were no further on in catching a killer and it would appear that most of the cats they'd spoken to had alibis that just didn't stack up. She felt that Marlon was now at the centre of so much confusion that the sooner she was able to have a few things out with him the better. 'You've been really helpful,' she said. 'We'll leave you in peace, but one last thing – will you be making Marlon an offer for the fairground site to build your Wild West town?'

'I guess I have to wait for the dust – or should I say sand – to settle on that one,' said Wilt. 'I don't want to lose Minnie by being too keen, but it would be great if I could make it happen one day.'

Bruiser was waiting by Miss Scarlet when Hettie and Tilly left Wilt to his paperwork. He was able to confirm that Crazy Paws had played cards with Matty and Lill on the night of the murders and Hettie was satisfied that they had no further business at the showground. 'We'd better head back into town to see if we can find Marlon,' she said. 'He's got a number of questions to answer, and so has Monica for that matter, but we'll be treading on eggshells with her. By now, Monty's body will have been moved back to his wagon for this vigil thing they're arranging.'

'I think it's rather a nice idea,' said Tilly. 'I've always thought it was sad that bodies are put in fridge drawers at the undertaker's, like being kept in a filing cabinet. Much nicer to be in your own home where your friends can visit and have a cup of tea and a cake with you.'

'Make sure to remind me to put a clean tablecloth on our desk to lay you out on when your time comes,' said Hettie, 'and we could put an advance order in with the Butters for cream horns for your friends to enjoy.'

'An' maybe some of them mini pasties,' added Bruiser, jumping onto the bike.

Tilly giggled and clambered into the sidecar, followed by Hettie. With the lid secured, the three cats took off along the road from Gobbles Point in search of some home truths.

Chapter Twenty-Two

Bruiser dropped Hettie and Tilly off at the fairground and took Miss Scarlet back up to the villa. The motorbike was running a little bit rough and he had decided that some TLC from his toolbox was required.

Hettie and Tilly walked through to Marlon's office by the dodgems, but there was no sign of him and the office was padlocked. 'I suppose we'd better go and see if he's at the wagon park,' said Hettie. 'I can't see us getting very far with him today if he's surrounded by the Meakin clan.'

The wagon park, situated behind the fairground, was a long way from the sombre affair that Hettie and Tilly expected to find. The gathering Meakins had clearly started a wake and, in spite of their funeral clothes, a good time was being had by all. A barbecue and beer tent had been set up and there was a small band of musicians offering toe-tapping tunes; in the middle of it all stood Monty's wagon, festooned in flowers. Marlon sat by the door, nodding to those who filed past him to pay their respects to his son.

As Hettie and Tilly approached, the jollity suddenly stopped and all eyes turned on them. It was as if the scene had frozen and turned into a painting. The stillness was threatening and it was very clear to Hettie and Tilly that their presence was unwelcome and would not be tolerated. Marlon got to his feet and strode through the crowd towards them. 'This is not a good place for you to be,' he said, taking Hettie by the arm and marching her out of the park, leaving Tilly to follow. 'This is family and no strangers are allowed.'

Hettie pulled her arm away from Marlon indignantly and stood her ground. 'It seems to me that the word "family" is something to hide behind as far as you're concerned,' she said. 'If you want us to get to the bottom of who murdered Monty and your brothers and sister, it's time you started telling the truth.'

'What do you mean?' asked Marlon. 'And I'm not sure anyone asked you to get to the bottom of these murders. It was different when we thought some of the family had gone missing and we thank you for finding them, but the rest of it is our business and we don't need you poking your noses in, so I suggest you get on with your holiday and leave us to grieve in our own way.'

Hettie's hackles were up now and even Tilly was seeing Marlon in a very different light. 'I might remind you that we have spent the last two days of our so-called holiday trying to catch a murderer. Now you say all that matters is that carnival you've set up in the wagon park. You have a very funny way of show-ing your grief.'

'It's tradition,' said Marlon. 'It's the way we do things and it's what keeps the family together.'

Hettie laughed in Marlon's face. 'Not according to your youngest brother, who has defected to the Wild West show. He doesn't seem to think the family is very together, and neither does Mary for that matter. They both have a very dim view of your so-called traditions, and even Minnie seems to prefer to keep herself to herself, so not much unity there either. In fact, the general view is that you haven't made a very good job of things since taking over from your father.'

'That's unfair,' hissed Marlon. 'You don't know what you're talking about.'

'So now's the time to enlighten me. You could start by telling me why you lied about being at the Sailor's Sloop until midnight and why you didn't tell me you'd rowed with Monica and Monty?'

Marlon looked like a cat caught in headlights. He turned from side to side before answering. 'We can't do this here,' he said. 'Let's take a walk along the beach.'

Marlon strode out before Hettie could argue. Avoiding the fairground, he walked down onto the sand and waited at the shoreline. The beach was emp-tying as everyone was heading back for dinner, leaving the solitary figure of Pete to collect up the now empty deckchairs. The sight of him reminded Hettie that she still had to talk to him, but her conversation with Marlon was much more pressing.

When they reached him, it was immediately obvious that he was crying; his shoulders shook and he looked entirely wretched. Tilly's heart went out to him and even Hettie cast a sympathetic eye. 'I'm sorry,' he said. 'I just can't deal with any of this, and you're right – I've made a complete mess of everything. I'm not like my father and I don't want to be, and I'm sick of standing up for him and keeping his secrets. It's all too much. If I had my way, I'd walk into the sea and never look back.'

'I can see that families can be suffocating,' said Hettie, 'but secrets are better out in the open. We are strangers and will probably never see you again once we've returned to our town so, if you need to unburden yourself, now might be a good time to do it.'

Marlon stared out to the horizon and Hettie and Tilly flanked him. All was silence except for the gentle lapping of waves as they broke on the sand. Eventually he turned away from the sea and walked towards the pier, where a small fishing boat was pulled up on the sand. He clambered into it and invited Hettie and Tilly to do the same. 'This was Maxwell's,' he said. 'We had some good times on this boat, me, Maxwell and Micky. We used to go out night fishing, but I was always the odd one out because they both knew that I would be their boss one day. When my father died, everything changed. I was suddenly the one giving the orders, telling them what they could and couldn't do and it felt like I had no one on my side until Monica came along. She was a distant cousin from my mother's side of the family and it was always assumed we would marry. My father arranged it with her father when we were both kittens. It worked out well and when Monty was born I had a son to pass the fair and all the responsibilities on to. But I've been living with a terrible secret that my father passed to me on his death bed. He told me that he'd murdered his brother Milchip because Milchip was the rightful heir to my grandfather's fairground, which meant that everything I thought was going to be mine was a lie. My father said he'd adopted Mary because he'd killed her father – her mother had died in a wagon fire several months before Milchip, so Mary had no one. The rest of the family was told that Milchip had got in a knife fight with another showcat over a pitch, but it just wasn't true. My father challenged his brother to a fight to the death and that's what happened.'

'So do you think any of this has something to do with the murders?' asked Hettie gently.

'Maybe,' said Marlon. 'Last week I found a note pushed under my office door. It said something like "Isn't it time you told the truth and gave back what your father stole."'

'Do you still have the note?'

'No, I burnt it straight away, but then I started thinking about it and I realised that I would have to tell Monica and Monty. I felt almost relieved – maybe this was a way out for us.'

'What do you mean?'

'Well, with the fair not doing so well it occurred to me that we could escape all of this and have a proper life away from it. I thought that if Monica, Monty and me could start again somewhere new, we could be happy.'

'Is that what you talked to Monica about that night at the Sailor's Sloop?'

'Yes, and she hit the roof. I told her what my father had told me and she was just so angry because I'd kept his secret for so long. She said I should go back down to the fairground and tell Monty that someone was going to steal his birthright away from him and that it was all my fault, so that's what I did.'

'And how did Monty take it?'

'Really badly. He called me a liar and said he wanted nothing more to do with me and that he'd be leaving the fairground in the morning. He said he didn't want to be associated with a family who murdered to get what they wanted, and he threatened to tell Mary as well. Then he ran off back into the fairground and that's the last time I saw him alive.'

'Do you have any idea who the note might have come from?' asked Hettie. 'Presumably it was paw-delivered and didn't come through the post?'

'I thought it might have come from Mary at one point,' said Marlon. 'We hadn't been getting on so well because of the issue over the slots on the pier. I suddenly realised that if things had been different and Milchip had lived, then Mary would have owned everything as Milchip's heir. Then I thought that Mary likes an easy life without responsibilities and if she had something to say she'd just say it and not bother with a note under my door.'

'So do you think Mary knows the truth about her father's death?'

Marlon shook his head. 'I doubt it. As far as I can tell it was just between my father and Milchip. I had no idea until he was dying.'

'Did your Uncle Milchip have any other family who might have known about the murder?'

'My father was his only brother, so I don't think so. As far as I know there were no witnesses to the fight, which is why my father got away with it so easily.'

'What about your mother?' asked Hettie. 'Would Milo have told her what he'd done?'

'I just don't know about that and I wouldn't dare discuss it with her. She might not look it, but she's a formidable cat. I think as a family we respected my father but were frightened of my mother. The female Meakins had the money to start with and financed all the fairs over the years. The male cats traditionally did the fighting and talking, the female cats ruled the roosts and counted the money – that's the way it's been for over a hundred years.'

'Where does Monica sit in all of this hierarchy?'

'She was a Meakin even before we got together. By producing an heir in Monty, she's become a very significant member of the family and would, in time, have taken my mother's place, but none of that will happen now.'

'How does she feel about all this?'

'I just don't know,' said Marlon. 'She's hardly spoken to me and she's moved into Monty's wagon to sit with him until the funerals. After that, I don't know what she'll do but we're both going to have to give up everything we've worked for. Now my father's secret is out, we have no right to anything unless Mary wants to keep us on. Everything really belongs to her.'

'Will you talk to Mary about all this?'

'I'll have to, but after the funerals, when the family have all returned to their different parts of the country. I'm just trying to get through the next few days without involving any of them in this nightmare. The funeral traditions will have to go ahead and it's down to me to organise it all.'

'There's clearly someone who's out to destroy you and your family,' said Hettie. 'I understand that strangers like us are not welcome at this time but we would like to continue with our investigations, if only to bring whoever murdered Monty to some sort of justice. We don't need your permission, but we would like your blessing.'

'You have it,' said Marlon, 'and I'm sorry not to have been straight with you. I would be grateful if you could find the cat who took Monty and my brothers and sister from me, but I would also ask you to keep the things I've just told you confidential until after the funerals. Now, I really must get back to the wake as I'm supposed to be hosting it.'

Marlon walked away across the sand, leaving Hettie and Tilly still sitting in Maxwell's boat. Hettie looked across the beach, hoping to catch sight of Premo Pete as he was the last one left on Tilly's list to interview, but his deckchairs were now neatly stacked by the kiosk and Pete was nowhere to be seen.

'I wonder where Pete lives?' said Hettie. 'We shouldn't forget that he was out and about around midnight when we got back from the Wild West show with Wilt the other night. We need to ask him what he was up to and I want to know if he really was seeing Mary. She's suddenly become a much more important suspect in our investigations.'

'And he was talking about death long before anything happened,' added Tilly.

'Come on,' said Hettie. 'Let's go back up to the villa and find Bruiser. Hopefully he's sorted Miss Scarlet out. I'm starving and if Minnie hasn't managed any dinner for us we'll have to go out for some. To be honest, I don't fancy sharing the dining room with the Devon Meakins, and goodness knows how it will be when the Londoners arrive tomorrow.'

'I'm beginning to feel a bit homesick,' said Tilly, following Hettie out of the boat. 'I'd give anything for one of Molly Bloom's mixed grills or a Butters' pie. Everything has got a bit strange and nasty round here and I don't think we fit in up at the villa. It was horrible when all those Meakins were staring at us in the wagon park.'

'I feel the same, but I honestly think we are getting really close to cracking this case,' said Hettie. 'After what Marlon had to say, it's clear that Milchip's murder sits at the centre of all this and it's down to who knows what and why they've suddenly decided to strike now. I just wish Marlon had kept that note – if there ever was a note.'

'You don't think he's still lying do you?'

'To be honest, I'm beginning to think that just about everyone we've spoken to in the last couple of days has been lying to us, but sooner or later one of them will slip up. The important thing is to make sure they don't kill again.'

Chapter Twenty-Three

Bruiser was putting his tools back in Miss Scarlet's boot when Hettie and Tilly joined him in the car park at the villa. 'She's soundin' much better now I've tuned 'er up,' he said. 'She'd got sand in 'er fuel pipe from the crash but I've flushed it through so we're good to go again.'

Tilly clapped her paws, pleased that Miss Scarlet was feeling better. 'Thank goodness you could fix her,' she said. 'You're so clever. I don't know what we'd do without you.'

'Mercifully that's something we don't have to worry about,' said Hettie, offering her own back-pawed compliment, 'but food is now high on the agenda.'

The three friends made their way into the villa and were about to climb the stairs to their room when Minnie accosted them. 'I'm afraid dinner is off tonight,' she said. 'I've got to go down to the wagon park to cater for the Devon Meakins, as they're insisting on eating espresso. I just hope it doesn't rain. Anyway, I've laid out an afternoon tea for you in the dining room with mother's freshly baked scones. For your dinner later, I suggest you go to Catrina's Fish Bar at the end of the prom. She does a lovely hake bake, which I can highly recompense, and the best banana fritters in the whole of Suffolk. You'll have to book a table, but I've left her number stuck on the noticeboard next to the payphone. I know it's a lot to ask, but I won't be back till late as Monica has got me down to sit with Monty, so could you look in on Mother later to make sure she doesn't need anything?'

'Of course we can,' said Tilly. 'Would she like some supper brought back from Catrina's?'

'That's very kind,' said Minnie, 'but she's doing herself a boil in the bag curry with rice, as she's seen it on the TV. Just another fad, but she likes to think she's a bit of a trendsitter. Last week it was Smash potato mix, but only because she likes the aliens in the advert. She made a cottage pie with it and it went everywhere. I'm still having to scrape it off my carpet slippers.'

Hettie could only admire Minnie's playful banter under the circumstances. Her approach to life was a breath of fresh air compared with the miserable attitudes shared by the rest of her family, and the fact that she'd brightened up her funeral clothes with a cheery red cardigan spoke volumes.

Minnie bustled out of the front door, relieving the villa of her energy, and Hettie, Tilly and Bruiser made their way into the dining room to enjoy their cream tea. There were cheese and fruit scones, so Hettie put three of the cheese ones aside to take up to their room for a late supper; the rest she laid out on the table by the window, and Tilly boiled the kettle that had been left for them to make the tea.

'Shall I go an' phone up the fish bar?' suggested Bruiser. 'We don't want ta miss out on dinner.'

'Good idea,' said Hettie. 'I'll put some jam and cream on a scone for you.'

'Don't forget it's jam first,' said Tilly, favouring the Cornish way of doing things.

'Just as well there are no Devon Meakins here at the moment,' said Hettie. 'More than our life's worth to do that in front of them.'

'I do wonder about the cats of Devon,' said Tilly. 'Putting cream on first just doesn't work because it gets stuck to the jam and makes a terrible sticky mess.'

'Well, if anyone knows about sticky messes it's you. Your T-shirts are testament to that.'

'I'm sure I don't know what you mean,' said Tilly, wiping some cream off her whiskers with the back of her paw.

'We're all booked in fer eight,' said Bruiser, returning to the table to claim his first scone. 'That was the earliest she could do.'

'Eight o'clock is fine,' said Hettie. 'It'll give us a chance to find Premo Pete and have a word with him. After dinner we'd better go through Tilly's notes to see if there's anything we might have missed. We should talk to Monica, too, but if she's stuck in Monty's wagon watching him grow paler by the minute, I don't see how we can – and anyway, I don't regard her as a main suspect.'

'I'm feeling a bit sorry for Marmalade, Maxwell and Marty,' said Tilly. 'I'm sure Davy Button is looking after them at his undertaker's, but it all seems to be about Monty.'

'I suppose he was the heir apparent and much more important, being Marlon's son,' suggested Hettie. 'This showcat business is like some weird cult – clearly they're a law unto themselves. I wouldn't want to be Marlon if they find out about the deception between Milo and Milchip Meakin.'

It was a point to ponder on but the tea and scones were far too good for any further distractions. The three cats made short work of Minnie's afternoon tea, taking the three cheese scones back to their room before setting out to find Premo Pete. 'I think we should head down to the kiosk,' suggested Hettie. 'Maybe the cat who serves the ice creams knows where Pete lives as he sets up next to her.'

Hettie joined the queue at the kiosk and Tilly and Bruiser sat on a bench on the promenade to wait for her. It was a lovely sunny evening and perfect for a stroll along the beach. 'It's such a shame,' said Tilly. 'This is a wonderful place for a holiday and I feel so sad about the fairground. The beach won't be the same without it.'

'Maybe Marlon can save it. 'E just needs ta get some cats in ta work it.'

'I don't think that's going to happen after what he told us this afternoon.' Tilly went on to explain to Bruiser what they'd found out about Milo and Milchip, bringing him up to speed on the case.

'Blimey,' said Bruiser, 'that's a real mess, so I s'pose we're lookin' for the cat that sent the note. Shame 'e didn't keep it.'

'That's what we thought,' said Tilly, 'and here comes Hettie. I wonder if she's found out where Pete lives.'

Hettie looked triumphant and seemed to be carrying three iced lollies in her paws. 'The cat in the kiosk insisted I buy something before she'd part with Pete's address so I got us three strawberry Mivvis.'

'Ooh, lovely,' said Tilly, ripping the wrapper off hers. 'I love biting the strawberry lolly bit off so I can get to the ice cream. Where does Pete live?'

'In a beach hut up the other end of the promenade. It's called Pete's Place, evidently, and she says you can't miss it as it's painted up like the fairground.'

'Maybe Marmalade painted it for him?' said Tilly. 'It would be lovely if she had.'

'Let's go and see. We need to find out if Pete really is sweet on Mary Meakin and what he was up to on the night of the murders.'

The three cats sauntered along the beach, giving themselves time to finish their ice lollies. They noticed that Catrina's Fish Bar was just before a row of beach huts at the end of the promenade. The café looked jolly with its red striped awning and tables inside and out, and the smell of freshly cooked fish and chips was irresistible.

Pete's hut was easy to find as he was sitting on a deckchair in front of it smoking a pipe. The kiosk cat's description was accurate and the decorative swirls and beautifully painted figures were unmistakably the work of Marmalade Meakin.

'Well, well,' Pete said, 'if it's not our hero and 'is two friends! Saved any kittens today?'

Bruiser nodded hello and Hettie cut to the chase. 'I expect you know by now that four members of the Meakin family were murdered two nights ago?'

'I'd 'eard that somethin' 'ad gone on,' said Pete. 'Bad business closin' the fairground, though, 'specially in the middle of the season. I've 'ad a lot of complaints from me customers about there bein' no fair. It's what some of 'em come for.'

'Would you mind if we asked you a few questions about that night?' asked Hettie. 'You may have seen something that would help.'

'Fire away,' said Pete, 'but I don't see what I can tell you. I'm packed up an' back in me hut by dusk every night.'

'But that night we saw you just before midnight up by Sandscratchers Villa.'

'Did you now? Well, if you saw me I must 'ave been there, but I didn't see no murderers. I must 'ave been takin' a late night stroll.'

'It would help if you could remember exactly what you were doing that night,' pressed Hettie. 'We need to eliminate you from our enquiries.'

'That don't sound too friendly. You're soundin' like one of them detectives off the telly.'

'That's probably because we are detectives and there's a killer out there we're trying to catch. If you could tell us what you were doing that night, we'll leave you in peace.'

'What if I didn't want to say what I was doin'?' asked Pete. 'What do yer think you could do about it? As far as I can see, what I was doin' is nothing ta do with you, or anyone else for that matter.'

Hettie was getting tired of going round in circles. 'Were you with Mary Meakin?'

Pete's attitude changed immediately at the mention of Mary, and he suddenly became aggressive in his reply. 'Why? What's she been tellin' you? Trouble with 'er is she lets 'er mouth run away with 'er an' she makes things up when it suits 'er.'

'Actually,' said Hettie, 'Mary hasn't told us anything about you, but we did hear that you were walking out with her.'

'Walking out, yer say?' said Pete, throwing his head back and laughing. 'Well wouldn't that be a fine thing? You're way off course there. Me, a humble deckchair attendant, walkin' out with a mighty Meakin?'

'If you weren't with Mary that night, perhaps you can tell us what you were doing until just before midnight and after?'

'As I've said, I don't 'ave to tell you anythin' and you're startin' ta bother me. I've answered some of yer questions so now I suggest you sling yer hook an' go an' bother someone else.'

As Hettie seemed to have hit a brick wall with her questions, Tilly decided to have a go. 'You told us there were going to be deaths and that we would be involved,' she said. 'I was wondering how you knew that?'

Pete smiled. 'Like I tells you before, I gets these messages now an' then. It runs in me family. There's days when I just seems to be one jump ahead – useful if you're playin' cards, but not so good if somethin' bad is goin' ta happen.'

'So does your gift run to knowing who might have killed the Meakins?' Hettie asked.

Pete shook his head. 'Isn't that supposed ta be your job?'

Hettie realised that they were getting nowhere with Pete. The clock on the Spa Pavilion Theatre said it was five minutes to eight and Catrina's Fish Bar awaited them, so they left Pete to his evening and headed for the café. Catrina had reserved them a table outside on the promenade, and all three cats agreed that on such a lovely warm evening it was an idyllic location. They sat down to study the menu and Tilly insisted on reading it out. 'I'll start with the different sorts of fish,' she said, scrutinising the small print. 'We can have battered cod, haddock, rock eel, hake or pollock served with small, medium or large chips. There's battered sausage, beefburgers or king prawns, cod or haddock fishcakes, sprats in breadcrumbs and cod goujons. The side orders are chips, mushy peas with mint sauce, curry sauce, buttered baps and Catrina's mayonnaise dip, and today's specials are hake bake, fish pie and salmon en croute, whatever that means.'

'I think they just stick pastry round it,' said Bruiser. 'I 'ad one of them once at a bikers' convention. Come ta think of it, they stuck everythin' in pastry that day – makes stuff easier ta eat if yer don't 'ave a plate, like them vol-au-vent things yer get at parties.'

'They make me cough,' said Tilly, 'and there's hardly any filling in them.'

'When the two of you have finally finished discussing things wrapped in pastry, perhaps we might order something to eat?' said Hettie. 'I'm going for haddock, large chips and mushy peas with a buttered bap.'

'I fancy the 'ake bake with extra chips,' said Bruiser.

Tilly studied the menu again. 'It's just all too lovely,' she said. 'I don't think I've ever had a battered beef burger and I might not like it, so I think I'll go for hake, medium chips and curry sauce, as that's a bit exotic – and I'll have to have a buttered bap as well.'

Before Tilly could change her mind, Hettie made her way to the service counter inside the café and placed their orders. She returned with some fizzy drinks on a tray and the three cats sat and waited for their dinners, enjoying the last of the evening sunshine. Catrina prided herself on a fast turnaround service and the meals arrived quite quickly. Hettie and Tilly's fish were huge and curled in a golden batter on their plates; Bruiser's hake bake took up the whole of his plate, with a separate bowl for his chips.

'I don't think Minnie could have competed with that dinner,' said Hettie, sitting back from her empty plate and wiping her whiskers on her serviette. 'With the chaos up at Sandscratchers, I think we should book ourselves in here for dinner tomorrow as well.'

'The London Meakins are arriving tomorrow,' said Tilly, dipping her final chip into her curry sauce. 'I hope they're going to be nicer than the Devon ones.'

'Let's just hope they spend their time down at the wagon park. At least that way we shouldn't see much of them.'

'What do yer reckon to Pete then?' said Bruiser. ''E wasn't much 'elp but I think 'e knows more than 'e's sayin'.'

'I agree,' said Hettie, 'but I think Maisie was wrong about him being sweet on Mary. Maybe we should try and talk to Mary again. After what Marlon told us about Milo and Milchip, we could approach her in a different way.'

'What do you mean?' asked Tilly.

'For a start we could ask her what she knows about Premo Pete. We could even say there were rumours about her and him. I'd also like to know what her plans are now, with the fairground being closed. She must have realised that Marlon will have to sell up or pass everything on to another branch of the family – unless she knows the truth and is biding her time before she claims the lot. When we spoke to her she hinted that none of the family were what they seemed, so she must know something.'

'It was the same with Matty,' added Tilly. 'He said we should ask Marlon about murder, so he obviously knows something – maybe he's more friendly with Mary than he's saying? They're both outsiders in the family.'

'If we could just get someone to start telling the truth, we might actually get somewhere. There are so many questions to be answered about this case. We don't even know where the Meakins were killed – and why was Monty's murder so different from the others? I've no doubt that he was killed in the ghost train and the others were moved there after they were dead. He must have disturbed the killer as he or she was posing the bodies, so are we to assume that he was never an intended victim and was just in the wrong place at the wrong time? Perhaps we should go back to our room and review everything we know to see if we've missed something.'

Hettie paid up for the dinners and booked a table for the following evening. They walked back along the sand as darkness began to fall, oblivious to the cat lurking in the shadows, watching them as they returned to Sandscratchers Villa.

Chapter Twenty-Four

All was quiet when Hettie, Tilly and Bruiser let themselves into the villa. Hettie and Bruiser made their way up to their room and Tilly volunteered to check on old Mrs Meakin to see if she needed anything. The dining room was exactly how they'd left it after finishing their afternoon tea. Tilly made her way into the kitchen and was pleased to see that Mrs Meakin was fast asleep in her chair by the Aga. There was an empty plate on the kitchen table, suggesting that she'd enjoyed her boil in the bag curry; the radio was turned down low, offering a late night play, and Tilly was satisfied that the old cat was in no need of assistance.

She made her way up to number six, where Bruiser and Hettie were waiting for her to open her notebook to review the suspects in the case. 'Where would you like me to start?' asked Tilly, settling herself on the sofa next to Hettie.

'Let's incorporate the suspects into the timings of the night that the Meakins were murdered,' Hettie suggested. 'Obviously some of the information we've been given is unreliable, but we'll just have to try and wade through what is and isn't possible. We know that the fair closed at ten, and so did the Wild West show, so let's start by seeing where all the suspects were at that point.'

'OK,' said Tilly, turning to the page where she'd listed the suspects. 'In no particular order I've got Wilt Dinsney. We know that he was at his show until it finished, as he was in the finale, and he helped us out of the bunker between ten-thirty and eleven. We arrived back at the villa with him just before midnight.'

'That doesn't give him any time to kill anyone,' said Hettie, 'unless the murders took place much later that night. That's a complicated scenario, though, as it would mean that all the dead Meakins would have gone back to their wagons and then been murdered. It makes much more sense for them to have been killed shortly after the fair closed when they were all together, which gives Wilt a cast-iron alibi – even though he stands to gain by the fair closing. Who's next?'

'Quince and his gang. He admitted that they were in Felixtoe beating up the cowboys just after ten, and we saw them at the Wild West show during the interval at around nine. They ran us off the road coming back from Felixtoe between ten-fifteen and ten-thirty.'

'They must 'ave cleared out fast after beatin' up them cowboys,' Bruiser pointed out. 'No time fer them ta kill the Meakins as well.'

'And out of all the cats we've spoken to, I think what Quince had to say to us was entirely believable,' said Hettie. 'They were obviously spoiling for a fight that night, but stabbing four cats to death just doesn't seem to be their style.'

'I've got Premo Pete next,' said Tilly. 'He wasn't really helpful, but we did see him near the villa when we got back with Wilt that night and Maisie seemed to think that he was seeing Mary in secret.'

'We need to look at Mary in a completely different light after what Marlon had to say. Pete seemed totally bemused at the thought of him and Mary being an item, so it seems that Maisie might have got that wrong. Also, I can't immediately see why Pete would want to kill the Meakins. He'd have nothing to gain by it. In fact, he seems to lead a charmed life with his deckchair business – but he was acting suspiciously that night when we saw him.'

'I was wondering whether Pete was seeing Marmalade?' suggested Tilly. 'She must have liked him to paint his hut, and that would connect him to the fairground, but it doesn't make him a killer.'

'That's a good point,' said Hettie, 'and several cats have told us that Marmalade had lots of admirers. Maybe Maisie got it wrong and it was actually Marmalade that Pete had his eye on.'

'What about Maisie?' said Bruiser. 'She's not 'appy about any of them Meakins except Monica. Maybe she made up the thing about Pete an' Mary ta cover 'er tracks? She could easily 'ave slipped out of 'er wagon that night.'

'Yes,' agreed Hettie, 'and she did mention that she'd like to burn down the fairground after what happened to Micky and the way the family have covered it up. She's bound to hold a grudge, but is she capable of stabbing four cats in cold blood?'

'She does seem very angry about Micky's death,' said Tilly, 'but I can't see her posing those bodies in the ghost train – and she'd be away from her kittens for most of the night to do that. And I do like her.'

'Let's look at the cowboys next. We know they were in Felixtoe straight after their show and we also know that they turned up at the Sailor's Sloop around eleven, battered and bleeding after Quince had finished with them. I suppose they could have gone on to the fairground after Quince and his gang left them, but they would have had to kill the Meakins, then hide the bodies out of sight and go back later to pose them in the ghost train. If you were going to kill four cats, surely you'd do it and get the hell out? You wouldn't go back later to create an elaborate crime scene and risk being caught.'

'And why would the cowboys want to do that anyway?' said Tilly.

'Maybe Wilt paid 'em so 'e could get the fair closed down to build 'is Wild West town?' suggested Bruiser.

'That's always a possibility, but I don't think he'd stoop that low and I think he genuinely cares about

Minnie and wouldn't want to hurt her by killing off her family. I'm still a bit concerned about Matty Meakin in all of this. He was in Felixtoe with the cowboys, he decided to make his own way home after the fight and he hates his family. He would have had time to kill the Meakins and dump them in the ghost train, then return later to lay them out.'

'But he said he stayed with Buffalo Lill that night,' said Tilly, consulting her notes.

'That alibi is only as good as Lill sticking up for him, and he did seem to know that Marlon was in some way connected to a murder. Maybe he got wind of the Milo and Milchip situation from Mary and decided to send the note to Marlon to muddy the waters? Let's take a look at Mary and what we now know about her.'

Tilly had a page full of notes on Mary Meakin and quickly read through them before presenting the facts to Hettie and Bruiser. 'Mary said she left her wagon around ten that night to go and build a fire on the beach under the pier, where she cooked sausages. That means she was around the fairground at the time it closed. She also refused to say if she was with anyone, so she doesn't really have an alibi – but Quince said he saw her lighting the fire, so at least that bit is true and he didn't say she was with anyone. I also made a note of the fact that she used to run the ghost train so she'd know all about that and she'd be used to setting nasty things up in there. Then I've written down the row you told us about between her and Monica and how Monica said she wasn't a proper part of the family – but that was after the murders, of course.'

'Yes, but we know they didn't get on because of Marlon's plans to close the slots down and give Monica more space for her café,' Hettie pointed out, 'and then comes the revelation about Milchip's murder and the fact that Mary should be the rightful heir, not Marlon. There are probably more than enough motives in all of that to make a cat commit murder but it would have to rely on Mary knowing that Milo had murdered her father.'

'If she did know,' said Bruiser, ''ow come she didn't just face Marlon with it? It's a bit drastic ta go on a killin' spree when she was in the right.'

'And how did she find out about her father's murder if it was all hushed up by Milo?' asked Tilly.

'The obvious answer to that is old Mrs Meakin,' Hettie said. 'She clearly has been the matriarch of the family and my guess is that Milo told her years ago that he'd murdered Milchip. Maybe in her old age she inadvertently blurted it out to Mary. She obviously has lapses of memory, as she'd forgotten that Micky was dead.'

'I suppose we should think about Marlon and Monica,' said Tilly. 'Now we know that Marlon met up with Monty as the fairground was closing and Monica doesn't have a solid alibi either, they've got to be suspects – and they all rowed about the impact of Milchip's murder.'

'From what we know about Monica, she must have seen red after Marlon dropped his bombshell, but if she murdered anyone surely it would have been Marlon? Why kill his brothers and sister? Then there's Monty. I still can't see either of them killing their only son.'

'There's one suspect we 'aven't said much about,' said Bruiser. 'Minnie 'as taken all this in 'er stride. She says she was with 'er mother that night, an' we know she was 'ere at midnight, but she could 'ave gone down the fair at ten, killed 'em and stuck 'em in the ghost train, an' been back up 'ere just as we was comin' in with Wilt.'

'That's true,' said Hettie, 'and we know that she doesn't have much to do with the fairground and the rest of the family. She could have done it all for Wilt so that Marlon would have to close the fair and sell to him.'

'But she seems so proud of her family,' Tilly objected, 'and she tells Wilt off if he says unkind things about the fairground and how old-fashioned it is – and she seems really sad about Marmalade.'

'Well, we've been through the list and I'm not sure we're any the wiser,' said Hettie, filling her catnip pipe. 'I think we should stick the kettle on for some milky teas and have those cheese scones.'

Tilly responded by filling the kettle in the small sink and switched it on. There was a sudden distant rumble of thunder and Hettie crossed to the window to close it. 'Looks like that storm out at sea is coming in at last,' she said. 'Hopefully it won't be quite so hot tonight.'

The three cats watched as a blue line of lightning arced across the sea and lit everything up around it. A deafening crack of thunder followed and the rain wasn't far behind; in seconds, it was lashing the windows, making it impossible to see anything. The lightning came again and fizzled across the villa, throwing their room into darkness, and the kettle died in an instant.

'Oh bugger!' said Tilly. 'Now the power's out. I hope Mrs Meakin is OK.'

Hettie lit a match, which flared briefly before going out. The thunder gave a deafening roar before the lightning once again offered a reply. 'Come on,' she said. 'We'd better go down and check on the old cat. She won't have slept through this.'

'I'll check the fuses while we're there,' said Bruiser. 'The storm might 'ave knocked 'em out.'

They made their way to the top of the stairs but froze momentarily as the sound of screams reached them. Bruiser bounded down, followed by Hettie and Tilly. He was first into the kitchen as Premo Pete lifted the knife to finish his work. Old Mrs Meakin had no screams left as she cowered in the corner next to the Aga, her paws protecting her head as she waited for the blade to claim her.

Bruiser pounced on Pete, knocking the knife out of his paw. Hettie retrieved it from the floor as Pete fought back and Tilly rushed forward to Mrs Meakin, doing her best to offer some comfort while Pete and Bruiser locked jaws in a vicious cat fight. Eventually Pete broke free and managed to pull open the back door. He dived into the storm and Bruiser gave chase.

Hettie was in two minds about whether to follow Bruiser but opted to stay with Mrs Meakin. The old cat was in shock and Hettie was keen to find out what had happened to make Pete turn on her. She and Tilly pulled Minnie's mother gently to her feet and settled her back in her chair. The light from the Aga revealed the resistance she'd put up. The kitchen looked like a whirlwind had passed through it: pans, plates and all manner of provisions were scattered and broken and the old cat sat in the middle of the devastation, alive but barely present as she rocked herself backwards and forwards in her chair.

Tilly's vision was not so good in the dark but with the help of the glow from the stove she managed to put the kettle on it. Hettie's eyes were much keener and she searched for mugs, teabags and sugar. She found milk in the big upright fridge and Tilly made sure that Mrs Meakin got the lion's share of the sugar.

Outside the storm raged on as Premo Pete made good his escape. The terracing below the villa that led to the promenade was wet and slippery as the rain tumbled down in instant waterfalls, unseating rockeries and uprooting summer bedding plants. Pete slid to the bottom and bounded across the promenade onto the beach, heading in the direction of the fairground. Bruiser followed at a distance, waiting to see what the cat would do next.

Pete stopped at the entrance to the fairground to catch his breath and Bruiser seized his opportunity, pouncing and knocking him to the ground. 'That's far enough,' he hissed, forcing his weight down on top of the other cat. 'You got some explainin' ta do.'

The fight seemed to have gone out of Pete as he lay in a deep puddle with Bruiser restricting his movements, and all around them the cacophony of the storm raged. Pieces of fairground machinery were being picked up and tossed in the air; the picket fence that surrounded the fair had come loose and was battering what had been Marmalade Meakin's donut stall; and to make matters worse, the tide was coming in at an alarming rate, swallowing up the sand in a broiling sea.

Aware of the danger they were both in, Bruiser hauled Pete to his feet, dragging him away from the fairground and back to the promenade, which was also by now deep in water. The lightning was all around them and Bruiser pulled Pete towards one of the colonnades, hoping for shelter. Pete bided his time, showing no resistance, but as they reached the safety of the shelter he made one last bid for freedom and wrenched himself away, splashing across the promenade and onto the sand. The incoming tide claimed him in seconds and Bruiser watched, helpless to do anything to save him. The power of the waves lifted

Pete up and spat him out three times before he finally disappeared in the undertow that sucked his final breath from him.

As if the storm knew that it had done its job, the wind suddenly died and the thunder rolled away into the distance. The torrential rain morphed into a fine drizzle, and only the anger of the sea remained as witness to the devastation.

Bruiser shivered as he stood in the shelter, and not from cold: witnessing the death of another cat was never something he accepted easily; it was a life taken before its time and – in this case – without explanation. Why had Pete turned on old Mrs Meakin? What was it in Pete's life that had made him take such a violent action and was he responsible for the other murders? All these questions were running through Bruiser's mind as he climbed, exhausted, back up to Sandscratchers Villa.

Chapter Twenty-Five

Mrs Meakin blinked as Tilly passed her a hot, sweet, milky tea. She curled her long claws around the mug and sipped the drink slowly; bit by bit, the sugar did its work and the old cat regained her composure. Hettie stood back, not wishing to crowd her, and wondered whether she should leave her in Tilly's capable paws while she went to look for Bruiser. The decision was made for her when Mrs Meakin began to speak.

'I'm grateful to you two gals,' she said. 'I really thought I'd had me time there for a minute. That's what you get for telling the truth, but I never thought he would turn on me.'

'Are you talking about Pete?' asked Hettie, stepping forward so that the old cat could see her in the light of the Aga.

'I called him Milchip after his father,' she said. 'He was my first born, but they took him away because I'd been promised to Milo. Milchip raised him with Mary, you see. I didn't know that until tonight. He came here to tell me that he was Milchip's son and his rightful heir, and that he was going to take over the fairground and the pier because he'd found out that Milo had murdered his father. I told him that if Milchip was his father then I was his mother and he flew at me. He said he'd spent every day of his life wanting to be part of a family and that Milo and me had denied him that. When Milo brought Mary back here, I didn't know that her brother had come too and lived like a homeless cat on the beach. If I'd known that, I would have given him a home and a job. I've spent years wondering what happened to my baby boy.'

'And do you think he was responsible for murdering Marmalade, Maxwell, Marty and Monty?' asked Hettie, as gently as she could.

Mrs Meakin shook her head. 'No, there's only one cat to blame and that's me. Too many secrets, too many lies, and in the end everyone suffers. I should have stayed with Milchip. I loved him and he loved me, but my father insisted and that was that. Milo knew that I preferred his brother – that's why he killed him. With Milchip dead, he got to inherit the rides and he used my money to buy this place from old Gervaise Smith. If Milo had known that I'd born Milchip a son, he'd have killed me as well.'

'How did Pete find out about his father being murdered?'

'I think Mary must have told him. They were as thick as thieves lately. I thought she was just sweet on the deckchair cat. I didn't realise that he was her half-brother.'

'But how did Mary find out about her father's death?' asked Tilly.

'She must have overheard Marlon and me talking after Micky's funeral. Marlon told me that Milo had confessed to Milchip's murder on his death bed. I told him to keep it to himself as it would set the family against each other and no good would come of it, and I was right.'

At this point the front door of the villa banged shut and Minnie Meakin rushed into the kitchen, followed by Bruiser. Both cats were drenched to the skin and Bruiser was bleeding from several injuries. 'Mother!' Minnie shouted. 'Are you all right? And what's happened to the lights? Surely you haven't been sitting here in the dark? How was your boil in the bag curry?'

Hettie and Tilly stepped back to allow Minnie to get closer to her mother. Hettie looked enquiringly at Bruiser, who slowly shook his head, indicating that Pete had met his maker. He was obviously in no mood to relive the horrific event and turned his attention to the fuse box in one of the kitchen cupboards. The main fuse had blown due to the lightning strike and he quickly replaced the fuse wire. Suddenly the villa was full of light again.

'For goodness sake, Mother,' said Minnie. 'Whatever have you been doing in this kitchen? I left everything ready for you – there was no need to make all this mess and one of my best plates is broken. It looks like Mount Verouka has erupted in here with all this porridge, devastated coconut and sugar everywhere.'

Hettie came to the old cat's rescue, pointing out that Premo Pete had tried to murder her. 'What?!' said Minnie. 'The cat with the deckchairs? Why on earth would he want to murder my mother?'

'That's quite a long and involved story,' said Hettie. 'We need to attend to Bruiser now so we'll leave your mother to explain everything, but if we could trouble you for some plasters and antiseptic cream we'll take them up to our room.'

Minnie looked more bewildered than usual and pulled a first aid box out of one of her kitchen drawers. She passed it to Hettie, who ushered Tilly and Bruiser out of the kitchen, leaving old Mrs Meakin to rewrite her family history for the sake of her daughter.

Chapter Twenty-Six

Daylight brought with it the true impact of the storm. Hettie, Tilly and Bruiser had had very little sleep. After attending to Bruiser's wounds, they'd sat up and talked long into the night about the demise of Premo Pete and the implications regarding the fairground murders. There were still questions to be answered and Hettie was frustrated by the fact that Pete was no longer available to give an account of how – or indeed if – he'd murdered the Meakins. 'The sooner we get to speak to Mary, the better,' she said, sitting up in bed and drinking the first milky tea of the day that Tilly had made for her. 'She just might be more helpful when she learns that Pete was trying to kill old Mrs Meakin. If she did tell Pete about Milo murdering her father, then she also might know what he did about it. I won't be satisfied until I know how those Meakins died and what really happened to Monty in that ghost train.'

'Just look at all this,' said Tilly, staring out of the window. 'There are bits of the fairground floating in the sea. One of Marmalade's lovely painted horses from the gallopers is lying smashed up on the beach along with Pete's deckchairs and the ice cream kiosk is upside down on the promenade.'

'That storm was a real bad'un,' said Bruiser. 'Stuff was flyin' everywhere. I'm surprised the pier didn't collapse. It's gonna' take some clearin' up, that's for sure.'

'I wonder what the wagon park looks like this morning?' pondered Hettie. 'Maybe Monty and the Devon Meakins have all been washed out to sea – and has the Wild West showground survived? Thank goodness the villa is high up on the cliff, otherwise we'd be bailing it out this morning.'

There was a knock on the door and before anyone could answer it Minnie barged her way into the room with a tray. 'I thought you'd all appreciate a nice bacon sandwich in your beds this morning,' she said, putting the tray down on the table. 'I can't thank you enough for what you did for Mother last night, and fancy that deckchair cat being a Meakin! I can't abide secrets at the best of times but what Mother told me last night was a real revolution. To think that my father was a murderer! It buggers belief.'

'How was everything in the wagon park when the storm hit?' asked Hettie eyeing up a bacon sandwich on the tray. 'The fairground looks like half of it's been washed away.'

'It was terrible down there,' said Minnie, sitting on the spare bed and making herself at home. 'Good job the wagons sit high on their wheels, but all the fencing was flying about and all those flowers Monica dressed Monty's wagon with disappeared in the first gust of wind. The Devon Meakins made a run for it when the storm died down – they're all holed up in their wagons in the villa's car park now, drying off, and the London Meakins will be arriving any minute. Not the best day to come to Felixtoe. Some are saying it's worse than the storm of '53. I dread to think how Wilt's showground looks this morning. The milk cat said that the whole of the golf course is under water, so goodness knows how things are at Gobbles Point.'

To Hettie, the fact that the golf course was under water was the first bit of good news of the day, along with the bacon sandwich.

'Maybe you should ring Wilt to see how things are out there?' suggested Tilly as she put the kettle on, assuming that Minnie would be keen for a cup of tea.

'I've tried that,' said Minnie, 'but all the telephone wires are down. I've even tried calling Marlon in his office at the fairground but there's just a nasty noise on the line. He's got a lot of explaining to do. As far as I'm concerned, he's not worth the steam on my tea at the moment, keeping all those secrets and running the fair when it wasn't his to run. And poor Mary! Don't even start me on that one. Anyway, I came up here with your breakfasts to find out what happened to Premo Pete? Mother's frightened that he's going to come back and have another go at killing her.'

'That's not going to happen,' said Hettie. 'Bruiser chased him away. He went into the sea and drowned last night.' The simplicity of her statement surprised even Hettie when compared with the account that Bruiser had given, but she had no intention of putting him through it again in the cold light of day.

'Well, I suppose it's case closed as they say on the TV,' said Minnie, gratefully accepting a milky tea from Tilly. 'I assume he did the murders? The sooner we get these funerals over with, the better I'll like it – then all the Meakins can go back to where they belong.'

'Aren't you sad about the fairground?' asked Tilly. 'What will happen to Marlon?'

'I am a bit sad about the fair,' said Minnie, 'but I haven't had much to do with it lately and I do love my villa – nothing is going to take that away as it was Mother's money that bought it originally. As for Marlon, he's made his bed and now he's going to have to lie in it. If he'd told the truth, my brothers and sister would still be alive and Monty might have gone to work for Wilt and had a proper future. I suppose Mary and Pete might have made a good job of running the fairground, but goodness knows what will happen now. I'm still finding it hard to believe that Deckchair Pete was my half-brother. Anyway, you need to get on with your breakfasts and I'd better go and supervise Mother. It's kippers this morning from her boil in the bag range – she's gone mad on conveyance foods. Will you be in for dinner?

It's going to be like feeding the five thousand later when the Londoners arrive.'

'We thought you'd be busy so we've booked a table at Catrina's again for tonight,' said Hettie. 'We had a lovely meal there last night before the storm came.'

'Sensible,' said Minnie. 'If things get bad I might even join you.'

She swept out of the room, leaving Hettie to pounce on a bacon sandwich and take it back to her bed. Tilly passed one to Bruiser and sat on the sofa to eat hers. The sandwiches were very good but soon over and, although Hettie was tempted to curl up and go back to sleep, they still had some work to do. 'I think we should go and find Mary,' said Hettie, wiping the bacon fat off her whiskers with the back of her paw. 'The more I think about it, the more I reckon she holds the key to this whole case.'

Tilly stood up and went to the window 'Oh look!' she said. 'There's something going on down there on the beach.'

Hettie and Bruiser joined her to see a group of cats gathering at the shoreline, close to the pier. 'Come on,' said Hettie. 'Let's go and see what's happening.'

The three cats threw on some clothes and made their way down to the beach. As they grew closer to the sea, it was obvious that something had come ashore. There in the sand was the body of Premo Pete. Bruiser turned away, not wanting to relive the horror of the night before, and he and Tilly walked towards the pier. Hettie stayed by the shoreline and stared at the corpse, wishing it would rise up and tell her what had happened the night the Meakins were murdered. The pathetic bundle of fur didn't look capable of killing anything and Hettie was reminded that death was a great leveller. She turned towards the pier to catch up with Bruiser and Tilly and bumped into Mary, who'd abandoned her slots to see what was happening. She pushed past Hettie and froze at the sight of her brother's body, then forced her way through the crowd of cats circling the corpse and threw herself on top of it. She sobbed into the wet fur, cradling her brother's head, and the onlookers backed away when they saw her distress. Hettie moved closer as Mary vented her anger on the dead cat. 'You stupid, stupid boy,' she said. 'This was never goin' to end well. You should have listened to me and bided your time, and now look at you. How could you do this to me?'

She was becoming hysterical and began to pound the body with her paws. Hettie stepped in and pulled her away from the corpse as gently as she could. 'You need to leave him now,' she said. 'There's nothing more you can do for him. We'll call the undertaker, who'll look after him. Let's go and find you a cup of tea. I think we need to have a chat about Pete.'

'But why 'as 'e drowned?' cried Mary, allowing Hettie to lead her away. ''E surely wasn't out in that storm, was 'e?'

'I'm afraid he tried to stab Mrs Meakin last night,' said Hettie. 'He ran down to the beach and was carried away in the storm. There was nothing Bruiser could do to save him.'

'Stab Mother!' said Mary. 'Why would 'e do that? You got that wrong.'

'I'm afraid we caught him in the act,' said Hettie. 'Mrs Meakin had just told him that she was his real mother.'

'What?!' said Mary. 'You are jokin' me? We both 'ad the same mother and Milchip Meakin was our father.'

'That bit is true,' said Hettie, 'but Mrs Meakin told us that she loved Milchip and gave him a son before she married his brother Milo. That son was Pete.'

'I just can't get me 'ead round this,' said Mary. 'I think I need to 'ave a sit down.'

'Is the café open today? We could go there and talk some more.'

'Maisie's in there cleanin' up the mess from the storm. The winders leaked an' she's moppin' up, but she'll let us sit in there I expect.'

They caught up with Tilly and Bruiser at the entrance to the pier. Bruiser offered to go to Davy Button's funeral parlour to arrange the collection of Pete's body, while Hettie, Tilly and Mary made their way to the café. Maisie greeted them at the door, keen to know what was going on at the beach. Mary and Tilly settled themselves at one of the tables while

Hettie explained that Premo Pete had died in the storm, offering no further details.

'That's awful news,' said Maisie, abandoning her mop and bucket. 'Who's going to do the deckchairs now?' It was an obvious question, but Hettie was keen to speak to Mary rather than to pass the time of day with Maisie and suggested that a cup of tea might be welcome. 'Of course,' Maisie said. 'You all look like you've had a shock. I'll go and stick the kettle on and finish mopping the floor. Bear with me.'

Maisie disappeared into the kitchen and Hettie went to sit with Tilly and Mary. 'I think this would be the right moment to tell us exactly what happened the night the four Meakins were killed,' said Hettie. 'Now that Pete is dead, you might find it easier to talk about it.'

'I didn't kill no one,' said Mary. 'Before I starts, I just want ta make that clear.'

'We understand,' said Hettie. 'Shall we begin when the fair closed that night? You said you left your wagon around ten to light a fire on the beach. Were you on your own?'

Mary considered her response carefully before replying. 'No,' she said. 'I'd arranged ta meet Pete. It was 'is plan ta get all the Meakins down there for a barbecue after they'd finished work for the night. I often did that if someone was 'avin' a birthday. It backfired a bit as Marlon an' Monica were goin' out, so I just invited Maxwell, Marmalade, Marty an' Monty, but Monty didn't turn up – not till later, anyway.'

'So why did Pete want them down on the beach?'

'I thought 'e was goin' ta tell 'em that 'im an' me really owned the fair 'cause Milo 'ad murdered our dad, but instead 'e pulled a knife on 'em an' stabbed 'em.'

'Didn't you try to stop him?'

Mary shook her head. 'How could I? I thought 'e was goin' ta do for me as well. It was all so quick, an' 'e did say that if I didn't 'elp 'im get rid of the bodies, I'd go the same way.'

'So what happened next?'

'Well, there was just so much blood, an' Pete was covered in it so 'e went into the sea ta wash 'imself. The tide was comin' in an' that 'elped ta wash some of the blood away on the sand. When Pete came out of the water 'e said we needed to 'ide the bodies somewhere in the fairground. I think I was in shock, 'cause it all seems like a bad dream when I thinks about it now, but I suggested the ghost train as it was the ride I used ta run. Pete left me with the bodies an' went off ta find somethin' ta move 'em in. I was frightened that Monty might turn up so I hid behind one of them groynes by the pier. Pete came back with a wheelbarrow an' we loaded Maxwell an' Marty in it an' took 'em ta the ghost train. I took Marty's keys out of 'is pocket an' we let ourselves in an' put the lights on. Pete told me ta make the bodies look like they was part of the tricks in there. I said I wouldn't, so he cut Maxwell's 'ead off in front of me an' slashed Marty's throat. 'E said I'd get the same if I didn't do as 'e said. 'E left me an' went ta fetch Marmalade's body. When 'e came back 'e bumped into Monty, who'd seen the light on in the ghost train.'

Mary was suddenly silent, as if she was reliving the next part of her story in her head and Hettie and Tilly waited, knowing what would come next. The silence was broken by Maisie bustling through from the kitchen with a tray. 'I thought you'd all like a toasted teacake to go with your tea,' she said, putting the tray down on the table. 'They've got to be used up today and I'd hate to waste them. I can't see me being ready to open later, so you may as well enjoy them. I'm taking some home for the kittens – they love them. Is there anything else I can get you before I get on with swabbing the decks?'

Hettie was pleased to see the teacakes but found their arrival quite bizarre at such a crucial moment in Mary's account of what had happened in the ghost train. 'Thank you, that's very kind,' she said, hoping the cat would return to her mop, 'but I think we have everything we need at the moment.'

Instead, Maisie drew everyone's attention to the window. 'Oh look,' she said. 'They're taking Pete off the beach and Mr Bruiser is helping – such a lovely cat. That Davy Button has been busy lately, hasn't he? Such a pride in his profession. Couldn't do enough for me at Micky's funeral. Mind you, it didn't go down too well with Marlon that I had him cremated, but

Micky once told me that he had an aversion to worms so I had no choice, really. I wonder if Pete has any family? He's always seemed like a bit of a loner to me.'

Hettie was frantically trying to think of a way of getting rid of Maisie so that Mary could continue with her story when the telephone rang in the kitchen. 'Oh good,' said Maisie. 'Sounds like we're back on again. I'd better go and see who that is – it's probably Monica to see how things are.'

She left them in peace and Hettie resumed the conversation as Tilly poured out three cups of tea. 'You were about to tell us what happened to Monty in the ghost train?'

'It was terrible,' said Mary. 'First thing I knew was when Pete dragged Monty in an' tied 'is paws behind 'is back with some of the bandagin' from one of the mummies. Then 'e takes 'im to where we 'ave the 'angin' murderer an' strings 'im up. I shouted at 'im ta stop but 'e pulled out 'is knife from 'is belt an' every time Monty swung towards 'im 'e stabbed 'im till 'e was dead. There was so much blood.'

It was with some satisfaction that Mary's account of Monty's death tallied with Hettie's own supposition, but the telling of it was horrific and far worse than she had feared. It was clear that underneath the self-contained cat in charge of deckchairs lurked a very angry and sadistic character. 'What happened next?' she asked.

''E threatened me again with 'is knife an' said I 'ad ta do what 'e told me. We put poor Marmalade and

Marty each in one of the coffins, an' Pete stuck Maxwell's 'ead in the wall with the skulls an' I 'elped 'im put the shroud an' chains on the rest of 'is body. We stuck the barrow outside the back door an' locked up the ride. I went back to me wagon an' Pete went across the beach. I suppose 'e went back to 'is beach hut but I didn't see 'im ta speak to again.'

'If we hadn't tried to solve the murders, what would yours and Pete's plan have been?'

'Well, as far as I was concerned there wouldn't 'ave been no murders,' said Mary. 'When I found out that Milo 'ad murdered me father an' stolen 'is rides, I was goin' ta 'ave it out with Marlon 'cause 'e was tryin' ta close me slots down an' I thought that me an' Pete was owed some compensation for all the lies an' secrets, but Pete stuck a note under Marlon's door tellin' 'im 'e knew the truth an' 'e should give back what 'e stole. Pete was 'opin' that Marlon would come clean an' 'and the fair over ta me so me an' Pete could run it together, but Marlon did nothin' an' that made Pete really angry.'

'How do you feel about everything now? Do you still want to take over the fairground after everything that's happened?'

'Truth is,' said Mary, 'I never wanted ta take it over. All I ever wanted was a family who'd accept me and include me in everything. When Monica came along all that stopped, an' when I over'eard Marlon talkin' with 'is mother about Milo murderin' my father, I turned ta Pete 'cause 'e was my proper family.'

'How did Pete come to live here?' Hettie asked.

''E came with me after my father was killed, but Milo didn't want 'im so 'e bought 'im the deckchair business an' 'is beach hut. It was Marmalade's, actually – she'd painted it up lovely but Milo bought 'er a wagon instead where she could do all 'er paintin' for the fair. Pete was pleased at first an' we saw each other all the time. The rest of the Meakins 'ad no idea that Pete was my brother – or 'alf-brother as things 'ave turned out.'

'So what will you do now?' asked Tilly, giving Hettie a chance to take a bite out of one of the teacakes.

'I just don't know,' said Mary. 'I've been stewin' over it since the murders. Now it's all out in the open an' Pete is gone, there's nothin' left for me here. When Marlon finds out what I done ta help Pete with the killin's, 'e'll 'ave me 'ung, drawn and quartered. I just can't get all that horror out of me 'ead. Every time I try an' close me eyes, the faces of them dead Meakins just stare back at me. I 'ave ta keep checkin' me paws ta see if they're covered in blood.'

Hettie's paws were now covered in butter from her teacake and she was conscious that it wasn't entirely appropriate, bearing in mind that Mary was in such abject misery. She found herself desperately looking for something to say and it was Tilly who came to her rescue. 'The London Meakins are arriving today for the funerals – maybe you could start a new life with them?'

'Go back to me old life, yer mean?' said Mary. 'I'm not sure they'd want me an' after all this I feel like sellin' up me slots. I've done with fairs an' Sandscratchers. I might just move into Pete's hut if it's still standin' after the storm and live out me days cookin' sausages an' watchin' the waves come an' go. I s'pose you're goin' ta tell on me now yer know everythin'?'

Hettie thought for a moment, weighing up the situation. As far as Pete was concerned, justice had been done, but the tragedy of the story began with Milo Meakin murdering his brother; all the subsequent misery stemmed from that one act. Of all the cats involved, Mary was quite simply another victim. 'No,' she said, getting to her feet, 'we won't be telling anyone and we wish you luck in whatever you decide to do.'

Hettie and Tilly left the café and met up with Bruiser back on the sand, which was now busy with beachcombers out to salvage treasure from the storm. The sun was high in the sky and the band of dark storm clouds that had hovered on the horizon for days had been replaced by a deep blue above a sparkling sea. It was as if Mary Meakin's testimony had cleared the air and brought some hope for the future.

The three friends sauntered down the beach, finally free of the case that had baffled them for days. They were pleased to see that Catrina's Fish Bar had survived the storm but the door of Premo Pete's beach hut had been blown further down the beach. Bruiser went to collect it as Hettie and Tilly took the opportunity to take a look inside. The hut was sparsely furnished, with a striped hammock, a table and transistor radio, a collection of catnip pipes in a pint mug, a jar of catnip, and a book half-read with a deckchair ticket marking the page. 'Look,' said Tilly, 'he was reading one of Miss Crispy's. It's a bit sad that he'll never know who did it.'

'He certainly made up for it by killing all those Meakins,' Hettie pointed out. 'Even Miss Crispy's body counts couldn't compete with Premo Pete.' She was about to leave the hut when she noticed a bag on the floor under the hammock and stooped to pick it up. 'Well, well, well,' she said, 'a bag full of money. There's too much here for deckchair hires. I bet these are the takings from the fairground on the night the Meakins died. Marlon said the money had disappeared.'

'What should we do with it?'

'That's a difficult one,' said Hettie. 'I suppose we should give it to Marlon, but all things considered it belongs to Mary, really, and after what the family and Pete have put her through she deserves it.'

'Speak of the devil,' said Tilly. 'Here she comes.'

Mary was surprised to see Hettie and Tilly so soon after leaving the café, and even more surprised to see Bruiser attempting to refit the door to Pete's hut. 'I was wonderin' if the hut was still 'ere,' she said. 'Thank you fer fetchin' the door. I've decided to move out of me wagon an' try me luck down 'ere on the beach. I might even rent out a few deckchairs when I've sold me slots – only really fit fer them collectors these days, I s'pose.'

Hettie shared a look with Tilly before passing the bag of money to Mary. 'This might help you to get your business up and running.'

Hettie, Tilly and Bruiser walked away, leaving Mary Meakin staring after them, holding a bag of hope for her future in her paw.

'What shall we do with the rest of our day?' asked Tilly.

'Let's take a vote on it,' said Hettie. 'I suggest we have lunch instead of dinner at Catrina's, then go back to the villa, pack up our things and head for home. Those in favour raise your paws.'

Three paws shot up instantly and they headed for Catrina's Fish Bar.

Chapter Twenty-Seven

It took several weeks for Hettie, Tilly, Bruiser and Miss Scarlet to get over the Felixtoe case. Returning to their town and the comfort of familiar surroundings and friends did much to erase the horrors of the Meakins' murders. The summer rolled on, with plenty of sunny days, happy gatherings, picnics and barbecues, and it was at one such gathering on the Butters' lawn that news came from Felixtoe with an unexpected parcel.

Tilly had taken up a new hobby, much to the consternation of all those around her. The bow and arrow she'd bought as a souvenir from Wilt Dinsney's Wild West Show had been in constant use, as Bruiser had kindly made her a target and hung it on his shed door at the bottom of the garden. The thought was a lovely one, but he'd done it mainly to protect the cats around him: Tilly's aim was nowhere near as true as that of Buffalo Lill.

On this particular afternoon, Tilly had announced that there would be a contest and that she, in a Robin Hood-like fashion, would challenge all comers to an archery competition. Those all comers were Hettie, Bruiser, Betty and Beryl, who no doubt would have preferred to sit quietly in their deckchairs and enjoy the sun.

Betty and Beryl had decided to make Tilly's tournament more of an event by putting on an afternoon tea, and Bruiser had gone as far as hanging some bunting in the trees that surrounded the garden, much to Tilly's delight. 'I think we should have the first round before tea,' she said. 'I'll go first as I'm more used to it.'

She drew the bow and aimed the arrow at the target, letting it fly through the air and narrowly missing the window in Bruiser's shed. It was at this point that everyone was grateful that the arrow had a sucker on the end of it. 'That wasn't a real go,' Tilly said. 'I was just testing out the distance from the target and I hadn't licked the sucker, so that doesn't count.' She took aim again and this time managed to hit one of the outer rings. 'That's twenty-five points for me,' she said triumphantly, as Hettie chalked up the score on the blackboard that the Butters used for their specials.

Betty was next and missed the target altogether as the arrow fell from the bow in front of her. Tilly offered her another go, but Betty declined on the basis that she had to put the kettle on for tea. Beryl followed and made a little more progress, but her arrow still fell short, which freed her up to butter the scones she'd so recently pulled from the oven.

After three contestants Tilly was the top scorer, but Bruiser and Hettie were still to come. Bruiser took aim and fired his arrow, scoring twenty-five points to put him level with Tilly, much to her annoyance. Hettie triumphed by hitting the bull's eye before her arrow bounced off the target and onto the grass. She was about to give herself fifty points when Tilly protested. 'I'm afraid you'll have to be disqualified,' she said, snatching the chalk out of Hettie's paw. 'Better luck in round two.'

'You only said that because I scored fifty,' said Hettie, 'and I don't see how you're allowed to judge a competition that you're taking part in.'

'I'm allowed because it's my bow and arrows,' said Tilly, 'and we don't have a judge who's not taking part.'

'I'm happy to stand down from the tournament,' offered Betty, seizing her opportunity to absent herself from the game. 'I'll be your judge in the next round, but we'd better get on with the tea before the wasps have it – it's nice and hot at the moment. Perhaps Tilly would like to remind us of what's on offer?'

Tilly abandoned the chalk and crossed the lawn to the trestle table, which was groaning with lovely things to eat. 'We've got salmon and cucumber rolls, cheese rolls, minced beef and onion pasties, prawn cocktail baskets, marmite mini bites, cheesy sausage rolls, sardine samosas and cheese and potato puff bakes. That's the savouries. The puddings are strawberries in a chocolate cup, custard tarts, cream horns, obviously, a peach and jelly lattice flan, scones and...'

Tilly's list of afternoon tea was abruptly curtailed by the appearance of Squeak, Lavender Stamp's new postcat. 'Sorry to interrupt,' she said, 'but I've got a parcel for Hettie and Miss Stamp says it has to be delivered today because it's in her way at the post office.'

'Leave it by the back door and come and have some tea with us,' said Beryl. 'There's plenty to go round and we're having an archery competition.'

Squeak didn't need asking twice. She put the parcel down and joined everyone at the trestle table. Betty poured the tea as the plates were piled high and eating took priority over anything to do with bows and arrows. When all the cats were full to bursting, Tilly decided that it was time to resume her competition and noticed that Squeak was eyeing up her bow and arrows. 'Would you like to have a go?' she said. 'We have a spare place in the competition now that Betty is going to be a judge – unless you have to get on with your deliveries?'

'No, I've finished for the day,' said Squeak, 'and I'd really like to have a go.'

Tilly passed the bow and one of the arrows to Squeak, who spat on the sucker, took aim and fired at the target, hitting the bull's eye. The arrow remained firmly there and Betty chalked up a score of fifty, while Hettie, Bruiser and Beryl applauded the newcomer. Tilly took aim, hoping that Squeak's strike was beginner's luck, but as the scores mounted up it was clear that the postcat would be crowned as the tournament champion, with Tilly coming third behind Bruiser.

Slightly disgruntled, Tilly waved Squeak off, giving her the bow and arrows as her prize and declaring that next summer she might consider taking up croquet. After helping Betty and Beryl to clear up the tea things, Bruiser left to meet Dolly Scollop for a trip to the cinema and Hettie and Tilly retired to their room with their parcel and the leftovers from tea that they'd earmarked for their supper. 'It's quite a big parcel,' said Tilly, giving it a sniff, 'and it's flat and square. It must be something you've ordered and forgotten about. I hope it's not a target for my archery, as I've moved on from that now.'

Hettie laughed at the predictability of Tilly's short-lived fads. 'According to the postmark it's from Felixtoe, and I certainly haven't ordered anything from there so the only way to find out is to open it.'

Tilly obliged by running her claw along the Sellotape and ripping the brown paper off the parcel. 'Ooh look,' she said. 'It's a lovely painting of a fairground and it's just like a Marmalade Meakin.'

'That's because it is a Marmalade Meakin,' said Hettie. 'She's signed it, and there's a letter with it.' Hettie slit the blue envelope open and pulled out the letter along with a bundle of five pound notes that floated to the floor.

Tilly leaned the painting against the sideboard and gathered up the money. 'There's fifty pounds here,' she said, waving it under Hettie's nose. 'Who's the letter from?'

Hettie turned to the final page. 'Minnie Meakin. Why don't you read it out for us while I put the kettle on?'

Tilly sat down on her blanket and squinted at the very small paw writing. She started to read while Hettie made the tea.

'Dear Hettie, Tilly and Mr Bruiser,

I hope this letter finds you well. We are still all at sevens and sixes here in Felixtoe, but us Meakins settle our debts so I have enclosed fifty pounds which I hope you will accept with our gravity for everything you did for Mother and the rest of us. We discovered the painting in Marmalade's wagon when we were clearing it out and I thought you might like it.

As you got to know so many of the family when you were here, I thought you might like me to unindate you with our news. Monica left shortly after the funerals to start a new life with the Devon Meakins and has opened a café in Torquay. Maisie has taken over the café on the pier and is making a really good job of it. Mary has bought up a whole row of beach huts, which she hires out, along with a deckchair business, and has sold her slots to Marlon (we now call her Mary Queen of Huts). Wilt has done a swap with Marlon and is building his Wild West town on the beach where the fair used to be and he has put Matty and Buffalo Lill in charge of the building work. Marlon has moved all the rides into the big top at Gobbles Point and intends to open it as a vintage fairground museum to include the slots he bought from Mary. He doesn't seem that bothered about Monica leaving; in fact he's quite progmatic about it, and Mary has agreed to help him out when the museum is open, so they've buried their defences.

Mother has gone back to eating meat full time and given up her vagrant ways, and has taken up golf which is proving a little dangerous for the other players. She's already been banned from the clubhouse for swearing at the fourteenth and is on a final warning regarding her behaviour with a six iron in one of the bunkers. She does look very nice in her plus fours, though, and she's knitted her own harlequin socks.

Wilt and I are planning an autumn wedding which you will all be invited to. He's taking me on a round the world curse for our honeymoon, which I'm absolutely emphatic about. If any of you ever fancy a seaside break, you will always be welcome at Sandscratchers Villa, free of charge.

I must dash, as the arbour is playing up again and there's a definite smell of burning.

Until next time,
Minnie Meakin'

'Well, that sounds like a satisfactory end to the Meakins' saga,' said Hettie. 'You should write it all up as your first novel.'

'I think I'll stick to reading other cats' books,' said Tilly. 'As Minnie would say, I'm not really suited to a litter tray life.'

Acknowledgements

I have many happy memories of being taken to the Goose Fair in Nottingham as a child back in the late '50s, when fairgrounds were very different from the ones we have today. In researching this book it's been a joy to learn more about the families who ran them. I would particularly like to say thank you to Thomas Rowland and Sue Perry from Dingles Fairground Museum in Devon for a wonderful behind-the-scenes insight into the running of a fairground, and to Thomas for sharing his family history with me. It is quite sad to think that, by the time you read this book, Dingles will have closed and the rides on display will have been scattered across the country and beyond to new owners; it was really special to be able to see them together in a proper setting at Dingles.

Those of you who have visited Felixstowe on the Suffolk coast will no doubt recognise several of the locations in the book. My thanks go to the owners of the Cliff Top Café for providing the perfect setting for Minnie Meakin's guest house, and to Cobbles Point for accommodating Wilt Dinsney's Wild West Show.

I would also like to thank my editor, Abbie Headon, for her advice, dedication and – crucially – a shared sense of humour: Catriona Robb for dotting the eyes and crossing the milky teas; Jason Anscomb for another splendid cover; and to Pete Duncan and all at Farrago Books for their continued belief and support for the series. Finally to Nicola, my first reader and lifelong companion along the road.

About the Author

Mandy Morton was born in Suffolk. After a short and successful music career in the 1970s as a singer-songwriter – during which time she recorded six albums and toured extensively throughout the UK and Scandinavia with her band – she joined the BBC, where she produced and presented arts-based programmes for local and national radio. She more recently presents The Eclectic Light Show on Mixcloud.com.

Mandy lives with her partner, who is also a crime writer, in Cambridge and Cornwall, where there is always room for a long-haired tabby cat. She is the author of The No. 2 Feline Detective Agency series and also co-wrote *In Good Company* with Nicola Upson, which chronicles a year in the life of Cambridge Arts Theatre. A complete retrospective collection of Mandy's music entitled *After The Storm* has recently been released on Cherry Red Records.

Twitter: **@hettiebagshot** and **@icloudmandy**
Facebook: **HettieBagshotMysteries**

Preview

Six Tails at Midnight

Hettie, Tilly, Bruiser and the Butter sisters set out across the snowy fens to spend Christmas at The Fishgutter's Arms. Snowed in with no hope of rescue, they find themselves sharing Christmas with some unwanted guests.

Will the ghosts of Christmas Past reek vengeance on the present?

Can our feline detectives dig themselves out of a spooky festive fiasco?

And will the sausage rolls and sherry last until midnight?

Jump on board for a cat-a-strophic sleigh ride into a snow drift full of Christmas spirits.

COMING SOON

Also available

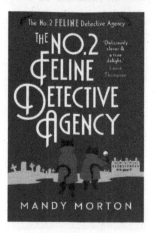

The No. 2 Feline Detective Agency begins

Hettie Bagshot has bitten off more than any cat could chew. No sooner has she launched her detective agency than she's thrown into her first case.

Furcross, home for senior cats, has a nasty spate of bodysnatching, and three former residents have been stolen from their graves. Hettie and her sidekick, Tilly, set out to reveal the terrible truth. Is Nurse Mogadon involved in a deadly game? Has the haberdashery department of Malkin and Sprinkle become a mortuary? And what flavour will Betty Butter's pie of the week be?

In a haze of catnip and pastry, Hettie steers the case to its conclusion, but will she get there before the body count rises – and the pies sell out?

OUT NOW

Also available

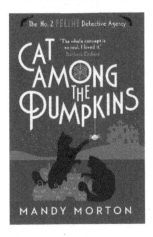

The No. 2 FELINE Detective Agency

'The whole concept is
so real, I loved it.'
Barbara Erskine

CAT AMONG THE PUMPKINS

MANDY MORTON

Gunpowder, treacle and shocks

As All Hallows' Eve approaches, Hettie Bagshot of The No. 2 Feline Detective Agency has more than just a ghost and a warlock tart on her plate.

Upon discovering the body of Mavis Spitforce, Hettie and her trusty sidekick Tilly set out to investigate an old crime and a spate of new murders. Why was Mavis Spitforce dressed for Halloween? Can Irene Peggledrip really talk to cats from the spirit world? And what's the connection to the legend of Milky Myers, suspected of murdering his family on Halloween, longer ago than anyone can remember?

As the November fog closes in, can the tabby duo unearth the truth, and stop the murderer before they strike again – and will there be enough samosas to go round?

OUT NOW!

Also available

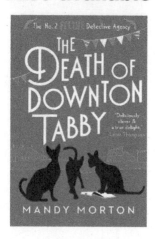

Hettie and Tilly are on the case

The town is celebrating its first literary festival, and The No. 2 Feline Detective Agency has been hired to oversee security.

When the body of the most popular author, Sir Downton Tabby, is found in a secluded part of the grounds, however, Hettie and her faithful sidekick Tilly are plunged into crisis as a serial killer stalks the festival.

As the duo turn their attention to investigating the death of Downton Tabby, will there be an author left standing? Will Meridian Hambone sell out of her 'Littertray' T-shirts? And will there be enough crime teas to go around?

OUT NOW!

Note from the Publisher

To receive updates on new releases in The No. 2 Feline Detective Agency series – plus special offers and news of other humorous fiction series to make you smile – sign up now to the Farrago mailing list at farragobooks.com/sign-up.